Abo

Anwen John lives with her wife in the beautiful, historic city of Canterbury. She started writing when she took early retirement following a cancer diagnosis. This is her first book. Anwen's short stories have been published in print and eBook anthologies, and broadcast on radio. She shares some of her writing on her website, anwenwrites.net.

The Canterbury Cullings

Anwen John

The Canterbury Cullings

Vanguard Press

A CIP catalogue record for this title is available from the British Library.

ISBN 978-1-83794-542-9

This is a work of fiction. Names, characters, businesses, places, events and
incidents are either the products of the author's imagination or used in a
fictitious manner. Any resemblance to actual persons, living or dead, or actual
events is purely coincidental.

Vanguard Press is an imprint of
Pegasus Elliot Mackenzie Publishers Ltd.
www.pegasuspublishers.com

First Published in 2025

Vanguard Press
Sheraton House Castle Park
Cambridge England

Printed & Bound in Great Britain

Dedication

To Andie.
My wife, my soulmate, my rock.

Acknowledgements

I would like to thank my wife, Andie, for her support during the months when this book was being written, and for encouraging me to write it in the first place. Andie's feedback as my first editor was invaluable.

I would also like to thank the wonderful group of family and friends who were so generous with their time in reading and giving feedback on the first several chapters of the book. Your encouragement meant so much to me.

On 29 May 1982, at Canterbury Cathedral, the Archbishop of Canterbury, Robert Runcie, and Pope John Paul II knelt side by side in silent prayer at the Altar of the Sword's Point, the spot at which another Archbishop of Canterbury, Thomas Becket, had been murdered in 1170.

This morning, a man knelt alone.

Geoffrey Rochester stared at the kneeling man. He was puzzled, then angry to find someone in the cathedral. How did he get in? What was he doing there? It was Geoffrey's job to open the cathedral and he took this breach of security very seriously. He marched up to the kneeling man and put a hand on his shoulder. The man fell back as far as his hands, bound to the altar, would allow. It was then that Geoffrey realised the kneeling man was dead and saw that his eyes and eyelids had been removed.

Geoffrey screamed.

Chapter 1

Detective Chief Inspector Bethany Harper, known to all as Beth, walked into the Murder Squad room at East Kent Police Station in Canterbury, carrying two of Marge's finest coffees. Marge's Manor was a three-minute walk from the police station and was one of those rare cafes which still served plain old filter coffee. Her bacon and cheese baps were renowned across the whole of Kent, so you had to get in early or late to avoid the office crowds collecting their breakfast on their way to work.

The first coffee was for her – the crank that started her engine every morning. The second coffee was for Detective Sergeant Terry Corfe, due to join the team this morning in his first DS position. Her team had been looking forward to getting more help, so Beth thought she should start off on the right foot with a proper coffee.

Beth was surprised to see Terry at his desk before her, and made a mental note to set her alarm a little earlier tomorrow to miss that office queue at Marge's. Her team were great, and Detective Constable Clarissa Griswold had met Terry at Reception and settled him in to his new desk. Beth was sure the team would have kept any horror stories to a minimum on Terry's first day.

"Good morning," Beth breezed. "Welcome to Canterbury Murder Squad."

"Thanks, Ma'am. It's great to be here. I've heard a lot of good things about this team."

"Flattery is always a very good way to start, Terry. Do you mind if I call you Terry?" Terry shook his head. "Excellent. Well here you go, Terry – have one of Marge's lush filter coffees!"

As Beth was about to elaborate on this local gem, her phone rang.

"DCI Harper. Good morning, Sir. Yes. Yes. Yes of course, Sir, we'll be there in five minutes." She put the phone down on Superintendent Donald Campbell.

"Okay team. They've found a body at the cathedral. It looks like a murder. I want you all over there as quickly as possible. Grab your coffee, Terry, you're with me."

Terry did as instructed, his mind whirring. This was his first murder case and what a case it was – a body discovered in the UK's oldest cathedral, recognised across the world. *No pressure,* he thought, as he walked a little faster through the double doors to catch up with Beth.

"We'll take your car," she said, when they walked into the large car park behind the police station. Terry identified his car by pointing his remote control at the Dacia Jogger and Beth spotted three children's car seats in the back. *That's a large family for a twenty-eight-year-old,* she thought.

It was a brief journey from the police station to the cathedral, but long enough for Terry to tell Beth about his life; he met his wife Leah when they were both first-year undergraduates at Loughborough University – he was studying criminology, she was studying psychology. They were married two weeks after graduation and lived in Loughborough for the early years. Three children later – six-year-old Harry, four-year-old Hugo, and two-year-old Hayden – with another baby due to arrive in three months' time, they realised they needed more support, not least with babysitting, so they returned to East Kent and bought a house in Margate, a short drive from Terry's family in Ramsgate and Leah's family in Broadstairs. "This will be the last baby," declared Terry. "I think if we're being honest, we'd like a little girl but we can't keep trying until we get one, so we'll draw the line at being parents of four!"

Terry was about to ask Beth about her home life when the cathedral car park appeared and a uniformed PC directed them towards the crime scene.

The main entrance to the cathedral was through a light glass door, which stood behind a heavy wrought iron gate known as the southwest door. The team had arrived before them; Beth knew that walking to the cathedral was much quicker than driving, but always travelled by car to make onward journeys, such as visiting bereaved families, as timely as possible.

Beth and Terry were met by the first officers on the scene, who briefed them on what they'd found, and what they hadn't found; including the fact that the victim had no ID on him. The body had been found tied to the Altar of the Sword's Point, a modest altar sitting underneath an imposing sculpture bearing two swords and their shadows representing the four knights who murdered Thomas Becket.

They were also met by Matthew Rye, the Receiver General, the cathedral's equivalent of a Chief Operating Officer, the Very Reverend Emma Draper, the first permanent female Dean of Canterbury, and Geoffrey Rochester, a senior member of the Close Constabulary. All present had seen the victim in situ. Matthew was very pale, with one hand on his hip and the other hand on his stomach, which Beth presumed was an attempt to keep his breakfast in place. Emma, on the other hand, had seen some horrors in her younger days that would have prepared her for an event like this. According to one of Beth's colleagues, shortly after Emma graduated from Oxford University, she became a young missionary supporting civilians during the civil war in Rwanda, so she looked and sounded in control of the situation, calmly telling Matthew and Geoffrey what needed to be done next, for both the cathedral's visitors and staff. Geoffrey was still very pale and shaky.

"I'm so sorry that you're all having to go through this experience," said Beth. "But we need to ask you a few questions and then take a statement from each of you. Can I start by asking if any of you recognise the victim?" The question was answered with a unanimous "No".

"Geoffrey, I understand you found the body this morning when you opened the cathedral. Who locked up the cathedral last night?"

"Philip Crossfield did the security lock-up, but you'll need to check with the head of housekeeping about who locked the doors after they'd finished their shift at eleven p.m.," replied Geoffrey. "I phoned Philip earlier. He confirmed that there was nothing unusual at the Altar of the Sword's Point when he checked the building after locking the doors, and he saw nothing suspicious when he was doing his rounds. He's as shocked as we are."

"Yes, of course," replied Beth. "Clarissa, please arrange for statements to be taken as quickly as possible, then get hold of all CCTV footage from the time the southwest door was locked last night. Thank you." As soon as Clarissa had sympathetically moved the cathedral staff along, Beth told Terry, "Come on, it's time for you to meet Mac the Knife!"

Forensic Pathologist Jane McDonald, affectionately known as Mac the Knife, was leaning over the victim's body, having cut him free of his shackles. She heard Beth approach, and sprang up far more quickly than might be expected of a woman of fifty-four.

Beth introduced her to Terry.

"Terry, this is our regular pathologist, Jane McDonald. Jane, this is our new sergeant, Terry Corfe."

Jane stretched out a warm welcoming hand and said "Welcome to the team, Terry. Please don't sing at me!"

Beth chuckled quietly as the reference to a popular singer of the same name went whistling over Terry's head.

"Good to meet you, Jane," said Terry. "I'm looking forward to working with you."

Mac smiled and turned to Beth, who asked, "What do we know so far?"

"So far, the cause of death is not obvious – no blows with a blunt instrument, no stab wounds or bullets – so we'll need to get him to the mortuary to find out more, but the lack of blood suggests that if he was stabbed or shot, it didn't happen here. Also, there are what I believe to be post-mortem mutilations to the face – the victim's eyes and eyelids have been removed. Come and see." Beth stepped forward and checked on her new sergeant, but there was no need; Terry clearly had the stomach for this job, and he too bent over the body to see more.

"Grim," muttered Beth. "Okay, thanks for the update, Mac. I'll see you at the post-mortem," and Beth left her to her body.

Beth looked carefully at the crime scene. There was very little detail to note; as Mac had mentioned, there was no blood on the scene, the murder weapon – whatever it might be – had not been left at the scene, and there were no marks on the floor near the body to suggest how a dead body could have been taken to the altar; so, was it possible that the victim had walked there and been killed at the scene? And was the scene itself significant? Did the killer believe they were acting on behalf of another? The knights who killed Thomas Becket believed they were acting on behalf of Henry II; perhaps the killer believed they were acting on behalf of God himself? Beth recognised the scale of the challenge ahead and steeled herself.

She walked around the cathedral, stopping for an update with every member of the team. One of the Detective Constables, Dave Roberts, had recognised the victim as local loan shark Jimmy Wheeler and gave Beth an update on all he knew about him. She thanked him, found Terry and said "We've got an ID on the victim. We need to head over to see his family. Let's go." As she said this, she spotted Donald Campbell with East Kent Police's Deputy Chief Constable, DCC Ian Merryweather. Both were deep in conversation with Matthew, Emma and Geoffrey. Beth caught Donald's eye and gave him a quick update on the situation. He told her he'd update the DCC as soon as they'd finished talking to the cathedral's 'Top Team', and asked her to come and see him in his office before she left every day, to keep him updated on progress with the case. Beth nodded, then left the building with Terry to carry out one of the most difficult jobs in policing – breaking the news to the family.

Chapter 2

The Speaker of the House of Commons stood and announced, "So we proceed to the statement by Dr Julian Jefferson-Briggs."

Julian Jefferson-Briggs, MP for Canterbury and Secretary of State for Health and Social Care, moved from the green bench to the despatch box, cutting a handsome and distinguished figure with his grey hair and his Savile Row suit. He hadn't always wanted to be an MP; he'd trained as a doctor many moons ago, and had worked in both the NHS and then the private sector before deciding, at the age of forty-eight that he wanted to do something that would benefit far more people than the few who could afford his fees. Ten years later, he became part of the government and felt that he was making some real progress in improving the lives of his constituents and the wider population.

Julian had studied at Oxford University, one of the world's leading medical schools. In addition to learning his craft, he had excelled at gymnastics, and soon became a leading member of the Oxford University Gymnastics Club. It was there that he met the love of his life, his soulmate, Elizabeth. In the forty years they'd been together, his love and passion for her had not diminished, and it was that love that would make his statement so very difficult.

The minister began, "Thank you, Mr Speaker. With permission, I'd like to make a statement on the government's plans to tackle the tragedy of suicide in this country today.

As the House will know, today is Suicide Awareness Day, and it was on this day three years ago that our beloved only child, our twenty-two-year-old son, Matthew, died by suicide. This government is determined to prevent as many families as possible from living through the deep grief of the loss of a loved one by suicide."

Julian paused to take a sip of water, then went on to outline the government's plans and take questions from fellow MPs. After an hour and a quarter, the Speaker drew questions to a close, allowing only points of order to be raised – the parliamentary equivalent of The Guardian's Corrections and Clarifications column.

Elizabeth Jefferson-Briggs had watched her husband deliver his statement and respond respectfully to all questions. She found the beginning of the statement very emotional, and was full of admiration for Julian being able to deliver those lines without tears, a feat she knew she would never be able to achieve. She was glad that she had caught the London train that morning to support him.

When the points of order began, Elizabeth slipped quietly out of the Strangers Gallery, a series of pews above the House of Commons where all members of the public are able to watch debates, and walked to Julian's office to wait for his return. When Elizabeth switched on her phone, she thought it was malfunctioning – the endless pings when text messages were delivered, the many renditions of the opening bars from Elgar's Pomp and Circumstance Marches for all voicemails received. Since Matthew had died, her message count had reduced considerably, so she was intrigued as she started working through the ones delivered in the relatively brief time she'd been sitting in the Strangers Gallery.

Elizabeth was listening to the final voicemail as Julian walked into his office. She stood and hugged him tightly. "You did wonderfully well, darling. I was very proud of you out there. But we have to go back to Canterbury immediately. They've found a body in the cathedral and the poor chap was murdered. The city needs its MP to be visible at this time, and I need to be at the cathedral to support the team." Elizabeth took her role as a Non-Executive Member of the Chapter at Canterbury Cathedral very seriously – the Chapter are responsible for all aspects of the day-to-day management of the cathedral, and Elizabeth's previous senior role at an Energy Multinational headquartered in London brought corporate expertise to the team.

"A murder?" said Julian. "At the cathedral?"

"Well, as I understand it, they're not sure if he was actually murdered at the cathedral or if his body was just moved there. Either is a very bad look for us commercially," replied Elizabeth.

"Oh darling, be careful no one hears you say it's a bad commercial look for the cathedral, even though we know it is."

Elizabeth bristled and picked up her bags.

"Come on, we're wasting time," she replied.

Julian did as he was told. He packed a laptop and some papers in his lockable briefcase and made for the door. As he got there, he turned and said to his wife fondly, "Come on, darling. The good people of Canterbury need us. Let's go home."

Chapter 3

According to Google maps, the drive from Canterbury Cathedral to Jimmy Wheeler's house in Ickleford would take forty-five minutes. Long enough, thought Terry, to find out more about this intriguing new boss of his – what lies beneath the smart trouser suit, Doc Martin boots, and rucksack so casually slung over her shoulder? Why colour her hair what looks like an unusual shade of dark orange – he thought Leah would probably call it 'burnt orange'. The slightly padded waist told its own story.

But how to approach it without crossing any lines?

"So do you live near the office?" he asked.

"Would you like to know a bit more about my out-of-office life, Terry?" asked Beth.

"Transparent?" asked Terry.

"A little," replied Beth. She was an intensely private person and would be happier if she only had to discuss personal issues with family and friends, but she understood people well enough to know that it was necessary to share personal details with colleagues in order to build good working relationships. And so, she delivered a quick and well-practised potted history to the young man she was already warming to – he had visited the squad room a few times between getting his job offer and starting with the team this morning, and she saw from his easy manner with his soon-to-be colleagues that he was likely to be a very good fit with the team. And with her.

"I was born and raised in Cardiff forty-two years ago. My parents were killed in a car crash when I was twelve-years-old, so my mum's sister, Aunt Kate, and her husband Gareth gave me a home, which was pretty good of them considering they had no children of their own, and had no experience of raising a hormonal teenager in grief, but they did a wonderful job and I feel very lucky to have had them in my life.

When I was eighteen, I moved to Canterbury to study history at the University of Kent. East Kent Police did a recruitment drive at the Uni a few months before graduation, and I love this city so I decided to stay and apply for a job with the police. It was the best move I ever made.

I'm single. My only long-term relationship lasted for eight years and finished four years ago. Her name was Jemima and she was lovely, but the pressures of being the partner of a police officer, especially an ambitious police officer, can be considerable and, for some, unbearable. So she left me. I'm sure I don't need to tell you this, Terry, but you have to prioritise Leah and the boys. Of course, there will be times when we will need to work for long hours, or work unsociable hours, but make your family your priority and leave the office on time whenever possible.

I live in Faversham, a beautiful town just ten miles from Canterbury. I lived on my own until three years ago, when Kate was told she had terminal cancer, and Gareth died of a heart attack a week later. It was then I asked Kate to move in with me so I could keep an eye on her.

The last four years have been tough, Terry, really extraordinarily tough, but the job has been a godsend. Having something I love to focus on, when people I love are leaving me, is exactly what I needed. So, I've carried on working hard, getting the results, and finally getting the Chief between Detective and Inspector, and that helps. Well, that and Marge's coffee, of course." The last sentence was delivered with a smile to signal an end to Beth's turbo-charged run through her life.

"Wow. You've certainly faced some challenges in your life, Ma'am. Thank you so much for sharing all that. Your story has just pushed you right up in my estimation. Not that it counts for much, of course, but thank you."

"You and I are going to work together closely for what I hope will be a long time, so being open with each other is important," replied Beth. She dipped into her pocket and pulled out her personal smartphone. "Now, you will go right up in my estimation if you tell me you like Two Tone," she said, slotting her smartphone in the docking station and finding her favourite Madness playlist. "Oh, and to quote the great Helen Mirren in Prime Suspect, 'Don't call me ma'am – I'm not the bloody queen!' The rest of the team call me Guv. Can we go with that?"

"We most certainly can, Guv, and I love Two Tone. My parents played nothing else in the house when we were growing up. They even named me after Terry Hall!"

Beth nodded her approval.

Chapter 4

They were halfway through Wings of a Dove when they found Jimmy Wheeler's house. They parked directly outside the beautiful, large, detached period property on a small side street off Ickleford's small main road. As they were walking up the path, the front door flew open and a wiry blonde woman ran towards them. "Have you found him?" she asked frantically.

"Are you Dawn Wheeler, Jimmy Wheeler's wife?" asked Beth.

"Yes. I reported him missing last night. He wasn't home by midnight and he hadn't told me he'd be staying out, so I knew something was wrong. I phoned your people and they said it was too early to report him as a missing person, but we Googled it and that's not right. We called again, they took some details and I asked if they'd share the details with other police forces within forty-eight hours, like it said on the internet, and they said they would; so have you found him?"

"Let's move inside, Mrs Wheeler," said Terry, gently.

When they got inside, they were met with more questions from a woman who looked very like Jimmy, standing as tall as him with quiffed black hair just like his.

"How many people have you got out looking for Jimmy? Where have you started looking? Have you spoken to his friends?"

"Can I ask who you are?" asked Beth.

"I'm Jimmy's sister, Jackie Wheeler," she replied. "We're twins. There's something wrong, I can just feel it."

"Please, sit down. I'm afraid I have some bad news," said Beth. Dawn let out a guttural cry, and Jackie moved quickly to put a protective arm around her, just as she had done since they became best friends at primary school. "The body of a middle-aged man has been found in suspicious circumstances in Canterbury Cathedral. We believe that man to be your husband, Jimmy Wheeler."

When Beth shared this news, both Dawn and Jackie shrieked "No!" and hugged each other tightly, wracked with tears.

"I know this is very difficult for you, but we need to investigate his death as quickly and thoroughly as possible, so it would be a great help to us if we could ask you a few questions. Are you ok with that?" Beth directed the question to both women. Dawn nodded in agreement. Jackie paused, and then nodded too.

Beth fired off her first question.

"Can you think of anyone who would want to harm Jimmy?"

"He worked in finance," Dawn replied. "It's a difficult job, dealing with people who have money worries, but Jimmy always did his best to help his customers. He was a really good friend as well – if you were his mate and you needed anything, he'd be there like a shot, so I can't think of anyone who would want to hurt him. If anything, you'd think everyone who knew him would want to keep him safe, because he'd always be there for them."

Beth hadn't heard the expression 'working in Finance' used to describe a loan shark before, and Dawn's description of her husband didn't match the update Dave Roberts had given her. Dave had encountered Jimmy on at least three occasions during his time in CID, and each one involved a serious physical injury on a third party, which could never be tied to Jimmy. Clever Jimmy.

"Has Jimmy spoken with you recently about any worries he had, any threats he'd received?" asked Beth, but when Dawn broke down sobbing, and Jackie avoided her gaze, she realised that they weren't going to find any answers today.

"I want to see him," said Dawn. "Can we go and see him now?"

"We can, but before we do, I need to tell you that there's been some trauma to Jimmy's face." Beth steeled herself to deliver the detail. "His eyes and eyelids have been removed, so the process of formally identifying the body is going to be a very upsetting one. Who do you think can do that?" asked Beth.

The news silenced both Dawn and Jackie. And then Jackie recovered. "His eyes and eyelids have been removed? What the fuck is going on here?" she shouted. "This isn't just a murder, it's a mob job."

Dawn put a calming hand on Jackie's arm. "I'll identify him," she whispered quietly.

Jackie took a breath and said, "I'll come with you."

"Thank you. We're parked outside. Please come out and join us when you're ready," said Beth, and she and Terry made their way to his car. En route, Beth took out her work phone and called Clarissa. "How's everything going at the cathedral?" asked Beth.

"Not too bad. SOCOs are getting on very well, but there's a dispute going on between the cathedral team and the Superintendent regarding how quickly they can open up the cathedral to the public. The staff want to reopen today, if you can believe such a thing, but the Super says the crime scene investigators will take as long as is needed, and until they're ready, the cathedral will have to remain closed to the public. The DCC is backing the Super, but the local MP and his wife are on their way and phoned the Dean a few minutes ago. They're supporting the cathedral staff, so how long the Super will be able to hold out, I do not know.

One bit of bad news is that the CCTV system isn't working properly. Something to do with the lighting, apparently; the engineers are booked to come and look at the issue tomorrow. All of which unfortunately means that we have no footage of any after-dark activities in the building last night, but we'll check the footage taken during daylight, just in case."

"Ach that's rubbish news," replied Beth. "Okay, thanks for the update. We're bringing the victim's wife and sister in to identify the body. We should get to the mortuary in about an hour. Please let Mac know we're on our way so she can prepare the body, and please ask Jenny to meet us there."

Jennifer Fisher was a forty-year-old detective sergeant, who'd tried a number of jobs after leaving school but found nothing that really interested her until she joined the police and found her true vocation. She had an excellent ability to draw information from both suspects and victims, and Beth knew that Jenny would make an excellent Family Liaison Officer for the Wheelers.

Once Dawn and Jackie stepped into the car, Terry started the long drive to the mortuary. When they arrived, Beth showed all three the way to the relatives viewing platform, which allows relatives to see the victims whilst preserving forensic evidence.

"I don't want to see him from here," said Dawn. "I want to hug him and kiss him goodbye."

"I'm afraid that won't be possible at this stage, because the post-mortem hasn't happened yet, but as soon as that's done, and we have confirmed his ID, I'll ask the pathologist to arrange for you to see your husband close-up. I'm very sorry, Dawn, but that's all I can offer at this time."

Dawn nodded to indicate she understood that the investigation had to take precedence at this stage and said, "Okay, I'm ready."

Beth nodded to Mac who removed the cloth covering the victim's face. Dawn whispered "That's him. That's my Jimmy," and the Wheeler women sobbed.

Chapter 5

Beth had asked the whole team to get back to base for what would become a daily four p.m. debrief. As she walked into the squad room with Terry, she smiled at the assembled crew, thinking for the umpteenth time how lucky she was to work with every one of them: Detective Inspectors Fiona Richardson and Ki Wong; Detective Sergeants Terry Corfe and Jenny Fisher, who joined them via a secure video link from her car outside Jimmy Wheeler's house, and Detective Constables Clarissa Griswold and Dave Roberts. This was a top team with top investigative and technical skills, and all were committed to working together efficiently and effectively, although Fiona's ambition sometimes rubbed her colleagues up the wrong way. This is the team to catch a killer.

Taking her black marker pen to the whiteboard, Beth said "Ok, team, let's review what we know.

We know that the victim is Jimmy Wheeler, a local loan shark.

The victim was married and living in the village of Ickleford. He has a twin sister who looks a lot like him and, as Jenny found out, lives with their mum in a house at the end of the road where Jimmy and his wife Dawn live.

The victim's eyes and eyelids have been removed. Mac says that this was done after he died, which will be some comfort to his family.

And finally, at the post-mortem earlier, Mac confirmed that the victim hadn't been shot or stabbed, but there was a puncture wound on his back, on the right-hand shoulder. As you all know, 'Mac Doesn't Speculate', so she's sent a sample of blood and hair off to toxicology. I've got a meeting with the Super later, so I'll ask him to put some pressure on the tox team to get the results delivered as quickly as possible.

That's where we are currently. What are your thoughts?"

The team brainstormed a few ideas.

"Revenge killing from someone who's taken a beating in the past."

"Someone can't pay back their loan."

"He's having an affair and someone ain't happy about it."

"He's the first obvious victim of a serial killer."

That last comment chilled Beth to the bone; she'd been worried about the same thing, thinking that this was the beginning of a campaign that wouldn't end until she found the killer, and the pressure of more deaths sat heavily on her shoulders.

"Great thinking – thank you. So let's look at Jimmy the man. Dave, you've had a few encounters with him. What can you tell us?"

Dave cleared his throat. "In all of my dealings with him, he's shown himself to be a very violent man. Unlike many gangsters, he wasn't scared of getting his hands dirty. In fact, according to my sources, he preferred delivering beatings himself to getting one of his minions to deliver the blows on his behalf."

"And what about his personal life?" asked Beth. "I met his wife this morning, what else do we know? Has he got a girlfriend or a boyfriend? If so, who else knows about them?"

"I really don't know, but he did seem to dote on his missus, so I'd be surprised if he was playing away from home. Still, you never know," said Dave with a shrug.

"Okay, thanks Dave. Let's think about the removal of the eyes and eyelids. Why would anyone do that?"

"Maybe he saw something he shouldn't have and instead of telling the authorities, which a man in his position would never do, or just keeping quiet, he tried a spot of blackmail; so the removal of the eyes and eyelids are a warning to others, that if they see something that's none of their business, they should just walk on by?" suggested Dave.

"Good angle," said Beth. "Any other thoughts on this one?"

But there were no other suggestions. The whole team knew that murder with mutilation was rare, and they were dealing with an exceptionally difficult case.

"Ok. Let's go with the idea that he's spotted something illegal or unscrupulous for now. We need to know where he was in the days and weeks leading up to his murder. If he saw something dodgy, did he share that with someone?

Jenny – when I told Dawn and Jackie that Jimmy's eyes and eyelids had been removed, Jackie immediately said it was a 'mob job'. Can you find out what that's all about? I think she knows more than she was prepared to share in front of Dawn earlier, so if you can dig deeper when Jackie's on her own, she might open up to you.

Right. We have three areas to focus on tomorrow: Terry and I will look at Jimmy's personal life; Ki and Dave, look into his business dealings, checking in with Jenny as you go; and Fiona and Clarissa, start looking into everyone who had access to the cathedral from when it was locked up on the night of the murder, to the time Geoffrey Rochester found the body, and check if any of them had any contacts with or even knowledge of our victim.

And I know I don't need to say this, but for the avoidance of doubt, this case is high-profile and sensitive, so please tread carefully."

The team all nodded to confirm that they each understood their brief, and then started to peel away, leaving Beth alone in the squad room at six p.m. *Enough for one day,* thought Beth, as she packed a few files in with her laptop. *Time to see the Super, then home.*

Beth found Donald on his own at his desk.

"Come in," he said, looking up and smiling when he saw Beth sit down. "You've had quite the day. How are you and the team getting along?"

Beth gave him an overview of the day's events, and an update on the team's plans for the coming few days.

"It sounds as though you've covered all relevant areas for now. I'll feed back to the DCC, who's told me he's taking a keen personal interest in the case; that's not surprising given that it's probably the highest profile case he's ever had, and he's retiring in three months, but that means he'll want to go out in a blaze of glory so the pressure on you and the team, which is already intense, will be significant. I'll be as much of a barrier between you and the politics as possible, but I'm not sure I'll be able to absorb all the pressure, so just know that I am here to support you when you need it.

Also, I know that this case is grabbing headlines internationally by now, but the bottom line is that a man has died, and we need to find out who did it and why, to give his family the justice they deserve and to prevent any other deaths."

As she got up to leave, Donald said "Look, Beth, I know I don't need to say this to you, but this case is high-profile and sensitive, so please make sure the team tread carefully," and Beth nodded, thinking how easily she'd slipped into using the Super's language.

When Beth walked to her car, she took out her personal phone and called that familiar number. "Hello darling," said Kate. "I'm guessing that you're working on a very high-profile case that's been on all the news programmes today, national as well as local?"

"You might think that, Kate, but I couldn't possibly comment," smiled Beth. "I'm heading home and I'm going via Kathedral Kebabs if you fancied a large meat and chips?" Beth chuckled, as she saw in her mind's eye her aunt rolling her eyes and sighing at her niece's unhealthy lifestyle, one which she would never consider criticising outright.

"How very kind but no, thank you. I've just had a salmon and lentil dish, with a very nice side salad, so I just haven't got the room for a kebab at the moment, but you go for it and drive carefully. I'll see you in about half an hour."

Beth shut her phone off and smiled warmly. How good it felt after a tough day at work to be going back to a home full of love.

Chapter 6

Clarissa had first spotted Selwyn Du Pont when he was standing behind a pillar next to the Altar of the Sword's Point. Less than an hour after the victim's body was found, Selwyn was straining his neck to see what the police, SOCOs, and pathology team were doing whilst at the same time trying not to be seen himself.

Clarissa had introduced herself, asked if he was okay, listened sceptically to his "I didn't want to get in anyone's way," explanation for concealing himself from the throng of law enforcement staff, then took his statement and asked him to leave.

A tall man, broad man with a mop of shaggy ginger hair, Selwyn Du Pont had been compared to a Highland cow on more than one occasion. Now Canon Missioner at Canterbury Cathedral and a member of Chapter, he had been born into one of England's oldest families. Growing up, he had known privilege that few could even imagine, but as an undergraduate studying Theology, Religion, and Philosophy of Religion at Cambridge University, he did voluntary work with local homeless people, and saw hardship and suffering that shocked him to the core. A summer spent in South Asia introduced him to the effects of poverty on a much greater scale, and he vowed to spend his life in the service of others, to help ease the terrible consequences of poverty.

His first job was as a twenty-two-year-old curate in a coastal parish, where he met and fell in love with the vicar's daughter, twenty-one-year-old Mary, who helped run the local refuge for women and children who had suffered unimaginable abuse at the hands of their partners or parents. Twenty years later, they celebrated their wedding anniversary with Selwyn's appointment to work at Canterbury Cathedral. The couple, who had spent their entire adult lives in god's service, saw this appointment as a huge honour, and ten years later, it remained so for both of them. Mary was again an active member of the local refuge, Selwyn helped the homeless in Canterbury and the surrounding villages, and they both engaged in a lot of extra-curricular activities in their roles; they said they did this to allow colleagues with children to spend more time on family activities, but in truth, it was to help them dull the continuing torment of the cot death which had robbed them of their only child nearly twenty-two years ago, after so many years of hoping to be blessed with children themselves.

This morning, they had lingered over breakfast to give them time to digest the events of the previous day. They sat at their kitchen table, each hugging a mug of tea.

"It was Jimmy Wheeler," said Mary.

"I know," said Selwyn.

"No matter what he did, and we both know better than most how bad a person he was, no one deserves such a terrible end," said Mary.

"I agree," said Selwyn.

"Why put his body at the cathedral? And his eyes. Why on earth would anyone remove his eyes?" asked Mary, shivering.

"Selwyn, I don't feel safe here anymore," said his wife, tearfully. They lived in a large house on the grounds of Canterbury Cathedral, and Selwyn completely understood his wife's concerns.

"I know, my darling, but we are safe here," Selwyn replied. He moved his chair next to his wife and put his arm around her. "Look, I don't know why the murderer removed his eyes, but it does seem rather personal to me. Which makes those of us without his enemies safer, wouldn't you agree?" he asked.

"I want to move, Selwyn," said Mary.

"Oh darling, this is not the right time to think about this. These are very worrying times for the cathedral but we've got a Chapter meeting soon, so hopefully, we can steady the ship. And don't forget, our peppercorn rent is manageable on a stipend. Commercial rents are considerably higher and are too much of a challenge for us at this stage." Selwyn's father had died eighteen months previously, and his oldest brother Tarquin had inherited the family estate, including all the family money. Tarquin made the decision to stop the monthly allowance his father had been giving all his children. Some of Selwyn's siblings had been very vocal about that, but Selwyn and Mary knew their stipend was enough to keep them living a comfortable life, much more comfortable than so many of the homeless and abused people they helped, and any concerns they had about the withdrawal of funds was kept to themselves.

"What if the police find out about what happened, Selwyn?" asked Mary cautiously.

"Then, we will give them the facts," said Selwyn, with an enthusiasm that was entirely manufactured in the hope of reassuring his wife. "Now, I have a meeting to attend, then I have homeless folk to feed, and you have the victims of domestic abuse to support. Come along. I'll drop you at the refuge then I'll pick you up at six p.m. as usual." He gave his wife a long hug, then walked off muttering to find his keys. "Blessed keys. Where are they now?"

Chapter 7

At nine a.m., the southwest door of Canterbury Cathedral remained resolutely closed to the public, as the SOCOs recorded and recovered evidence from the crime scene.

Emma Draper had called an extraordinary meeting of the Chapter, to discuss the extraordinary situation they found themselves in. Her secretary had put out tea, coffee, and biscuits on the large oak table in one of the cathedral's meeting rooms in time to greet all nine members before taking her seat next to Emma, the meeting's Chair. The other eight members were evenly split between four clergy, and four non-executive members appointed due to the commercial experience they could bring to the running of the cathedral.

There were only three items on the agenda; firstly, an update on progress in the police investigation; secondly, how to manage the closure of the cathedral; and finally, how to manage the return to normality when the police finally agreed to reopen the building to the public.

Emma started the meeting by sharing the details of the video catchup she'd had with Superintendent Campbell at eight thirty a.m. that morning, in which he gave her some basic operational details from the investigation. She explained that at this time, his team would be focusing on the victim's history, as well as looking into the cathedral's security.

"Do you have any more detail on their interest in our security system?" asked Elizabeth Jefferson-Briggs. Elizabeth had been the IT Director for an international energy company headquartered in London, and was the cathedral's go-to on all IT strategy and high-level operational IT matters.

"I'm afraid Superintendent Campbell couldn't go into any detail," said Emma.

"Well I'm very happy to call him to act as the link person between the police and the cathedral on all issues relating to the IT side of our security," replied Elizabeth.

Selwyn Du Pont also offered his support. "And I would like to offer my support to the police by acting as the link person between the senior investigating officer and the cathedral, for operational, day-to-day queries. You, Emma, of course will continue to engage with the Superintendent, but if I can support you in any way, do please say."

"That's very helpful, thank you both. I'll call the Superintendent after this meeting to relay your offers and give him your contact details," said Emma, as both Elizabeth and Selwyn nodded their consent.

Secondly, on the largely academic question of when they could reopen the building, all nine members knew that it was a matter over which they had very little influence, as the police had made clear. The four members of the clergy present at the meeting had been deeply shocked by the discovery of the body, and were agreed that the police should be given the time they needed to thoroughly examine the crime scene in order to help bring the killer to justice. The four non-executive members on the other hand, believed that the police should be encouraged to conclude their investigations on that day. The most vocal member of that group was Elizabeth. "I've asked Julian to call the chief constable this morning to impress on him how important it is that the SOCOs are focused and efficient, in order to draw their work here to a close. Today. I'm sure the chief constable will understand and act on Julian's request."

"Thank you, Elizabeth," said Emma. "I'm sure the SOCOs are working as quickly and as thoroughly as they can, and I'm sure we all agree that the keyword there is 'thorough'. The priority is to find the killer, and if that means the cathedral is closed for an extra day or even two to gather evidence, then I agree with the other clerics here, we will have to live with that. All those in favour of this approach, please raise your hands," and by the slightest majority of five to four, the motion to support SOCOs taking the time they needed was carried.

"Thank you," said Emma. "Moving on now to Agenda Item three, this is going to require a very delicate approach. I had a Zoom meeting yesterday with Chapman and Burke, our regular marketing agency, to explain the situation and ask for their advice on how to ensure that the cathedral doesn't become a place that pilgrims would not want to visit, or that it becomes a place where those with a ghoulish disposition would want to make a beeline for to look at a crime scene. Their view was that pilgrims would not be put off visiting Canterbury Cathedral due to a murder – the body was, after all, found on the site of another murder, which we know took place in the building itself, so that should not prove to be a deterrent. With regard to the ghoulish, the agency believes that we should monetise this. Every additional visitor to the cathedral brings in additional income, so why discourage that? I can't deny, I am finding that quite unpalatable. What's the view around the table?" asked Emma.

"I agree with the agency," said Oliver Shepherd, a former Chief Financial Officer with a well-known British charity. "We've got an ever-growing list of maintenance and fixes that we need to address, so all additional income will be most welcome."

"Agreed," said Elizabeth. "There's no way to identify those who will visit in order to have a look at the crime scene, so there's no need to be sentimental about taking money which will be used for essential works."

"Does anyone else have a view?" asked Emma, looking in the direction of the clergy, but there seemed to be general agreement that more income in order to address some of the outstanding building issues would not be a bad thing, so Emma gave further detail on her meeting with the agency. "The agency's advice was to prepare a comprehensive communications strategy to be launched after the initial flurry of activity dies down – possibly as soon as next week – which draws the focus back to the cathedral's history and its purpose. They suggest the Archbishop should do the rounds of major TV and radio stations, as well as the most popular newspapers and magazines, to reinforce the positives of the cathedral. Are you all happy to allow the marketing team to take the lead on this, or do you have any suggestions? The Chapter will, of course, be given copies of all materials for final sign-off."

The vote was seven to two in favour of adopting the marketing agency's strategy, and Emma agreed to discuss the proposal for giving him a high-visibility role with the Archbishop, when he arrived in Canterbury later that day. The visit was, at the Archbishop's request, being kept from the press, because his priority was the wellbeing of the team at the cathedral, especially the three who'd seen the body. There would be plenty of time later for him to deal with queries from the press. For now, the press could deal with the police.

And with that, Emma drew the meeting to a close and asked her secretary to ensure the minutes were circulated to all members by close of play.

"Elizabeth, can I have a quick word before you leave?" asked Emma, as the group were moving towards the door.

"Emma," said Elizabeth. "What can I do for you?"

"Let me start by thanking you very much for all your hard work in the two years since you joined Chapter. Your support has been invaluable. However, going forward, can I ask you to either wait for the Chapter to convene and agree on a position on any new issue, or call me to discuss any issues on your mind, before going ahead and actioning them? I'm sure that Julian's influence with the chief constable will be helpful in future but today, the Chapter has agreed by a majority of five to four that for now, we should wait for the SOCOs to finish their investigations rather than try and influence a premature end to their work. I'm sure you understand and completely support the principle of collective responsibility, and I appreciate your co-operation in implementing this for Chapter."

Elizabeth bristled at this gentle rebuke, but managed a "Yes, of course Emma," before marching away to her car.

Chapter 8

By ten fifteen a.m., Beth and Terry were back in Terry's car on the road to Ickleford. They'd spent an hour checking the police database, and found a few convictions for petty crime when Jimmy was a teenager, which got him a few community orders, and a custodial sentence for breaking and entering when he was in his early twenties – a joint venture with two of his closest associates, Kevin Carter and Jeff Robinson, according to the database – but otherwise, his record was clean, so it was back to his home village to dig out some information from those who loved him, and those who might not.

Ickleford is a quintessential Kentish village – a small main road with small roads branching off; one corner shop with a little post office at the back; and one pub on the main road which served as a social hub for the village. In Ickleford, that pub was called 'The White Hart'.

Beth estimated that the population of Ickleford was eighty-four, Terry guessed three hundred and forty-seven. Beth's competitive spirit kicked in, and she made a mental note to call the local parish council later to get them to settle the matter.

Beth wanted to start the interviews with Dawn, to get an idea of what Jimmy, the man, was like. She then wanted to separate Dawn and Jackie. Jenny had told Beth that Dawn was like a limpet, staying at Jackie's side all day and all night. Jackie, it appeared, was very happy not to leave Dawn on her own. Why? Was she just supporting her old friend or was there something that Dawn knew that Jackie didn't want the investigating officers to know? Beth messaged Jenny on the way to Ickleford to ask her, on Beth's signal, to take Dawn out of the room they were all in, and to make the most of the break to find out if there was anything else Dawn wanted to share with the team. When this was happening, Beth and Terry would be interviewing Jackie. Beth was certain that Jackie had some information that would be helpful for the police, but that it wasn't something she would be keen to share with them. Like brother, like sister.

The journey took just short of an hour, as they waited for a herd of cows to make their way to the milking house. Those B roads were both a pleasure and a pain, but an unavoidable part of life in the countryside.

As they walked up the path to Jimmy's house, Jenny opened the front door and ushered them into one of two luxurious living rooms where they found Dawn, Jackie and an older woman, who appeared to have fashioned herself on Violet Kray, with her sixties hairstyle and twinset. "You know Dawn and Jackie?" said Jenny. "This is Shirley, Jimmy's mother. She and Jackie live in the house at the end of this road but they've both moved in here in the short term."

"We're here to support Dawn," said Shirley. "We hope you won't be dragging your feet on this investigation so we can all start to grieve properly."

Beth and Terry sat down without waiting to be invited.

"We have a whole team working as hard as possible on this investigation," said Beth. "We, like you, would like to find the killer as soon as possible, and that's why we're here this morning. We need to know as much about Jimmy as possible – Jimmy the husband, son, and brother; Jimmy the businessman – and we were hoping that you would be able to help us put together a good picture of who your Jimmy was.

Dawn, tell us a bit about Jimmy – what did he like to do when he wasn't working? Who did he spend time with? Did he go to the 'White Hart' or did he prefer socialising elsewhere?"

Dawn's face lit up as she took the opportunity to tell the police all about Jimmy's great philanthropic work.

"He'd look after anyone, but he was particularly generous with the little children. There's a children's home in the next village; he paid for their new gym, and he was their Santa every Christmas for the last six years." And then, she added quietly, "Jimmy and I tried for children for many years, but it just didn't happen for us. That was always a great sadness for both of us."

"That must have been very difficult for you," said Beth. "Your Jimmy sounds like a very generous man. Can you tell us a bit about his friends and his social times?"

Dawn was again very happy to share a lot of details about who Jimmy liked to hang out with and where. He would pop to the local pub every night for just one drink before going home for dinner, unless he had a business meeting.

"He worked very hard," she stressed.

He had a few friends, more acquaintances really, in their village and a few villages nearby, but his friends were mainly the mates he'd made when he was growing up on the Coxhall Estate, which Beth knew was one of Canterbury's most notorious housing estates, and most of them also worked for him.

"He did look after his friends, did Jimmy," Dawn said, proudly.

When it became clear that Dawn could talk about him until the sun set, but that no new information or great revelations would be shared, Beth signalled to Jenny that now would be a good time to move Dawn away from Jackie and Shirley.

"Let me make you all a cup of tea or coffee," said Jenny. "Dawn, could you give me a hand?" and Dawn dutifully stood and followed her into the kitchen.

"I'll help too," said Shirley, and followed both out of the room. Beth wasn't sure if Shirley wanted to keep an eye on Dawn, or if she didn't want to stay in the room with Beth and Terry and all their questions, but she was glad to have some time alone with Jackie.

"How are you bearing up?" asked Beth.

"As expected," replied Jackie, and Beth knew that getting any information from Jackie would be a considerably harder task than it was with Dawn. It was just a shame that Jimmy appeared to have kept Dawn in the dark about his business dealings.

"Jackie, if we're going to catch Jimmy's killer we need to know who would want him dead," said Beth, thinking that being blunt would be the best approach. "I know that you and him were very close, so did he tell you anything about any threats he might have had recently, or any run-ins he had with anyone who might have decided to take revenge in such a brutal way? I got the sense yesterday that you knew something that you were reluctant to share, but if you're worried or scared, we can look after you." This last comment was met with a raised eyebrow from Jackie.

"You all think Jimmy was a gangster, and he did have a few business dealings that could give him a bit of bother – he used to help people out by lending them some money, and he'd have to be pretty firm with them if they didn't pay him back when they'd agreed they would – but nothing that would end up with someone killing him," said Jackie, and Beth marvelled once more at the capacity of victims' loved ones to see them as helpful or generous, whereas everything she knew about Jimmy Wheeler screeched violent and cruel man.

"But he also had other business dealings, with people further up the food chain, and I really wouldn't put murder past any of them."

Beth's ears pricked up.

"That sounds like it could be really helpful," she said. "Can you tell me some more?"

"I really don't know too many details – Jimmy and I were very close, but business was business, and home was home, so he didn't share that much. All I know is that some posh boys from London had come to Canterbury one day, and put a proposition to Jimmy and he said no. The posh boys tried again, but Jimmy wouldn't be moved. What that proposition was, I do not know, but what I do know is that Jimmy wasn't scared of anyone, he never had been, but he seemed to be pretty scared of this lot, so I reckon if you find them, you'll be closer to finding his killer. Sorry. I really can't help you anymore."

"That's very helpful. Thank you for sharing it, Jackie. Look, I'm really sorry to have to raise this, but what do you think is the significance of what happened to Jimmy's eyes?" asked Beth.

The reply came from behind her.

"He missed nothing, did my Jimmy, so I reckon he saw something that someone else didn't want seen." Beth hadn't seen Shirley come back into the room, but welcomed the opportunity to get another perspective on Jimmy's life.

"Any thoughts on what that might have been, Shirley?" asked Beth.

Shirley shrugged.

"If we're going to find Jimmy's killer, we need to know as much about his life as possible, Shirley. I know some people find it hard to talk to the police, but if you want a quick end to this investigation, then the more help you give us, the more likely that outcome will be." Having had success using the blunt approach with Jackie, Beth hoped the same would apply to Shirley, who appeared to be weighing up the options.

"Go and speak with Kevin Carter," said Shirley. "Now, if there's nothing else, you can leave."

And leave they did, without having the coffee prepared by Jenny and Dawn, but with new information to help them move the investigation forward.

"Right, Terry, it's time we went to the pub," said Beth with a smile.

Chapter 9

Julian Jefferson-Briggs had spent the morning in his constituency office. He'd never known such a busy day, with endless phone calls and emails enquiring about the body at the cathedral, and about his announcement in Parliament the previous day – it hadn't taken the press long to track him to his office in Canterbury, when they couldn't find him in his office in Whitehall.

He told his office manager, Harry, and their part-time administrator, Freya, that all queries relating to the body in the cathedral should be directed to the murder squad, led by Detective Chief Inspector Bethany Harper, and all queries relating to the announcement of the Suicide Prevention Initiative should be directed to him or the Department of Health and Social Care team, led by Rosie Wright.

Julian shared his Department's press release about the new Preventing Suicide initiative with his constituency team so that both were aware of the facts rather than 'the truth as they see it', as Julian had once referred to press enquiries:

Preventing suicide in England: Gambling Suicide Prevention Initiative

Announcing new measures to support citizens with an addiction to gambling who may experience suicidal thoughts.

From: The Department of Health and Social Care and Julian Jefferson-Briggs MP

- Studies have shown that deaths from suicide are significantly higher among adults with a gambling disorder/problem compared to the general adult population.
- A new initiative – backed by five million pounds of government funding – aims to reduce suicide in this group by ten percent in the first year, and by fifty percent in the first five years.

In his speech to the House of Commons today, the Secretary of State for Health and Social Care, Dr Julian Jefferson-Briggs, unveiled a five-million-pound funding package to support those working with gambling addicts in order to reduce the rates of suicide within this group.

Working across the country, a Gambling Suicide Prevention team, led by Dr Charlotte Walton, will share knowledge and expertise with charities and voluntary sector organisations in order to provide targeted support for addicts experiencing suicidal thoughts.

In addition to this, the government will introduce legislation to regulate advertising and sponsorship by gambling companies, and will put measures in place to prevent those organisations from employing Members of Parliament to lobby on their behalf.

The Secretary of State for Health, Dr Julian Jefferson-Briggs, said:

"An addiction to gambling can ruin lives and, far too often, can take lives. We remain committed to the principles outlined in *'Preventing Suicide in England: A cross-government outcomes strategy to save lives'*, which was first published in 2012, and aim to build on its success with a targeted approach in relation to gambling addiction.

I have today announced a five-million-pound fund to support this work, which brings the total sum invested in this hugely important work to sixty-two million pounds."

"That's an excellent initiative," said Harry. "Should play well with the voters. What's the reaction been like so far?"

"I can tell you that the most negative reaction came not from the gambling companies but from my colleagues on the back benches, who can see their lucrative lobbying fees disappearing, and they are not happy, Harry. The gambling companies are concerned about the detail in the proposed legislation surrounding advertising and sponsorship, and I understand their legal teams are working together to agree a statement and present a united front. The only other reactions I've heard have been positive but of course, it's early days."

"How much do we know about the body in the cathedral?" asked Freya.

"Very little at this stage," replied Julian. "I had a call with the chief constable of East Kent this morning, and he was obviously very cautious when sharing information about a live investigation, but I understand that they've identified the victim and are currently looking into his history for a motive and any suspects. Nasty old business, isn't it. What's the general feeling in the city?"

"Nervous," replied Harry. "There's a rumour that the victim's eyes, ears, nose and tongue were removed which has made the murder of a local man a much more frightening prospect. I know that the overall crime rate in Canterbury remains low for a city of this size, but it has been increasing steadily over the past few years and people are starting to get anxious about it. I think it would be very helpful for the police to confirm or deny the rumours about the victim's facial features in order to calm the public mood, but there's also an opportunity here for you to speak with the home secretary and launch a Canterbury Crime-Reduction Initiative, one which has your name closely associated with it, and if we could do that before the local elections, that would be excellent." He lowered his voice and shrugged "And, of course, it will do your career no harm to be seen to be tough on crime."

"I agree that rumours are a curse during difficult times like these, and I will share that with the chief constable when I call him tomorrow morning for the next update. I also agree that a local initiative to tackle the rising crime rate is very important, especially as we'll be starting to campaign for the local elections at the end of next month. Leave that with me, and I'll buy the home secretary a Bellini when I'm back in Westminster," said Julian.

Freya asked when Julian planned on returning to his Westminster office to which the reply was "As soon as possible." At that point, his wife, Elizabeth, swept in.

"Good morning, Elizabeth," offered Harry cheerily.

"Is it," she barked in reply. "Julian. Can I see you in your office?" She threw open the office door and Julian, who'd seen this mood so many times before, dutifully followed her in, closing the door behind him in an attempt at noise reduction. He was met with a full forty minute update on the Chapter meeting, and how dare Emma talk to her in that way. She wasn't a child!

Julian had expected a fractious atmosphere in the days after the discovery of the body, and had a plan to calm the choppy waters around him; he suggested a long lunch at

Elizabeth's favourite Canterbury restaurant. It worked. As Julian and Elizabeth left the constituency office, Julian told Harry that he was available on his mobile for emergency calls only, and turned his attention to the fine bottle of red they would soon be enjoying.

Chapter 10

The White Hart was a beautiful pub, full of old world charm. It had an inglenook fireplace and oak beams on the ceilings and walls, but the one thing it didn't have today was many customers. A couple of Japanese tourists sat in one of the window seats, gingerly trying a plate of fish and chips, but otherwise, Beth and Terry were alone with Mark, the barman who was also the pub's landlord.

"What can I get you?" he asked cheerfully, when they entered through the heavy oak door.

"Just some information, thanks," replied Beth, as she and Terry flashed their warrant cards at him.

"Always happy to help the police with their enquiries," replied Mark. "What's this about, officer?"

"You may have heard that the body of one of your neighbours, Jimmy Wheeler, was found at Canterbury Cathedral yesterday. The post-mortem has confirmed that he was murdered, and I'm heading the team that's investigating this crime," said Beth.

"It sounds like a pretty violent attack," said Mark. "We heard someone had poked his eyes out? That was a massive shock. His murder? Less so. Did they poke his eyes out? And did they put his eyes in his mouth? That's what one of my regulars heard from a friend of his, who works for the Kent Online Daily."

"Sorry, Mark, we can't talk about the details of the case at the moment, but we will share as much as we can just as soon as we can. In the meantime, it would be a great help to us if you could tell us as much as you know about the person Jimmy was, who his friends were, and any business dealings you were aware of," said Terry. "Did you see him in here often?"

"Jimmy used to pop in here most nights at about seven p.m. to 'get out from under my feet while I make his dinner', according to Dawn. He'd order one drink, a whiskey and ginger – ale, not beer – and take a seat at the end of the bar to sup it. He'd leave between seven thirty p.m. and seven forty-five p.m., never any later than that because dinner would be on the table at eight p.m. and he needed to choose and open the wine before then. He was crazy about that wife of his, and did everything he could to live up to her expectations of life in a Kentish village."

"Did he have many friends in the village?"

"I think his friends were mainly over in Canterbury. I think they all grew up together on a pretty tough estate so there were strong bonds. He used to bring a few of them in here when they were visiting him and Dawn, say for a Bank Holiday barbecue. The two I remember most clearly were Kevin and Jeff. They were both perfectly well behaved when they were here, but you know when you get that vibe off someone not to get too close or there'll be trouble? Well, that's the vibe I used to get off both of them

63

but Kevin in particular. That said, we only really saw his friends about two or three times a year, so it was no bother.

He didn't really have any friends in the village, I don't think. He'd perch at the end of the bar and talk to whoever stood or sat next to him, but only general chit chat about the football or snooker; Jimmy was a big snooker fan. I think the one person Jimmy was as close to being a friend to in the village was Guy Fanshawe, but you'd need to speak to him about that."

"What can you tell us about Mr Fanshawe?" asked Terry.

"He's lived in the village for about six years now. He comes here most nights, arriving at seven p.m., and he used to take a seat next to Jimmy if there was one free. Guy works in London for a big financial company, and his commute always gets him back here for seven, so he'll pop in for a pint or two on his way home. It's a habit he's carried on since lockdown, even when he's working from home. Like I said, Jimmy mainly talked about football or snooker, but with Guy, they would often move away from the bar and grab a table to talk. I don't know this for a fact, but I think they knew each other before they both arrived in Ickleford."

"Do you know much about Guy's job?" asked Beth.

"Nah, people are very chatty, especially when they've had a few sherbets, but there's some stuff they never talk about, and the detail of his job is one of Guy's private matters."

"Do you know much about Jimmy's business dealings? It's not cheap to live in a village like this," asked Terry.

"I know that he was 'flush with his funds' as my grandmother used to say. Him and Dawn didn't have children, or, according to my missus, couldn't have them, but they both loved kids and spent a lot of money on the children's home in the next village. So yes, very generous with the young ones, and always the first to put his hand in his pocket when he brought his friends in.

My grandmother was talking about pawn brokers being flush with their funds but I guess we can include loan sharks in that." Mark saw a hint of surprise on Terry's face when he said that. "Yes, we knew what he did for a living, and we'd heard that he could be very handy with his fists with those 'clients' who missed a repayment, but none of that happened in here so none of it is really my business."

"That's all very helpful. Thanks Mark. Is there anything else you can think of that could help with the investigation?" asked Beth.

"Nope. that's it I'm afraid. That's all I know about Jimmy Wheeler, the man who was murdered and had his eyes poked out. Christ, that's really awful. I hope you catch the sick bastard soon."

"Okay. Well if anything else comes to mind, please get in touch with me or Terry," said Beth, and they both handed Mark their business cards. "And many thanks for your help. We'll probably be back soon to try that fish and chips!" she said, as Terry held open the heavy door.

And with that, two new customers walked in and Mark made a beeline for them.

"Well, that was interesting," said Terry. "So, some top level take aways are: If Jimmy was having an affair, he was doing it during working hours because he seemed to be at home with his wife from seven forty-five p.m. nearly every night. He may have moved home geographically but his heart still seemed to be on the Coxhall Estate in Canterbury. He pretty much kept himself to himself in this village, apart from one resident with whom he had more than just a passing acquaintance in the pub; Guy Fanshawe. And his reputation as a thug was well known to everyone who knew him apart from to his family."

"There are none so blind as those who will not see," said Beth, and she and Terry stared at each other.

"Well now, there's another angle on the eye removal. Very interesting. Well done, Guv! When will you hold the first press conference to share details of the case? Rumours like the ones Mark mentioned are bound to happen when facts aren't available to the public, though I'm not too sure how much detail we want to release about Jimmy's mutilations, otherwise we'll have every fantasist in Kent and beyond on the phone confessing to his murder."

Beth was about to reply when her phone rang. It was Clarissa. "Morning Guv. Traffic have phoned. They've found an abandoned car on the B257. It's registered to a James Wheeler of Ickleford. They've got a car transporter booked to pick it up late afternoon, but there'll be a traffic officer with the car until it arrives, so if you'd like to have a look, you've got a few hours to get over there. I've emailed the location's co-ordinates over to you."

"That's great; many thanks Clarissa. Can you ask traffic to send us all CCTV footage for the nearby roads from five p.m. on the day of Jimmy's murder? We're heading towards his car right now," said Beth, as she plugged the co-ordinates into her phone's satnav and filled Terry in on the development.

Chapter 11

The Coxhall Estate was a collection of eight blocks of low-rise flats. Each one had four floors; two of the blocks had once had shops and cafes and fast-food stores all across the ground floor, but most of those were now boarded up. The mood on the estate was as grey as the concrete used to build the blocks, and no matter how good the mood of its visitors on arrival, The Cox, as its residents called it, soon wore them down.

"Right," said Ki Wong. "Let's get to work. What's the flat number for the first known associate?"

Dave Roberts smiled at his friend's efficiency. Ki was always one to get straight to the heart of the matter. His parents had moved from Guangzhou to Canterbury when Ki was three months old and his brother was five. The move had been prompted by the disappearance of his maternal grandfather, who was vocal in his dissent against his country's government.

On arrival, Ki's parents worked in local shops and restaurants, but soon took out a business loan to fund a restaurant of their own in the St Dunstan's area. They worked hard, working long hours day and night, leaving the boys in the care of Ki's maternal grandmother. Their hard work was rewarded with a decent lifestyle in a beautiful city where they all felt safe.

His parent's work ethic was shared by both Ki and his brother, who, at the age of sixteen, followed his father into the kitchen at their restaurant. Ki was expected to join his mother front of house, but he wanted something different. Something that made a difference. Ki was very close to his grandmother, who kept her husband's memory alive by telling him stories of his grandfather's activism, and as he got closer to leaving school, Ki realised that working for the police force in his new home would meet his need to make a difference to the lives of others, and would also, in some small way, send a signal that a society needed to be policed and protected by a state which cared for its citizens, and not put them in fear of their lives.

"Block two, number eleven. Kevin Carter. Jimmy's best mate from school and his wingman on The Cox," said Dave, who had spent the best part of the morning doing his homework.

Ki and Dave made their way to number eleven but their knocks went unanswered. The same applied to Jeff Robinson at number twelve in Block one.

"Well," said Ki. "This is turning into a productive morning. How many more known associates did Jimmy have, and how many of those live on The Cox?"

"Two more associates, Gary Nixon and Mikey Curtis, both of whom live in this illustrious estate," replied Dave. "Next up, Gary; Block four, number nine."

This time, their knocks did not go unanswered. The door to number nine opened to reveal an elderly woman, immaculately presented.

"Who is it, Nanna?" bellowed a young man in one of the rooms behind her.

"Hello, my dears," said Nanna. "And who are you?"

Ki and Dave presented their warrant cards.

"Good morning, madam," said Ki. "We're looking for Gary Nixon. Is he in?"

"It's a couple of coppers, Gary. Are you in?" asked Nanna.

A strapping young man appeared in the hallway behind her.

"What do you want?" asked Gary. "I haven't done anything."

"We just want to have a chat with you about Jimmy Wheeler. We understand you used to work for him?"

"He did," said Nanna. "His dad, my son Martin, god rest his soul, was a good mate of Jimmy's. When he was knocked down and killed on the road, Jimmy told me he'd look after Gary, and that's what he did from that day to this. And your lot never caught the driver who killed my boy," she said accusingly.

"You okay to make us all a cup of tea, Nanna?" asked Gary. When Nanna nodded, Gary held his arm out to invite Ki and Dave into their beautifully-decorated living room. "Sorry, Nanna's not over dad's death. Someone said to me at his funeral, and I'll never forget these words, 'natural

order dictates that parents should die before their children'
and she's living proof of that, god love her.

Anyway, I'm guessing you're here about Jimmy's
murder? I don't know anything about that, or anything
about anyone who might know something about that, so
I'm not going to be much help to you, but if there's
anything I can do to help you catch that scum, I'll be happy
to help, so if you have any questions, ask away."

"That's great. Thanks very much, Gary. Can you tell
us what you did for Jimmy?" asked Ki.

"Just a bit of this and a bit of that, depending on what
he needed doing that day. Pick up his suit from the dry
cleaners. Go and buy some flowers for him to take home
to Dawn. Make sure people saw my biceps so they didn't
start any trouble. But mainly just driving him around
Canterbury and the villages to his business meetings. He'd
drive from home to here, then I'd drive until he was ready
to go home. He said a chauffeur-driven car showed people
that he was a real player, not some two-bit loan shark –
those are his words, not mine."

"What time did he leave you to drive home on the
night of his murder?" asked Dave.

"Same time as always," replied Gary. "We'd get back
here at around six p.m. and he'd drive straight home from
here."

"Did you go to any of those business meetings with
him?" asked Ki.

"Nah, never," replied Gary. "If he was in a meeting, I was in the car. If he was in the office, I was in the room next door."

"Where is his office?" asked Dave

"It's his flat here on The Cox. Block two, number twelve. He bought it as soon as he had a few quid in the bank, but I'm not sure why he was holding on to it – sentimental value, my Nan says."

"Ah right. So he lived next door to Kevin Carter. Don't suppose you know where we can find Kevin today? He wasn't at home when we knocked earlier," said Dave.

"Sorry. No idea. We're all at a bit of a loose end at the moment, without Jimmy telling us what needs doing."

Dave nodded empathetically.

"Do you know anything about the loans side of the business?" asked Ki.

"Nothing," said Gary. "I was just a driver."

"Right. So these business meetings of his. Were they always business, or were some of them pleasure?" asked Dave.

"He used to take some of his business associates out to lunch, but I don't think that's what you're asking me, is it? I'll just say this – he loved his Dawn and I never saw him ever look at another woman in that way," said Gary.

Dave paused before asking the next question. "You knew Jimmy probably as well as anyone, Gary. Do you know of anyone at all who wanted to hurt him or said they wanted to kill him?"

"To be honest, I heard a load of people say they wanted to hurt him over the years. Not so many said they wanted to kill him but for those who did, we none of us took them seriously. He could really look after himself, could Jimmy. Well, that's what we all thought," replied Gary and clenched his fists to control his emotions.

"Okay. Last question, Gary," said Ki. "Have you heard about the posh boys who came down from London?"

"Posh boys? A lot of Jimmy's business meetings were with blokes in posh suits and fancy shoes, but I couldn't tell you any more than that. I wish I could help you more. Jimmy was very good to me and I want to do right by him and get that murdering bastard off the streets," replied Gary.

"You've been very helpful, Gary. Thank you very much for your co-operation. If you hear anything about the murder, or Jimmy's business dealings, anything at all that might help us catch his killer, then please get in touch with me or Dave," said Ki, as he and Dave handed Gary their contact cards.

"Here's your tea," said Nanna, as she walked into the room.

"Sorry, Nanna, but these gentlemen have got to go now. I'll have a second cuppa though," said Gary.

"I'll join you darlin'," said Nanna, with a warm smile.

Chapter 12

It took just twelve minutes for Beth and Terry to reach Jimmy's car.

"God, he was nearly home," said Terry, as they parked up and he stepped out of his car. Beth was already at Jimmy's car, wearing disposable gloves, trying every door and the boot, but they were all locked and as his keys hadn't been found on his body, nor had they been dropped anywhere near the car, there was no way in.

They'd found Jimmy's silver Range Rover Sport in a layby, big enough for three cars on the main road leading in to Ickleford.

"That's a Lord of the Manor car," said Terry. "Ties in with what Mark told us earlier, about Dawn having firm views on what life in the countryside should be like. Might be worth checking to see how happy Jimmy was, living in the country rather than in the city with his friends."

"Good angle," said Beth, as she peered into Jimmy's car. "The inside of this car is pristine. No scuff marks anywhere so it doesn't look as though he was taken by force. There's no blood in there, as far as I can see, so it doesn't look as though he was killed or mutilated in this car. So what happened? How did the killer get him to stop his car and voluntarily get out? A 'business' meeting, do you think? Was he meeting someone here who decided the only way to settle their debt was to get rid of the man who owned it? Or did he meet someone who wanted to take over his patch and was prepared to kill for it? Is that where the posh boys come in? Doesn't really fit with the description, but we can't ignore it."

"Great points. I think that someone who couldn't meet their debts any more is the most likely scenario, but the other questions are plausible and definitely worth looking into," replied Terry. "Guv, something's been niggling away at me all morning, and seeing this very expensive car has helped confirm it. I just think it's a little unlikely that a loan shark from a rough estate in a city can afford a luxury lifestyle in the country. Buying his own house on the council estate he grew up on, or in a more expensive estate nearby, is far more in keeping with the sort of money we're talking about here, don't you think?"

"Yes, I've been thinking much the same," said Beth. "He's either got a network that stretches hundreds of miles in order to make that sort of money, or he's got other business interests that we're not yet aware of. It's something to raise with Ki, Dave and Jenny at the four p.m. debrief. Talking of which, we need to head back to base because I've got a three p.m. meeting with the head of Organised Crime, and I need some lunch before then. For your information – and you'll thank me for this one day – Marge also does a lush sausage and onion huffkin, and I can hear one calling my name. Come on, Terry, let me introduce you to one of Kent's finest lunches."

They'd just started the journey to Canterbury when Beth's phone rang. "Hi Mac, lovely to hear from you. You're not calling to tell me that the Super's nag yesterday worked, and the tox report is back already, are you?" asked Beth, more in hope than expectation.

"Today, my dear, is your lucky day," replied Mac. "Yesterday, Donald and I performed a pincer movement on the toxicology team and yes, the report has been completed and sent to me. I have been called domineering. Me? Imagine such a thing.

Anyway, I can confirm that the victim died from a large overdose of oramorph, a liquid form of morphine. It's prescribed as a pain killer for severe pain. The most obvious use is for cancer patients, but it's also used to ease breathlessness associated with COPD and so on, so there's quite a supply out there."

Beth was familiar with oramorph, which Kate had been prescribed a few months earlier.

"Thank you so much for using your influence, or should I say your charm, to get that over to us this quickly, Mac. I owe you a plate of spag bol and a bottle of red!" replied Beth, before hanging up and giving Terry an update.

"God, finding the source of the drug won't be easy. It's legitimately prescribed to people who live in their own homes, and to people who live in care homes and, of course, for those who know where to look, it'll be available on the streets. But we can start by checking in with the Drug Squad to see what the market for opioids is like in Kent, then we can get in touch with the NHS to ask if there have been any break-ins at pharmacies recently, or if they know of any unusual prescriptions being issued or fulfilled. I'll get on to it when we get back to the office."

"Great, thanks Terry. Can you make Guy Fanshawe your priority this afternoon and ask Dave to help out with the oramorph angle? If Jimmy had just one friend, no matter how loosely associated they are in his home village, I'd like to know more about him."

"No worries Guv. There's Marge's Manor – do you want me to park outside and wait for you, or will you walk back to base?"

"Terry Corfe, know this. I buy Marge's food to build up my energy levels, which I then preserve until I need, not want but need, to expend some. I will see you here in two minutes," said Beth, as she jumped out with a smile.

Chapter 13

"Well that was pretty helpful," said Ki, as he closed the front door to Gary's flat behind him. "Let me give Jenny a ring to ask her if Dawn still has a set of keys to their old flat, and if she's happy for us to have access to it."

"Aye, that'll be the quickest way to get into his office," said Dave. "Then, shall we see if Mikey Curtis is home before grabbing some lunch at the greasy spoon in Block two? There were quite a few customers in there when we walked past earlier, so if they're all local, we could get some good info on Jimmy." Ki nodded, rolling his eyes at the thought of lunch at a greasy spoon in The Cox, and wondering if he still had that pack of indigestion tablets in the glove box of his car. "Great. Next stop Block six, number seven."

Ki knocked the door, then knocked again. As they were about to leave number seven, they saw the kitchen blinds twitch.

"Mikey, it's the police. Open up. We just wanted to talk to you about Jimmy." said Dave.

All quiet in number seven.

"Mikey," said Dave. "Dawn is heartbroken. Absolutely heartbroken. She needs Jimmy's killer off the streets so she can start to grieve properly. And Jackie and

Shirley are heartbroken too. If Jimmy could see them now he would be crushed. We need help to find his killer, Mikey. Can you let us in?"

As Ki and Dave stood in front of the door to number seven, they heard a key going into a lock and then they were looking at Mikey Curtis. A broad man, reportedly the same age as Jimmy, he had the face of a man twenty years older. His white vest revealed a number of tattoos, with names of past girlfriends sitting alongside images of naked women. Dave guessed they were not one and the same people.

"Come in if you're coming in," he said gruffly, then quickly marked his territory. "I'll do anything for Dawn and Jackie – we were all in the same class in primary school and we've been together ever since – but all I'm giving you is anything that might help catch the bastard who killed Jimmy, so don't bother asking me about anything else."

As Ki and Dave walked into the living room, a woman in a very short t-shirt and very little else, walked from the bathroom to the bedroom. *There's another name for his arm,* thought Dave, as he nodded and smiled at her genially.

"Who wanted him dead, Mikey?" asked Ki, knowing that keeping this brief and to the point was the best way to get the most useful information.

"No one that I know of. And that's the truth. He had a reputation as a tough guy, but he was fair and didn't make the enemies you think he would have," said Mikey.

"Who are the posh boys from London?" asked Dave.

Mikey looked puzzled. "No idea who you're talking about. I didn't work on that side of the business."

"What side of the business is that?" asked Ki.

"The 'none of my business' side of the business," replied Mikey.

"So what side of the business was your business, Mikey?" asked Ki.

"I worked with Jimmy on the loans," he replied.

"I heard Jimmy could be handy with his fists when people missed their repayments," said Dave.

"You don't want to believe everything you hear," said Mikey.

"Mikey, let's stop pissing about shall we?" said Dave. "Jimmy was a loan shark who made enemies. If one of those wanted him dead, they succeeded. So, who might want him dead, Mikey? Who owes him money but can't meet the repayments? Who's taken a beating and sworn that he or she would take revenge?"

"Know this," barked Mikey, with a menacing look in his eye, "Jimmy never, ever laid a finger on a woman, so make sure no one ever thinks that. But he might have given a few blokes a few slaps. You might want to have a word with Muhammad Khan. He wasn't paying his dues so Jimmy had a word. I hear Muhammad's been shooting his gob off since then, calling Jimmy all sorts and saying he'll get him back. Fuck sake. Like he's even half the man Jimmy was."

"Thanks Mikey. Where can we find this Muhammad?" asked Ki.

"He lives on The Cox. Block three, number two. But you didn't hear that from me."

Both Ki and Dave nodded their thanks.

"So what about people who can't pay back their loans? Anyone struggling and making threats?" asked Ki.

"Michelle Crossfield, Block three, number eight. Again, you didn't hear that from me. She's the only one I know of who's been shooting her gob off, saying the rates are fucking ridiculous and she's going to tell the press. Like anyone gives a fuck about people like us, who live on estates like The Cox. But I heard she'd been saying her money worries would be over soon, and her brother is an ex-army man with a short fuse, or so I heard, so it's worth having a word with her. Apart from them two, I honestly don't know of anyone else who might want to properly hurt Jimmy, or anyone who could. Now, if you don't mind, I have company so..." and with that, Mikey escorted Ki and Dave to the front door.

As they left number seven, Dave's stomach grumbled.

"Come on, time for a greasy spoon," he said, and Ki reluctantly followed him to the stairwell.

As they walked in to the greasy spoon, they found as many customers as staff. The young man behind the counter issued a cheery "Hello gents, take a seat and Mel will be with you shortly," nodding to the young waitress who smiled warmly at them, before finishing clearing a table which six hungry customers had just left.

The two remaining customers were an elderly pair who looked as though they'd been coming to the caff for many years. They looked up as Ki and Dave walked in, then went back to their all-day breakfasts.

Ki took a seat at a table and Dave went to the counter to flash his warrant card.

"We're investigating the murder of Jimmy Wheeler," he said. "We're gathering some background on the victim, and wondered if you could help us."

"Sorry, no. I didn't really know him," replied Counter Guy.

Dave turned to the waitress, who was back after taking a stack of dirty dishes to the kitchen. "We're looking into Jimmy Wheeler's background," he said. "Is there anything you can tell us about anyone who might have wanted to harm him?"

"Sorry, no," she replied. "I read about his murder in the paper this morning, but I didn't really know him."

"Really?" Dave directed the question to both Counter Guy and the waitress.

Ki watched as the elderly couple exchanged a 'course not' look.

"Yes, really," said Counter Guy, with a look Dave thought was fear.

"Didn't he ever come in here? When he was visiting his flat?" asked Dave.

"Look, I really can't help you," said Counter Guy, turning away.

"I met his wife a couple of times," said the waitress, looking nervous. "Poor love, she must be gutted, but I really didn't know anything about her husband that could be helpful to your inquiry, officer."

Dave joined Ki at their table, which Ki had deliberately chosen directly next to the two customers.

"Is there anything you can tell us about Jimmy Wheeler?" Dave asked them, hopefully.

"He was a rotten little bastard. Used to come in here a few times a week," said the elderly man. "If you took a loan from Jimmy, you'd better meet your repayments on the dot, otherwise he would make sure you never missed another one. My wife and I have lived on this estate for forty-five years and we've watched Jimmy and his mates grow up. Jimmy was always the leader, and he always liked using his fists, so he attracted the wrong 'uns on the estate from a young age. We told our boys to keep well away from the lot of them."

"Did anyone say they wanted him dead?" asked Ki.

"Pretty much everyone on the estate wanted to see the back of him," said the elderly man. "But I can't think of anyone who could or would actually kill him. This is real life, mate, not a film."

"What about Muhammad Khan?" asked Dave.

The elderly woman chuckled. "He's all mouth and no trousers, him. I've heard his threats towards Jimmy. I've also seen him run in the opposite direction like a rat up a drainpipe, when Jimmy or his mates were anywhere nearby. Ha! The idea that he could murder Jimmy is funny enough, but we heard the murderer took his eyes out and put them in a pickling jar next to one of altars. There's no way Muhammad would have the guts do something like that."

"We know that Jimmy kept his old flat and was in it several times a week. Did you ever see anyone suspicious hanging around his flat or his block?" asked Dave, who wasn't at all surprised to have that question met with a laugh from both diners.

"Fair do's," said Dave. "Well, if you can think of anything that could help our inquiry, will you give either of us a ring?" he asked, as both he and Ki handed over their contact cards, more in hope than expectation. This time, they were both surprised.

"No problem, officers," said the elderly man. "We live in Block two so we'll ask our neighbours if they can think of anything, because they're more likely to talk to us than to you, and if anyone does come up with anything, we'll be in touch."

Ki and Dave thanked them both for their help then turned their attention to the menu. Ki wondered where he could pick up a bottle of Febreze.

Chapter 14

Fiona Richardson was furious with Beth. Her thought process was clear. After graduating with an upper second in law from Cardiff University, she joined East Kent Police and was soon on their fast-track programme. She moved quickly through the ranks and became a Detective Inspector two years ago aged twenty-eight. She had set her sights on being the first woman Chief Constable in Kent, and was confident that things were progressing to plan, until she was given the task of looking at members of the cathedral's staff and management teams, to see if any of them had a motive to murder and mutilate a local loan shark. What had Beth called it? *'Sensitive'*, that was it. Well it was more than sensitive. Looking into the history of senior staff, including for example the wife of the local MP for god's sake, wasn't just sensitive, it could be a career-breaker if it wasn't handled correctly, and Fiona was sufficiently self-aware to know that she was not the most sensitive soul in the force. She had tried to view this as a dry run for the politics she'd have to deal with from Superintendent level up, but that hadn't eased her fury. Her best friend, Jody, had suggested that this should be viewed as an opportunity to appear on the radar of the great and the good, to get her name and face known among those who could help her career, and that she should stop viewing this in a negative light, start seeing the positives in the situation and start working on her inter-personal skills. Fiona had slept on it and, although she still had reservations, she decided to make an effort and try to take Jody's advice.

Fiona had done her homework and knew that Canterbury Cathedral is one of many buildings within the cathedral precincts. Since 1520, access to the precinct has been through the Christ Church Gate, a heavy wooden gate with heraldic shields on the outside, and a beautiful vaulted roof on the inside. After walking through the gate, the twenty-four-hour security office, known by cathedral staff as the Constables' Lodge, was found immediately on the left-hand side. The security at the cathedral is in the hands of the Close Constables, who have historically worked very closely with the local police, and it was this office that Fiona and Clarissa entered with warrant cards held high.

"Good morning," said Fiona. "Can we speak with the most senior member of staff here today?"

The middle-aged, slightly overweight man sitting in a comfortable, aged armchair, supping a hot mug of tea held his hand up. "That'll be me then," he said. "I'm Arthur. Arthur Lloyd. I'm the cathedral Sergeant in charge of today's shift."

"Hello Arthur, I'm Detective Inspector Fiona Richardson and this is my colleague, Detective Constable Clarissa Griswold. We're investigating the death of Jimmy

Wheeler, whose body was found at the Altar of the Sword's Point."

"Very nice to meet you both," replied Arthur, extending a hand to Clarissa then Fiona. Fiona bristled at the perceived slight. "I was in charge of the evening shift on the night that body was placed in the cathedral, so that's handy. What can I do to help you, officers?" he asked, hauling himself up from the chair.

"Thank you, Arthur," said Fiona. "Let's start with your normal security practices. Can you walk us through your security checks?"

"Yes, of course. We normally have a team of four constables working every morning shift, from six a.m. to two thirty p.m., four constables working every afternoon shift, from two p.m. to ten thirty p.m., and two constables working the night shift, from ten p.m. to six thirty a.m. Each team of constables has a half-hour handover with their colleagues before they start their shift.

One member of the morning shift opens the cathedral doors at seven a.m. and does a walk-around to check that everything's alright, and one member of the afternoon shift locks the doors at eight p.m., and also does a walk-around to check that everything's okay."

"That's interesting," said Fiona. "Do any of your team go in and check the cathedral after the housekeeping staff have finished their shift at eleven p.m.?"

"No, we don't. Once we've finished our checks at eight p.m. we won't enter the building again until seven a.m. the following morning, unless we're called there for any reason."

"Any reason such as?" asked Fiona.

"Oh, the ladies might need a hand carrying some of their rubbish bags out if they've overfilled them. You know the sort of thing," replied Arthur.

"So, going back to the security detail. During the day, we have two constables posted on the Christ Church Gate, meeting and greeting the public and answering their questions, and the other two on patrol around the precinct. There's an established route for this, and I can walk you around it if that would help? And I can walk you around the cathedral as well, showing you all exit and entry points as well as the internal doors and corridors."

"It would be a great help for us to get a good sense of the buildings within the precinct and the layout of the cathedral, particularly the routes leading to the Altar of the Sword's Point," said Clarissa. "Many thanks for the offer." She shot Arthur a beaming smile. He warmed to her immediately, sensing that her colleague might be more difficult to please.

"Delighted," he smiled in return. "Follow me."

Arthur took Fiona and Clarissa on an hour's walk around the grounds, ending the journey with a detailed tour of the cathedral. When they arrived back at the Constables' Lodge, he took his guests into his office, offered them a cup of tea, and asked if they had any questions.

"So apart from checking the building when you unlock its doors in the morning, and checking it again after your team have locked its doors at night, the security team doesn't enter the cathedral at all. Is there a reason for that?" asked Fiona.

"It's not that we wouldn't enter it at all," replied Arthur. "If there's an incident, we're called and we respond no matter where it is in the precincts. We just don't enter it as a matter of course. I'd say that's historical; as I understand it, for many centuries, anyone involved in the security of the cathedral had to get the Dean's permission every time they needed to enter the building. Isn't that weird? But as a result, I think out of habit, the security presence within the cathedral itself is kept to a minimum at all times, but especially when worshippers and visitors are inside."

"So, on the night of the murder, did you or your team notice anything unusual? Anything suspicious?" asked Fiona.

"Not at all," replied Arthur. "This has all come as a complete shock to every one of us."

"What about in the build up to the murder. Did you see anyone suspicious hanging around? Have you had any break-ins or attempted break-ins at the cathedral recently?" asked Clarissa.

"Nothing's been reported to me or the other Cathedral Sergeants about any suspicious activity in the past month. We had a meeting about this yesterday, so I can be certain I speak for all Sergeants. As for attempted break-ins, again no, nothing to report for well over two years. Sorry. This really isn't helpful," said Arthur, smiling weakly at Clarissa.

"We've taken a statement from Geoffrey Rochester who, as we know, found the body," said Fiona. "Geoffrey spoke with Philip Crossfield and told us that when Philip checked the building after locking the doors that night, there was nobody at the Altar of the Sword's Point and he saw nobody elsewhere in the cathedral. Clarissa has taken statements from the Head Housekeeper and the three cleaners who were on duty that night, and none of them saw a body at the altar or anything suspicious between the time they entered the cathedral at nine p.m., or the time they left at eleven p.m., but unfortunately, we can't confirm that for the time they left, because it was dark and the internal CCTV cameras weren't working, so we have no recordings for that time. If we assume that the body was tied to the altar between eleven p.m., when the cleaners left, and seven a.m. the following morning, when Geoffrey found the body, and I can confirm that SOCOs found no evidence of any forced entry, we can assume that either the murderer has a set of keys to the cathedral doors, or they were in the cathedral when Philip and, or, the cleaners were. Let's focus on the keys first. Do you have a list of all the keyholders?"

"There are only two sets of keys to the cathedral," said Arthur. "One set is permanently kept in that locked key safe on the wall, to the side of the filing cabinet, in case anything should happen to the other set, and that other set is only ever handed to a list of trusted staff and volunteers.

The keys are always signed out and signed back in again, so we have a full record of who has ever been handed the keys. I can email a copy through to you, if that would be helpful?"

"That would be excellent, thanks Arthur," said Fiona with a smile, and she extended her hand to shake his. *Interpersonal skills are easy,* she thought.

Chapter 15

Beth walked into the squad room for the four p.m. debrief with an unknown, smartly dressed woman in her mid-thirties in tow.

"Team, meet Andrea Walker. Andrea's a DI in the organised crime squad, and has got a lot of experience of untangling dodgy financial doings, which could be very helpful when we're looking at Jimmy's business dealings; so, her boss has very generously agreed that we can have some of Andrea's time. We need to use it wisely. Andrea, meet the team," said Beth, sweeping a hand across the room. "Details to follow," she said, with a smile.

"Okay, I've given Andrea an update on what happened yesterday, so she's joining us today to meet our motley crew – that's you – and get an overview of where we are with the case, after which she will only join the debriefs when she has uncovered new details, or we need to pick her colossal brain!"

"Right, updates. Terry and I were in Ickleford today. We met with the Wheeler family, including Jimmy's mother, Shirley, which was an interesting experience," said Beth, who went on to relay the conversations they'd had at the Wheelers and at the pub.

"One new angle on the mutilations," said Beth. "Shirley's view on the removal of the eyes matched our suggestion yesterday, that Jimmy had seen something he shouldn't, but another angle is this; there are none so blind as those who will not see. Did Jimmy know something that he should have acted on but didn't? It's something to bear in mind when we're thinking about motive."

"Now Terry, what more do we know about Guy Fanshawe?" asked Beth.

"It's been tricky to find out anything about him. Jenny asked Dawn for some background information, and she told us Guy moved to Ickleford a few months before her and Jimmy. He's been married to Cindy for ten years and they've got two children of primary school age. He and Cindy used to live in the St Thomas's area in Canterbury, which is the next area along from the Coxhall Estate, so the landlord's theory that Guy and Jimmy knew each other before they moved to Ickleford is feasible; but Dawn says she only met the couple when she and Jimmy moved to the village, so I guess this could be another area in which Jimmy kept Dawn in the dark.

We know that Guy drinks in The White Hart most nights, but only sat with Jimmy occasionally, rather than every time they were both in the pub. We also know that he and Jimmy would often have private conversations when they did meet up. The landlord said Guy worked for a big financial company in London, so I've called a number of the largest firms this afternoon but none had heard of him. I'll start working on some of the medium-sized companies tomorrow. Dawn didn't know anything about his job, unfortunately, but not surprisingly.

Guy's not on any of our databases, so I'd like to do a bit more digging into his business dealings before contacting him directly, because that's the area we'll get the best intel on the dealings he had with Jimmy. I can't imagine they moved away from the bar to talk about snooker."

"Sounds like a good plan, Terry. You can update us tomorrow on progress with finding Guy's employer. Give forensic accounting a ring to see if this is something they could help us with," said Beth, who then updated the team on finding Jimmy's car. "It was locked up when we arrived and, as you know, we didn't find anything personal on the body at the cathedral, including a set of keys, so we couldn't open it. However, once traffic got the car back to the pound, they handed it over to forensics, who found Jimmy's laptop and a phone in a laptop bag in his boot, and Terry sent them over to the Digital Forensics team this afternoon. There was nothing else in the bag so it looks like Jimmy was a man of the digital age. I'll chase the Digital Forensics team first thing tomorrow, to explain how urgent it is that we get as much information off both devices as quickly as possible."

Beth then told the team about the phone call from Mac, who confirmed that Jimmy died of an oramorph overdose.

"Oramorph? That's an unusual murder weapon," said Fiona. "Surely the chances of us tracing that drug is much higher than other drugs. Why not choose a non-prescription drug?"

"And using poison or drugs is a pretty uncommon method of murder; it accounts for very few deaths to compare with sharp instruments and physical assault," said Terry, trying to impress Beth with the research he'd done before joining his first murder squad.

"That's correct," said Beth. "Does that have an impact on who we might be looking for?"

"According to the Washington Post, women are seven times as likely as men to choose poison as their murder weapon," offered Terry, to glances of "Washington Post?" curiosity from the team. "I've been Googling," he offered with a shrug.

Dave cleared his throat.

"But then, how would a woman get the body from the murder site to the cathedral?" he asked. "That requires enormous strength."

"Maybe she had some help? Hindley and Brady? Fred and Rose West?" suggested Clarissa.

"These are great points; well done all. We need to bear these ideas in mind, but for now, let's move on to what everyone else has unearthed today," said Beth. "Ki and Dave – what did you find out at The Cox?"

Ki answered first. He told the team that Kevin and Jeff were not at home when they called, and gave them an update on the conversations with Gary and Mikey. "Jenny got us permission from Dawn to enter their flat, or Jimmy's office as it's now known, and brought us the keys but when we went in, there was nothing of any interest in there – no laptop or phone, which I presume is because they were found in the boot of his car, and no handwritten files, just some old furniture for them to sit on and a kettle to make tea, so we're no further on than yesterday. There was a proper office set up in one of the bedrooms though – no bed, just a desk, a couple of chairs, and an unlocked, empty filing cabinet. So, if I was a betting man, I would suggest that a trusted friend had been in to clean out the files before we arrived, although where they are now is an unknown. We also have a few names to follow up on," continued Ki. "Muhammed Khan took a beating from Jimmy and has been overheard threatening him, although one of the residents we spoke with laughed at the idea that he could follow up on any threats, and told us he normally ran the other way when he saw the Wheeler gang on the estate, but we'll do a background check and have a chat with him tomorrow. The other name is Michelle Crossfield," this caused ears to prick up across the squad room. "We were told that she's been looking to sell her story, and has said her money worries will be over soon, but the most interesting thing is her surname. Again, we were told that her brother was ex-army and it would be beneficial for us to have a chat with her, but if her brother is Philip Crossfield, and he is involved in the murder, he'd be stupid to put the body in his place of work although we've all seen stupid behaviours in our line of work so we'll be looking into Michelle and Philip tomorrow."

"Could be a double-bluff," suggested Clarissa. "You know – using the 'why would I leave a body in my place of work' line to his advantage."

"It's possible, of course," replied Ki. "But I'm not sure yet that Philip Crossfield has got the wit about him to consider that. But we'll be looking into it.

Now, the final point I'd like to make is an observation – Gary told us that he used to drive Jimmy to business meetings with men in sharp suits. That doesn't fit with a loan shark from a council estate, so who has he been meeting? I think that's a priority for us." As soon as he saw Beth nod, he said "Dave – would you like to take it from here?"

Dave cleared his throat and agreed with Ki's observation then went on to tell the team "We visited a greasy spoon on The Cox to get an impression of how the locals were taking the news about Jimmy," which was met with many a 'yes, of course that's why' and 'what did you order?' to which Dave replied, "We both had bangers and mash with an onion gravy and mushy peas, and it was delicious, thank you for asking! But back to the visit, the guy behind the counter and the waitress claimed not to know Jimmy, even though he's in there quite regularly every week, but the two diners were happier to talk to us," and he gave the team an update on the conversation in the caff.

"Okay, well, the reluctance to talk to us is to be expected, especially with Jimmy's reputation, but well done on the info gathering, and I'm glad you had a nice lunch into the bargain! It'll be interesting to see what you can dig up on any potential Crossfield link," said Beth, before moving on. "Okay, Jenny, what can you tell us about the discussions you've had with the Wheeler women?" asked Beth.

"Well, Dawn is always happy to share information about Jimmy but she doesn't appear to know anything about the business, or she won't talk about it – all questions from me are met with a 'oh I wouldn't know anything about that' – and she's never left alone; either Jackie or Shirley are always within earshot of her, which I suspect is their way of making sure she doesn't tell us anything that she might know. I have to say, I can't stop her when she starts sharing stories about how wonderful her Jimmy was.

Jackie and Shirley, on the other hand, seem to know a bit more about Jimmy's business, according to what Jackie told Beth about the posh boys from London, but neither will discuss the business with me. Also, when Jackie's with Dawn, Shirley's shadowing me and vice versa, so I haven't even had a chance to look for any evidence myself, but I know that uniforms had a look when they were there and didn't find any files. As Beth said, it looks like Jimmy was a man of the digital age, and kept everything on his laptop."

"Thanks Jenny. That confirms that I need to put the pressure on Digital Forensics tomorrow. If you can keep on trying to get any information out of either Jackie or Shirley – Jackie would be my best bet – that would be brilliant. Okay, Fiona and Clarissa, how did you get on at the cathedral?" asked Beth.

Fiona took the lead and gave the team an update on the security arrangements at the cathedral, including the fact that there are only two close constables working the night shift, and two sets of keys which are signed out and signed back in, and told them that the full log would be emailed over to her hopefully today, but at the latest tomorrow morning.

"As soon as we get the log, we'll do a background check on those who have accessed the keys in the past, and then we'll start looking at each of them for a motive," said Fiona, bringing their contribution to a close.

"Great work, thanks Fiona and Clarissa," said Beth.

"Okay. We've got a lot of work to do tomorrow. We need to find and talk to Kevin Carter urgently. Ki and Dave, can you please make that your priority then follow up on the Muhammad and Michelle connections? Can you also find out if Jimmy was happy living in the countryside, or if he just moved there to keep Dawn happy? I can't see Dawn harming her Jimmy, or paying someone else to do so, but if she wanted the lady of the manor lifestyle, and he was thinking of upsetting that, it's an angle we need to look into. We also need to know if Jimmy had a girlfriend, and if he did, has he had, or is he due to have, children with her, because that would give Dawn another very strong motive to harm him.

It's good to know that he left The Cox at six p.m. and, given the time it would have taken him to drive to the spot where his car was found, we can rule out the idea that he, or his body, were in the cathedral before Philip Crossfield locked up the building at eight p.m. that night," said Beth. "Fiona and Clarissa, can you check back in with the cleaners to ask if they always lock the doors behind them when they're in the cathedral, or could someone have entered the building when they were working in there? Terry and I will continue to look into Jimmy's history, and dig out as much information on Guy Fanshawe as possible.

Just one last point, mainly addressed to you, Andrea, and it ties in to the point Ki raised earlier. On our way back to the office, Terry and I were discussing how lovely the village of Ickleford is. Lovely, and pricey – I had a quick look at Zoopla's house price estimator earlier and, I know it can be quite random and sometimes way off the mark, but Jimmy and Dawn's house has an estimated value of six hundred thousand pounds, based on the five hundred thousand pounds they paid for it six years ago. Shirley and Jackie's house has an estimated value of five hundred thousand pounds, based on the four hundred thousand pounds they, or someone else, paid for it five years ago. Now, a council estate loan shark must be doing exceptionally well from the council estate dwellers of Canterbury, and much further afield, to be able to afford those house prices, so what else has Jimmy been up to? Has this got something to do with the posh boys from London that Jackie mentioned? But, that approach seems to be a few years after Jimmy found the funds to buy one, or probably two, houses in Ickleford for a combined cost of just under a million pounds. Andrea, can I ask you to look into Jimmy's other business dealings? There really has to be something more than the loan sharking funding his lifestyle. Ki, Dave, and Jenny will be able to support you. And you might want to start your investigations with Guy Fanshawe.

Terry, we need to check Jimmy's will to see who benefits, and we need to know who bought the two houses in Ickleford, and how they were financed.

Okay. Great work today, team. I really feel we're making progress in this case. I'm off to give the Super an update. I'll see you all in the morning – have a great evening, we've got another very busy day ahead of us tomorrow."

Chapter 16

The Wheeler house was silent. Jenny had gone back to the squad room after taking the keys to Jimmy's office to Ki and Dave at The Cox, along with Dawn's permission for them to enter the flat, and the Wheelers had refused the offer of another officer to support them.

"You tell those coppers too much, darlin," Jackie said to Dawn, stroking her fringe away from her eyes. "They don't understand our life, so they'll twist everything you say to make our Jimmy look bad."

"Sorry," said Dawn. "It's just that when I get a chance to talk about him, I could go on and on for hours and hours. He was amazing and I miss him so much, Jackie," as the tears started streaming down her cheeks again.

Jackie hugged her oldest friend. "I know, darlin', I know."

"Who did it, Jackie? Who wanted him dead? And why do such a cruel thing as take his eyes out? Why? What's that all about?" sobbed Dawn.

"I don't know, darlin, I just don't know. I know that some people owed him money, but I can't see any of them killing him to clear their debt. And as for the eyes, that makes no sense to me. I reckon there must be a madman running around Canterbury and our Jimmy was just in the wrong place at the wrong time."

Dawn seemed calmer at the thought that Jimmy's death and the mutilation of his body was not personal, just the act of a random stranger, and her tears slowly stopped.

"Come on you," said Jackie. "You're exhausted. Let me get your sleeping pills then I'll tuck you up and things will be a little bit easier in the morning."

As always, Dawn did as she was told, and within half an hour she was fast asleep.

"Is she asleep?" asked Shirley.

"Out like a light," replied Jackie.

Shirley poured them both a gin and tonic and they settled down on the largest sofa in the house. "She talks too bleedin' much," she said to her daughter.

"At least she doesn't know anything about the business," said Jackie.

"Nothing we know about," replied her mother. "But she might have overheard stuff that didn't mean anything to her, and could end up repeating it in front of that Jenny. The sooner we get the coppers out of our lives, the better.

Talking of coppers, Kev messaged earlier to say that the cops have been crawling all over The Cox today. Him and Jeff managed to avoid them, but they met that dopey halfwit Gary who offered them a cup of tea, and it was him who told them about Jimmy's office! Pillock. Kev said the coppers were in and out of Number twelve in about twenty minutes. They left empty handed so it's a bloody good job he cleared out all the business files and brought them to us before they had a chance to find them."

Shirley looked her daughter in the eye. "I think it's time for you to take over, love. You know that Jimmy wanted to keep the business in the family, he told Kev and Jeff to support the family if anything happened to him, and I'm here too. You're ready, love, and you need to move fast before anyone else tries to move in."

Jackie nodded. "Jimmy shared everything about the business with me. The only thing that worried me was those fucking posh boys from London, but I've told the police they need to look at them, so that should keep the cops and the posh boys busy and out of my hair. You're right, mum. I am ready. I'm going to The Cox tomorrow."

Chapter 17

The team had had a very busy morning in the office, doing background research on possible suspects from Jimmy's clients to cathedral keyholders, then Ki and Dave returned to The Cox. They looked for Kevin Carter and Jeff Robinson, but both were again impossible to find. Dave called former colleagues and his sources to ask them to keep an eye open for both of Jimmy's key associates, and let him know immediately if they saw either.

Michelle Crossfield was walking back from the shops when she spotted the two men outside her flat's door. "Whatever you're selling, I'm not buying," she said.

"Are you Michelle Crossfield?" asked Ki, as he and Dave flashed their warrant cards.

Michelle appeared to check them carefully, then said, "Yeah, I'm Michelle. I've been waiting for the coppers to arrive. You'd better come in," and led them through to a chaotic living room with toys on the floor, and clothes strewn on the shelves.

"Why were you expecting a visit from the police?" asked Ki.

"I heard about Jimmy Wheeler, and I reckoned the first people you'd be interviewing would be anyone who had a loan with him. And I knew it wouldn't be long before someone coughed my name," she replied.

"How much do you owe Jimmy?" asked Dave.

"Just over a grand," said Michelle.

Dave whistled. "A thousand pounds. That's quite a sum," he said. "Did you borrow it all in one go?"

"No," she replied. "It started with a hundred pounds borrowed to get us through Christmas last year, and the repayments were okay so I borrowed another hundred pounds for my daughter's birthday – presents, a party, you know how it is. Then I borrowed three hundred pounds to take my kids on their first ever holiday – they're five and seven already – but then the repayments were not okay and I struggled to pay them."

"So what did Jimmy do when you couldn't pay him his money?" asked Dave.

"First off, he just added the missed payments to my loan, and I paid back as much as I could every month, but then, once the loan hit a grand, things got nasty," Michelle replied.

"Can you tell us, in your own time, what happened when Jimmy got nasty?" asked Ki gently.

Michelle seemed reluctant to answer, but then said, "Well he's dead now, so he can't hurt me and his bunch of goons don't know whether they're coming or going, so I'll tell you. First off, he came to this flat and looked for anything that he could sell for a couple of quid, but when he saw I didn't have much worth taking, he started with the physical threats."

Ki looked her in the eye. "So he threatened you with physical violence?" he asked.

"No, not me," she replied. "I don't think Jimmy ever laid a hand on a woman, but he was always happy to show his fists to a man, so any man close to any woman in debt was in danger."

"Who did he threaten, Michelle, and did he carry out his threat?" asked Dave.

Again, Michelle hesitated.

"Look, love, we can do this down the station if you want," said Dave.

"My brother, Philip. He used to be in the army, so Jimmy thought it would be really funny for him to take a beating from a man who hadn't served in the forces," said Michelle, her eyes filling with tears. "The fucking coward jumped him from behind so Phil couldn't defend himself. He ended up in A&E with a fractured eye socket and two broken ribs. I'm glad the bastard's dead," she spat.

"You must have wanted revenge after that attack?" asked Dave.

"Oh please. Look at me – I'm a middle-aged mother of two with a weight problem. Do I look as though I could murder someone and chop their nose off?" she asked.

"And how about Philip?" asked Ki. "How did he react after the beating?"

"He didn't threaten to kill Wheeler, if that's what you're asking. He's not that type. Just because someone's been in the army, everyone thinks they're killers, but seeing what he saw on his tours of duty made him much less violent than your average drunk down the pub," she replied.

Dave paused before asking "So what's going to happen to your debt now? We heard you'd said your money worries would be over soon."

"Yeah, well, that hasn't worked out yet. I was going to sell my story to The Sun, but I haven't heard from them since Wheeler's body was found."

"How much were they going to pay you?" asked Ki.

"Well, we hadn't really gone that far. I was waiting for one of their journalists to phone me. I think the story would have been a good one, you know, *'Brave veteran attacked by filthy loan shark'* but I'm not sure I'll get a call now, so I'll just have to wait and see what happens to Wheeler's business."

"It would be a great help if you could let us know what's happening to your debt as soon as you find out. Will you call us to let us know?" asked Dave.

Michelle looked at Ki and Dave, then looked at their contact cards and shrugged. "Why not?" she said.

"Thank you," said Ki. "Michelle, do you know or have you heard of anyone who might have wanted to hurt Jimmy Wheeler, or kill him?" he asked.

"No, I haven't, but when you find him, I'll be the first one to buy him a pint," she replied.

"Okay. Well thanks for all your help, Michelle. Last question," said Ki. "Where can we find Philip?"

When they left Michelle's flat, Dave rolled his eyes and said, "The rumour mill is working hard these days.

We've had pickled eyes and now a nose removal. God knows what they'll come up with next."

When they got to the stairwell, they started their walk down four flights of stairs to Muhammad Khan's home, and as they were approaching Flat two, they saw a man fitting his description leaving the flat, and closing the door behind him. One of Dave's former colleagues had given them an update on his dealings with Muhammad – he was on the radar for small scale offences, including shoplifting some food, but the idea that he could be violent just didn't fit with her dealings with him.

Ki and Dave carried on walking until they were within touching distance of Muhammad, then held out their warrant cards. Muhammed looked as though he was about to run, but recognised that although he was fit and muscular, his stockier frame would not beat either police officer in a race, and accepted that he would be have to talk to them. "Alright? Do you want to come indoors, lads?" he asked with a broad Birmingham accent.

They entered the clean and orderly flat where Muhammed lived with his wife and three children. When they entered the sparsely furnished living room, Muhammed's wife stood and offered them all a cup of tea, which they declined, so she left them to it.

"Is this about Jimmy Wheeler?" he asked Ki.

"It is," Ki replied. "We hear you've had a run-in with him. Can you tell us about that?"

"Look, I borrowed a couple of hundred quid from him; the kids are growing up so quickly, they need new shoes and clothes and feeding them costs a fortune, then I got a couple of hefty bills and I just didn't have the money, and had nothing to sell, so I was desperate. That miserable bastard could smell it on me, so he offered a loan of five hundred pounds, we agreed terms, including a small increase every month until the debt was cleared, but after a couple of months, I couldn't meet the monthly increase so he came here, saw I had nothing for him to take to sell, then he gave me a beating. A bad one. In front of my wife. My bab was terrified and I will never forgive him for that," said Muhammad.

"Is that why you were overheard threatening him?" asked Dave.

"Ach, just empty threats from a man who was still smarting after a beating. I've been avoiding Wheeler and his gang as much as possible since it happened. I couldn't hurt another human even if I really wanted to – and I really wanted to hurt Jimmy Wheeler – but I just haven't got it in me," replied Muhammad.

There was a brief silence as that statement was being considered, then Dave asked "What's happening with your debt now that Jimmy's dead?"

"I've got no idea," Muhammad replied

"It would be a great help to us if you could let us know about that as soon as you find out. Will you call us to let us know?" asked Dave.

"Why not?" replied Muhammad.

"Thank you. Just one more question, do you know anyone who really wanted to hurt him and was able to do so?" asked Ki.

"Yes, I do," replied Muhammad. "But I'm going to need protection if I tell you who."

Chapter 18

Fiona and Clarissa walked from the squad room to the Constables' Lodge, enjoying some late autumn sun on their faces.

"So, why did you choose policing as a career?" asked Fiona. "I wouldn't have thought someone from a family like yours would have chosen the police as their public service role."

"The modern police force welcomes us all," smiled Clarissa, whose mother is the daughter of a Viscount, and whose family home is a large mansion set in hundreds of acres in the Kent countryside.

Clarissa went on to explain that when she graduated with a first in Philosophy from Cambridge University three years ago, her choice of career surprised many in her circle, but the rape of a close friend at university, and the way in which the case was handled by the police – not quickly, not sympathetically – affected Clarissa deeply, and she made the decision that complaining about the police investigation was not enough. The only way to effect change was from within, and so she became a police officer just a few weeks after graduation.

"I'm sorry to hear about your friend," said Fiona. "And very well done you, for deciding to do something to change things rather than just complain about them."

They finished the rest of their journey in silence and when they arrived at the Constables' Lodge, they presented their warrant cards. "We've arranged to meet Arthur Lloyd and...the head of housekeeping." Fiona struggled to remember her name, so Clarissa helped out "Rachel Bailey."

"Yes, Rachel Bailey here at midday."

"They're both waiting for you in the cathedral Sergeant's office. I'll show you the way," said the very efficient lodge administrator.

"Cup of tea, ladies?" asked Arthur, as they walked in, but both declined.

"Sorry, bit of a busy time for us Arthur," said Clarissa. "We've just got a few loose ends we need to tie up with you both."

"Fire away," said Arthur, as Rachel started to cry and clutched the cross hanging from her necklace. A small, devout, middle-aged woman, she apologised for her tears.

"I can't believe this has happened here," she said. "This was always such a safe, quiet space. Whoever did this awful thing has damaged our Cathedral and it can never be repaired. We will never feel safe here again."

"I'm so sorry that you feel that way," said Clarissa. "The sooner we catch the killer, the quicker we hope things will return to normal, and your support in helping us do that is very much appreciated." Clarissa paused to offer

Rachel a tissue. "So can I ask you, Rachel. When you and your cleaning teams go into the cathedral, do you lock the doors behind you, or are they unlocked for the whole time you're in the building?"

Rachel thought about it and replied, "We only unlock the southwest door when we go in to the cathedral, and we leave it open until we leave."

"Sorry to interrupt," said Clarissa. "But can I just check when you say you leave it open, do you mean unlocked or actually open?"

Rachel thought about the question and replied, "Mainly unlocked, unless there are more bin bags than normal, in which case we'll take them outside before the end of shift, and we'd leave the door open for that."

"Do you unlock any other doors when you're in the building?" asked Fiona.

"Only the internal doors. I should say that there's normally at least one of us in the Nave or thereabouts," said Rachel, and seeing a brief quizzical look on Fiona's face, explained, "It's the big area you walk into through the southwest door – so I wouldn't think anyone could get in without us seeing them, although I can't give you a hundred percent guarantee that's the case."

"Thank you," said Clarissa. "Have you or any of your staff noticed anything unusual or suspicious outside the cathedral recently? When you were arriving at, or leaving, the building in the dark, did you see anyone you didn't recognise hanging around, or anyone at all?"

"I've called every one of the housekeeping staff, and none of them have seen anything or anyone unusual, or anything suspicious. I'm so sorry I can't help you – I would love to say some of us had seen the killer and describe him for you to find on your computers, but we just haven't seen or heard anything that was out of the ordinary. Sorry," said Rachel, and started to weep quietly. Clarissa moved over to her side and offered her another tissue.

"Thank you, Rachel," said Fiona. "If you or any of your housekeeping team can think of anything over the coming days or weeks, you have our cards so please get in touch with one of us.

Arthur, if I can turn to you. Firstly, many thanks for sending over the log of those who'd signed the cathedral keys out and signed them back in. We were surprised to see how few names were on the list," she said. "Over the last two years, only seven people have signed for the cathedral keys; five are Close Constables, and two are housekeeping staff. If another member of staff or the clergy wanted to access any of the rooms normally closed to the public, or access the cathedral when it was locked, how would they do that?"

"Twenty-four-hour security, Fiona. They need access to a locked room, they come to the Lodge, and we go with them to unlock the doors," replied Arthur.

"Go with them every time, Arthur, or do the constables sometimes hand over the keys so the staff or clergy can open the doors themselves?" asked Fiona.

You could hear a pin drop in the room. Arthur looked uncomfortably at Fiona. "I think there have probably been times in the past when cathedral staff and clergy might have been given access to a set of keys, yes," said Arthur. "Not protocol, of course, but when staff are very busy or covering their colleagues on sick leave and so on, we all do what we have to do to keep the show on the road, don't we?" he ended with something resembling pleading.

"So, there are a number of people who could have made a copy of those keys to be used at a later date," said Fiona.

"Well, I suppose you could say that, but this is Canterbury Cathedral," said Arthur. "We trust our colleagues and we've never had a crime like this before."

"Well, you've had one now, Arthur, and the consequences are pretty significant, wouldn't you agree?" said Fiona, coldly. "Okay, please ask all constables to let you know urgently who has asked them to borrow the keys over the last twelve months and how long those keys were with them – long enough to make a copy, for example."

"Yes, of course," said Arthur. "I'm sorry." The apology was very sincere.

"Rachel, have you or your housekeeping colleagues been asked to share the keys with anyone else?" asked Clarissa.

"Only me and the Deputy Head of Housekeeping ever sign for the keys, I've never handed my keys to anyone else, but I'll check with my colleague Helena to ask if she has, and I'll let you know later today," replied Rachel.

"Well, please get that list over to us by tomorrow morning at the latest, Arthur, and if anyone can think of anything particularly unusual about any requests to borrow the keys, please include those in your email. Clarissa and I are heading back to the office now, so if you need us, we'll be on our mobiles and our landlines. Thank you both for your co-operation," said Fiona, as she swept out of the Sergeant's office.

As they walked back to the squad room, Fiona rolled her eyes at Clarissa. "For god's sake. I thought the security surrounding the keys was too good to be true, but this. I can almost guarantee that the constables will remember less than half of the requests so where does that leave us? Investigating all staff, clergy and volunteers? Jesus wept…"

Chapter 19

There was a buzz in the squad room when the four p.m. debrief started. It seemed that everyone there had some news that could move the investigation forward, including Andrea Walker.

"Okay, can we all settle down please," asked Beth. "Terry and I have worked closely with Andrea today, and she's joined us because she has some very interesting information to share. Andrea…"

Andrea Walker stepped up to the white board. "Thanks Beth. There are two things I would like to share with you today. Firstly, I don't know about you but when I heard the expression 'posh boys from London' I presumed Jackie was referring to city types in sharp suits, but when we contacted our colleagues in the Met, and explained the situation here, they suggested we look first at the Peckham Posh Boys, a gang from the Alan Turing Estate in Peckham Rye. They've got a good racket going there – loan sharking included – and our colleagues understand that they've been branching out to other, similar estates. We know that they've already established a presence in some of the Medway towns, so it's quite possible that their next stop on the journey from London to the east coast of Kent would have been in Canterbury, which would have brought them into contact with Jimmy Wheeler at The Cox. The leader of the Posh Boys is a nineteen-year-old calling himself 'The Shank' which, as I'm sure you all know, is slang for slashing or stabbing someone. He is, reportedly, a very violent and unstable young man, which would explain Jackie's comment about Jimmy being scared. I've shared the details with Beth, but if you need any more help on this front, please let me know and I'll put you in contact with the relevant staff at the Met.

The next thing I'd like to share is in relation to Guy Fanshawe. Guy used to work for one of the UK's largest banks before moving to one of the UK's largest venture capitalist firms. When he was there, he led the investment in an art gallery startup, which did very well. So well, in fact, that Guy decided to leave the world of finance and open his own gallery, in Chelsea. His gallery did quite well but not spectacularly, so Guy diversified, and he is now under investigation for his trade in paintings with less-than robust provenance – it would appear that he has a large and growing list of clients who have specific requirements and will pay handsomely for those paintings, no matter how they gain access to them.

What's interesting for us is this; Guy has invested in another art gallery, in Canterbury. Both Chelsea and Canterbury galleries have very knowledgeable managers and assistant managers, who are the first point of contact with clients who walk into the buildings, or email through queries, but unlike in London, Guy had a business partner here in Canterbury, who worked solely behind the scenes.

His name was James Wheeler, and our colleagues in London believe that this gallery is a front for money laundering. As such, we are working closely with our colleagues in London to gather evidence, and we will keep you updated on any information which impacts your investigation, otherwise I'm afraid we can't go into too much detail with you at this stage."

Beth moved to stand next to Andrea. "Thank you so much for the updates, Andrea. That certainly gives a new steer to our investigation. Does anyone have any questions for Andrea before she heads back to her office?"

Dave cleared his throat then asked, "So, Guy Fanshawe has gone into the money laundering business with Jimmy Wheeler. Am I the only one who finds this a little implausible? Why would Guy get involved with Jimmy for anything other than a pint at their local? Where would Jimmy get contacts like that from?"

"According to our colleagues in Organised Crime, it's been a long time since Jimmy Wheeler's criminal contacts were confined to The Cox. He had big ideas, and to fund his lavish lifestyle, he needed more than the interest he accrued from loans on The Cox – he needed big money so he networked with the big boys. We know for a fact that he has at least half a dozen contacts with significant criminals in East Kent. They, like Guy Fanshawe, will always need some muscle, and Jimmy and his gang could supply that. Also, if Guy needs a specific piece of artwork for one of his clients, we know that Jimmy, Kevin, and Jeff have all got form for breaking and entering, and we have to presume they have their own contacts who can provide this service as well – this is something that Andrea's team are looking into now. So there's his foot in the door, although I would like to know how Jimmy and Guy first met. Terry and I will look into that," Beth said. "Okay, if there's nothing else, then thank you for your time, and for sharing such valuable information with us, Andrea. If you need any information from us, please get in touch."

As Andrea walked out of the squad room, Beth turned to the team and informed them that Canterbury Cathedral Chapter had very helpfully offered the services of two members of their team to help with the investigation. Ki, who had studied for a BSc and an MSc in Computing with the Open University, was made the allocated contact point for Elizabeth Jefferson-Briggs, and Fiona became the allocated contact point with Selwyn Du Pont. Beth felt that both members of her team were sufficiently qualified and senior to keep the Chapter members satisfied, given the Super's words last night. "These people are very senior in their fields, Beth, and we need to show them we appreciate their time and knowledge by allocating suitably senior staff to work with them. And I know I don't need to say this, but our staff must be firm about what information they can and can't share with Chapter staff, and if Chapter staff take umbrage with that, please refer them directly to me."

"Okay," said Beth. "It's update time. In addition to working closely with Andrea today, Terry and I have been in touch with Jimmy's solicitor. According to her, Jimmy bought both houses in Ickleford and he bought them outright. We asked the solicitor if she knew where the funds would have come from, but she claimed to have no idea – she was Jimmy's personal solicitor and as she understood it, Jimmy had a different solicitor for business matters. Jenny – I have no doubt that Dawn will have no idea who the business solicitor is, but if you could please check in with all the Wheeler women, we might just get lucky. If not, and if we ever catch up with Kevin and or Jeff, they might be able to help, otherwise Terry and I will raise this with Guy Fanshawe when we speak with him, although when that will be in light of the organised crime investigation, I do not know.

His will throws up no surprises – the house at the end of the road, and a reasonable sum of money, is left in equal shares to his mother and his sister, there are small financial bequests to his associates, a generous financial bequest to the children's home that he and Dawn have been so supportive of over the years, and the rest, in its entirety, goes to Dawn.

Ki and Dave, how did you get on at The Cox?"

Ki spoke first and updated the team on their interviews with both Michelle and Muhammad. Everyone agreed that Philip Crossfield was a serious suspect, and Beth asked Ki to bring him into the station for a formal interview as quickly as possible. The team also agreed that Muhammad, although he was fit and muscular, and looked as though could look after himself, in reality he couldn't so he seemed an unlikely suspect, and they were all intrigued when Ki went on to inform them about Muhammad's request for protection.

"It's the Tanner brothers," said Ki, to gasps of surprise across the squad room.

Frankie Tanner was a very successful bookie with a very violent past. He'd served a number of prison sentences for assault, including one with an offensive weapon.

Frankie had started with one shop, on the Florence Nightingale Estate in Chatham where he and his siblings grew up, then he opened another on Chatham High Street. He now had eight shops, including ones on Canterbury High Street and at The Cox. Frankie's style was to open a new shop on a high street, then get to know the area and its criminal gangs well in order to open another shop on a council estate in the same city, where he was sure that he would find a relatively healthy income stream.

"It turns out that once Frankie has established himself on an estate like The Cox, he builds alliances with the local hard lads then his brother Billy, who has as violent a past as Frankie, moves in to set up as a loan shark. Frankie opened his shop on The Cox six months ago, and has been making friends and enemies there ever since. As soon as he heard that Muhammad had taken a beating from Jimmy, he approached him and invited him to join the Tanner gang, providing some muscle on the estate and further afield when needed. They made it clear that the invitation was not an invitation, but a statement of what was going to happen. According to Muhammad, the Tanners had been threatening Jimmy Wheeler, and it was made clear to him that one of his first duties on behalf of the Tanners would be physical violence against Jimmy, specifically to 'beat Wheeler to within an inch of his life'. Muhammad says there's no way he could physically hurt another human being, so he's, rightly, shitting a brick about this approach and he wants out. I told him I'd follow up on his request for protection, but a lot of this depends on Frankie Tanner's response to Jimmy Wheeler's death. He might think that there's no need to recruit Muhammad, in which case there might be no need for protection, but we'll have to wait and see. Dave – over to you."

Dave cleared his throat "Thanks Ki. I've followed up with a few of my sources this afternoon, and it turns out that the Tanners have approached both Gary Nixon and Mikey Curtis to go and work for them. Both said no – Mikey seemed to think they just wanted Jimmy's loan list then they'd part company, and pretty violently – but we don't know yet if they've caught up with Kevin Carter or Jeff Robinson. I know we haven't."

"Excellent work," said Beth. "Although, we really need to find Kevin and Jeff asap. Keep that as your priority, please. Okay, we need to get on top of this quickly. Jenny, can you please ask Dawn, Jackie and Shirley if they know anything about Jimmy's dealings with the Tanners and, if so, what contact was made. Can you also ask them about the Peckham Posh Boys, to confirm that they're the ones Jackie was referring to, and to ask what sort of contact they'd made. If The Shank has threatened Jimmy with physical violence, we need to know about it.

Ki and Dave, keep up the good work on The Cox and Terry and I will go and interview the Tanners on their own turf. See if a visit from a couple of coppers ruffles feathers or encourages others to speak to us.

Right. Fiona and Clarissa. How has your day been?" asked Beth.

Fiona took the lead on this. "Well, as we understood it yesterday, there was very tight security surrounding the cathedral building itself, but apparently not.

The head of housekeeping told us that they don't lock the southwest door when they're inside, and they sometimes leave the door wide open, so she couldn't be confident that, if someone wanted to enter the cathedral unseen after dark, they wouldn't be able to do so on her watch – the Nave is full of nooks and crannies, which makes it easy for someone to hide in the dark.

Added to that, we were told today that the keys that are signed out and signed back in are sometimes just handed to cathedral staff, clergy, and volunteers because they trust them. So, the list we were sent this morning is only some of the story. I have asked the cathedral Sergeant to interview all logged key holders to get as full a list as possible of everyone who borrowed the keys over the past twelve months, and how long they had them for – long enough to make copies? I am not confident that the list Arthur will send us will be complete, or will include even half of the little borrowers, but it's all we'll have to go on I'm afraid."

"That's a poor show from a security perspective," said Beth, rolling her eyes. "But not entirely unexpected. I'm sure all those who work at the cathedral are viewed as a very trusted team, but that makes the whole thing more difficult to investigate. Well done for unearthing the security lapse, Fiona and Clarissa, and good luck working through the revised list when it arrives.

And finally, how's it going tracing the oramorph?"

"Slowly," replied Dave. "I've been in touch with the local health commissioners and their medicines management team are looking into it for us, but it's a massive job, so it could take some time. I'll keep chasing them."

"Okay, great work as always, guys. We're really moving the investigation forward now. I'm off to give the Super an update then I'm off to the Shakespeare for a pint after work. If anyone is thirsty, the first round is on me."

Chapter 20

Shirley had messaged Kevin to tell him to be at Jimmy's office on The Cox at six p.m. sharp. There had been developments.

Kevin arrived as instructed, feeling a little wary about what he would soon be told. Ever since he was a small child, he'd known nothing else but being Jimmy's wingman, and he didn't know what life without his best mate would be like.

Jackie was at the office when Kevin arrived, and soon had the kettle on, ready for a brew.

Not the most emotionally open of men, Kevin found it hard to talk about Jimmy's loss, but he knew he had to ask, "How are you and Shirley coping? And how's Dawn doing?"

Jackie could do emotions, but this wasn't the time. She didn't have the bonds with Kevin that Jimmy had, so their relationship would be business, start to finish. "I'm okay, mate, thanks. Mum's bearing up and Dawn's a wreck, but we'll get through this."

There was a brief silence as they looked awkwardly at each other. "Jimmy told me everything about the business – the posh boys, the Tanners, the growing list of loan repayment defaults. He always said that if anything happened to him, he wanted to keep the business in the family, so he always told me and mum everything. Thanks for getting his paperwork over to us. We've managed to hide that from the coppers," said Jackie, smiling at the last comment.

"I know that you and Jimmy would do the collections on The Cox together, with Jeff, if things were likely to get tricky, and I know he paid you and Jeff to work for him. Things have changed a lot since the early days," she said. "The loans business has grown, but the other side of the business has grown even quicker, so I'm going to need to spend a lot of time with those clients. I want to make you an offer, Kevin. You look after everything to do with the loans – making the offers, collecting the repayments – and I'll pay you ten percent more than Jimmy did, plus I'll give you fifteen percent of the repayments you collect. We'll meet up every week to look through the loans book, but, unless you need some advice, the decisions will be all yours. What do you think?"

Inside, Kevin was bursting with excitement but couldn't let it show. "That sounds like a fair deal, Jackie. Thank you. I can assure you that I will look after the loans business well, just like Jimmy would have wanted."

"That's brilliant. Thanks Kevin. I'm going to need Gary to drive me around when I meet Jimmy's other business connections, but otherwise, him, Mikey and Jeff will be there to back you up when you need them. Can you message all three to ask them to come to the office so we can tell them about the new arrangements?"

Kevin did as he was asked, and as they waited for the others to arrive, Jackie asked him "Do you know who did this to Jimmy? Or why they killed him? Or why, and this is the bit that's eating away at both Dawn and mum, the killer would take his fucking eyes out? That's such a shitty thing to do, and it strikes me that whoever did it is totally fucking mental. If that person isn't some random psychopath, if it's someone specifically targeting Jimmy or his business, I need to know about it now, so I can protect myself properly."

"I have absolutely no idea who did this to him, Jackie. I know that a couple of the lads he'd slapped had been threatening him, but I don't think any of them would've been capable of hitting Jimmy, let alone killing him or taking his eyes out. I also know that he was worried about the Tanners, and that they'd threatened him with a good kicking, but that was the extent of it. No threats of murder that I've heard of. The Peckham Posh Boys came here a couple of times and their leader, The Shank, flashed his blade and said it would be his pleasure to cut Jimmy up one little bit at a time, but again, none of us took him that seriously and anyway, he would've put bits of him all over The Cox, not left him in the cathedral. So I don't know who did this to Jimmy, but I am looking into it, and I can assure you that I will find the fucker before the coppers do."

Chapter 21

The squad room was busy and buzzing the next morning.

The first phone call came at nine a.m. on the dot. Muhammad told Ki that Jackie Wheeler was now in charge of the Wheeler business, but that Kevin Carter was looking after the loans side of the business for her, with backup from Jeff Robinson, Gary Nixon, and Mikey Curtis. Asked how he knew this, Muhammad explained that he'd had a visit from Kevin that morning, just after his wife had taken the children to school. Kevin had been menacing and threatening, and Muhammad was genuinely worried for his safety. He asked if there was any progress on his request for protection, and Ki assured him he'd follow up on the request today. After ending the call, Ki updated the team on the new development, and Beth asked him to arrange for a search warrant to be issued for Shirley and Jackie's house as quickly as possible.

At 9.20 a.m., one of the police constables called Beth with an update on The Shank. He had been found badly beaten, and tied to a roundabout in the children's playground at The Cox at ten p.m. the previous evening, following an anonymous tip-off. He had been taken to the Emergency Department at William Harvey hospital in Ashford and the latest information was that he'd been patched up and moved to a ward for a few days' observation. Beth thanked her for her help, updated the team, then turned to Terry. "My sources say that the Tanners are expected at Frankie's shop on Sittingbourne high street at one p.m. today. That gives us enough time to head to Ashford to interview The Shank before we head down the M20 to interview the Tanners. Ki – let me know as soon as that warrant is ready, or if you need my input to obtain it. Many thanks, everyone," she said over her shoulder as she and Terry left the squad room for their first interview that day.

Shortly afterwards, Dave took a call from Michelle Crossfield who told him that as soon as she got home from taking the kids to school, she'd had a visit from Kevin and Jeff to explain the new arrangements for the repayment of her loan. They gave her a figure for her new monthly payments, and made it very clear that Jimmy Wheeler's old collection rules would continue to apply, so missing a payment would have very serious consequences. She told Dave that she felt sick because she didn't know how she was going to meet the payments, and she was worried about what would happen to Phil as soon as she missed one. Dave felt sorry for her, but he couldn't give her any financial advice, and since she was unwilling to give a statement on the record, he gave her the address and telephone number for the Canterbury Citizens Advice office, and advised her to get in touch with them that morning.

As Michelle's call came in, Beth and Terry were in Terry's car listening to Beth's favourite Specials playlist. "So," said Terry. "If Jackie Wheeler's taking over Jimmy's business, she knows more than she admitted to knowing when you spoke with her the other day. So what else has she been lying about? Do you think she knew full well who the posh boys were but tried to send us on a wild goose chase, looking for businessmen instead of that gang?"

"I wouldn't be at all surprised if she was trying to waste our time, and also make out that she knew nothing about Jimmy's business. Let me email Ki and Dave to ask them to check with Gary, to see if Jackie was at any of the business meetings he used to drive Jimmy to. Surely, she can't just walk into those meetings from today onwards – she must have had previous contact with his clients, or at least some experience or knowledge of them, and them of her?" asked Beth. After firing off her email, she called the Digital Forensics team to ask if they'd managed to pull any information from Jimmy's phone and laptop.

Terry heard a lot of "Yes," and "Ah, right," and "Oh, I see," during the call. When Beth eventually got off the phone, she sighed and said "I really need to go on an IT course so I can converse with our colleagues in Digital Forensics. Anyway, progress has been made.

Apparently, Jimmy watched a lot of American football on his laptop but did very little else with it, which suggests that all his business dealings are written down somewhere, most likely in the care of either Kevin, Jeff,

Jackie, or Shirley. We need that search warrant asap, and a warrant for Kevin and Jeff's flats too," and she fired off another email to Ki and Dave asking them to execute all warrants as soon as they had been granted, and explained what they needed to look for. "The phone, on the other hand, could be a treasure trove for us. There are a lot of names in his address book, most of which are already familiar to the tech guys from previous investigations, and there are a lot of messages too. The full list of numbers and messages will be emailed over to me this morning."

"That's a great development," said Terry, and started singing along to Ghost Town.

With that, the William Harvey hospital came into view.

Chapter 22

Philip Crossfield lived above the Chinese takeaway in one of Canterbury's less-salubrious areas. He was enjoying a lie-in on his day off when Ki and Dave knocked on his door. He threw on a rugby shirt and jogging trousers and made his way to the front door.

"Philip Crossfield?" asked Dave, as he and Ki showed their warrant cards.

"Michelle told me to expect you. Come in," replied Philip.

The three men walked up the communal stairs and into Philip's tired old flat.

"We'd like you to come to the station to give us a formal statement," said Ki. "Can you please grab anything you'll need over the next few hours, and follow my colleague to the car?"

Philip put on his socks and trainers, picked up his phone and his keys, and grabbed his coat. "Okay," he said. "Let's get this done."

The journey to the station was a quiet one. When they arrived, Dave offered Philip a cup of tea or coffee, or a glass of water, if he preferred. Philip chose the coffee, partly in an attempt to shift his brain into gear.

Ki did the formal introductions for the tape, then started with the very simple question "Where were you on the night Jimmy Wheeler was killed?"

"I was on the afternoon shift at work so I clocked off at ten thirty p.m. I went to McDonalds for supper, then I caught the 11.05 p.m. bus home. I got indoors just after 11.20 p.m." Philip replied.

"What bus do you catch to get home from town?" asked Ki.

"The number seventy-one" said Philip.

"Were you at home from 11.20 p.m. that evening to seven a.m. the following morning?" asked Ki.

"Yes, I was."

"Can anyone confirm that?"

"No. I live on my own and I went straight to bed when I got in, so the flat would've been quiet and dark."

"Did anyone see you arrive home? One of your neighbours, perhaps?" asked Ki.

"I didn't see anyone so I don't know if anyone saw me," he replied.

"Michelle told us about the money difficulties she got into with Jimmy Wheeler, and the consequences for you. That must have made you very angry," said Dave.

"Of course I was angry about being jumped from behind and beaten up, but I wouldn't kill someone for it. One thing being in the army taught me is how fragile life is and how much we should value it, so I never even joke about taking another life.

Why don't you ask some of my army colleagues about that – they know me better than anyone, and they know that when we were off base, I was always the one stepping in to calm things down if any of the lads got into a heated argument. I'm not a violent man, gents. I'm just not the guy you're looking for," said Philip, in a very sincere voice.

Ki left a brief pause before continuing with his questions.

"How long have you worked at the cathedral?" he asked.

"Nearly three months now," replied Philip.

"During that time, have you ever handed the cathedral's keys to anyone?" continued Ki.

"God no, never," came the reply. "Once I've signed for them, they're my responsibility and I take that responsibility very seriously."

"Okay. Did you know Jimmy Wheeler before Michelle borrowed money from him?" asked Ki.

"I didn't know the man. We'd never met or spoken, but I'm pretty sure I was in the same building as him once, a few months ago – the last week of September, I think it was. I'd heard that one of my old army mates was living on the streets of Canterbury, so I went to Canterbury Cares, the homeless shelter, one night to try to find him and offer him some help. When I was there, this bloke who looked like Jimmy Carr off the telly walked in and went straight over to one of the volunteers – he looked like one of the vicars from the cathedral, but it was all over too quickly to be sure. But he was a vicar, I think; he had the black jacket, black shirt and little white paper thing in his collar – and had a quiet word in his ear. I don't know what he said, but the vicar went mental and smacked him in the mouth. The whole place went quiet and we all just stared at the bloke on the floor. I mean, vicars never lose their tempers, do they. And I have never, ever seen someone who works for the church actually hitting someone else, not even in self-defence, so you kind of remember things like that, don't you. Anyway, the guy who looked like Jimmy Carr who was lying on the floor, just rubbed his mouth then smiled, got up, looked straight at the vicar and did that thing with his hand, moving it across his neck like he was going to slash the vicar's throat, and walked out. Unbelievable.

Anyway, Jimmy Wheeler looked a lot like the Jimmy Carr guy after he'd finished giving me a beating, and he was shouting in my face to tell my sister to pay him what she owed him or he'd see me again, so I reckon I had seen him but sorry – no contact until the beating, and no contact afterwards."

"Can you describe the member of the clergy for us?" asked Ki.

"Sure. Not a man you'd forget easily. He was taller than me, and very wide. If you look for a man with wild ginger hair you'll have him," replied Philip.

"Thanks Philip," said Ki. "Do you know, or know of, anyone who would be prepared to kill Jimmy Wheeler?"

"No, I don't. We don't mix in the same circles so I just wouldn't know that," shrugged Philip.

"But Michelle lives on The Cox and has had dealings with Jimmy. Are you sure she hasn't said anything to you that could help us move this investigation forward? Have you heard anything when you've been visiting her and the kids in their flat?"

"No, she hasn't and no, I haven't. Look, I came here voluntarily and I've tried to help you as much as I can," he said, showing them the palms of his hands. "I really can't help you any more, but if I do see or hear anything, I am more than happy to give you a ring to let you know," said Philip and both Ki and Dave gave him their contact cards.

"Okay, thanks Philip. Please give us the contact details for a few of your old army mates then I'll take you to Reception, where they'll arrange a car home for you."

"No problem. Give me a pen and a sheet of paper, and I'll give you some names and telephone numbers," said Philip, as he took his phone out and opened the address book. "And there's no need for a lift home, thanks. I'll pop to Marge's Manor for one of her huffkins then I'll get the bus back."

Once Philip had been escorted to Reception, Ki turned to Dave and asked what he thought.

"I think we need to talk to some people who know him, maybe someone in the line of command above him in the army, to find out if what he says about being a peacemaker is true. I don't know if I believe him – all that outstretched palms and the doing us a favour approach doesn't make me think he's innocent, it makes me think he's very well-rehearsed, but we'll see when we follow up with the army. In the meantime, that was a very interesting lead he gave us about the punching vicar," replied Dave.

"Yes, and I know who that punching vicar is," said Ki. "I saw him once when the kids were singing at a recital evening in the cathedral. Philip was right – once seen, never forgotten. The description was a perfect fit for Selwyn Du Pont, Canon Missioner at Canterbury Cathedral, and the man Clarissa found skulking behind a pillar on the morning Wheeler's body was found. I think we might just have ourselves another suspect."

Chapter 23

The William Harvey hospital was a collection of large, sprawling buildings set a few miles away from Ashford town centre. Since the Emergency Department in Canterbury hospital had closed, the William Harvey housed one of only two EDs in East Kent, which is why The Shank found himself in a bed in Ashford after travelling to Canterbury the previous day.

Beth and Terry walked on to Dickens Ward, the general medical ward for men aged eighteen years and over. They quickly spotted The Shank; the youngest patient on the ward with more tattoos than the other patients combined, it was his attitude that confirmed he was David Williams, aka The Shank, leader of the Peckham Posh Boys. The stare, the glare, the sneer when they walked up to his bed, drew the curtains and showed him their warrant cards.

"David Williams? Sometimes called The Shank?" asked Terry.

"Duh," sneered The Shank. "Who the fuck else looks cool enough to be The Shank?"

"You've taken quite a beating there. How are you feeling?" asked Beth.

The Shank shrugged.

"Who did this to you?" asked Terry, not expecting an answer. None came.

"Why did they tie you to a handrail on the roundabout at The Cox? I hear you were found in a crouched position, as though you were praying. What's that all about?" asked Beth.

The Shank shrugged.

Beth had picked up a bunch of grapes in the League of Friends shop on the way in, and popped one in her mouth. She offered The Shank a grape, but his look of disgust suggested he wasn't inclined to join her, so she put them down on the little table at the bottom of his bed.

"Shall I tell you what I think?" Beth asked. "I think you've been to The Cox a few times over the last few months, trying to muscle in on Jimmy Wheeler's business, but he wasn't having any of it and then, Shank, then Jimmy Wheeler gets murdered. So, anyone who's been threatening Jimmy, then becomes a suspect in his murder and, in my experience of this sort of situation, there are two ways things will go. Either the police will find the murderer, and the justice system in this country will treat the suspect fairly and safely. Or, and this is the bit I find most interesting, Shank, or the associates of the victim make their own decision about who killed their mate, and they go after the murderer to take their revenge. That often involves a punishment beating, although it could go as far as murder, and sometimes involves some form of symbolism. So here I sit, looking at a young man who's taken quite a beating, and who was forced into a kneeling position, as though he was praying, and I wonder whether this incident might be linked to Jimmy Wheeler's murder, whose body was found in a religious setting. What do you think? Does that sound like it covers the events of the last few days?" asked Beth.

"So, Wheeler got murked. Fuck all to do with me. You ain't got evidence so you can fuck right off," shouted The Shank.

"Calm down," said Terry. "The boss was just walking you through a scenario. If that's not what happened, then we can look at it again but you've got to admit, a man who had been threatening a dead man will be a prime suspect in his murder. Where were you that night?"

"No comment," said The Shank.

"What took you to The Cox last night?" asked Beth. "I don't think you were there to extend your sympathies to Jimmy's friends and colleagues."

"No comment," said The Shank.

"Oh, come on Shank," said Terry. "You're not being formally interviewed yet, so you can ditch the 'No comments'. Who was with you last night? I can't see you going to The Cox without muscle, so who was with you?"

"I don't need no fucking muscle. I can look after myself," he shouted.

Beth and Terry looked at the bruising on the young man in the bed then looked at him with raised eyebrows.

"Okay," said Beth. "It's obvious you're not going to talk to us today but you are obviously in danger, so here are our cards and if you want to talk, or if you think you need protection, give us a ring."

The Shank looked away, so Beth put the cards next to the grapes and they left the ward.

As soon as they were in the car, and Terry had set the GPS to guide them to Frankie Tanner's shop in Sittingbourne, he asked Beth what she thought about the encounter with The Shank.

"Well, we couldn't dig too deep today, thanks to the warning we had from Matron who, incidentally, bears more than a passing resemblance to Hattie Jacques don't you think, but I actually think the lad is scared," replied Beth. "It doesn't matter how hard you think you are, or how you talk, the bottom line is that a good beating will affect you, and I think it's affected him deeply. What did you think?"

"I think you're right – strip away the bravado and the guy has had a proper fright. Whether that will get him talking to us, I'm not sure. My worry is that once he's out of hospital, he will be back on The Cox looking for his assailants to give them a taste of their own medicine, if not worse, and the whole thing could escalate to a hellish degree. I can only hope I'm wrong. Do you think he killed Jimmy Wheeler?"

"I'm honestly not sure. I think he's got motive, he might have opportunity – it's something we need to check – but whether he's got it in him to actually kill another person then mutilate their body, I just don't know. His record shows that he's spent time in jail for physical assault, but that was for beating up members of other gangs, not murder and absolutely not mutilation. And he seems to threaten people with being stabbed or slashed, not murdered, which would be considerably more suitable if he was cultivating a hard-lad image. And also, where would he get keys to the cathedral from? Let's see what he says when we interview him under caution on his release. And let's see if we can find out who beat him before he gets a chance to look for revenge. Can you give PC Unwin a ring when we get back to base to offer help in identifying the assailants? We need to work closely with uniforms on this, if we're going to prevent any escalation or get a conviction on his assault," replied Beth.

Terry paused to consider what Beth had said, and then shared, "Oh and yes, I do think that Matron is the spitting image of Hattie Jacques. Please, don't tell my dad. He had a massive crush on her during the golden years of the Carry On films, and I wouldn't put it past him to come up with some illness or other to get admitted to Dickens Ward, then my mother will have words with you and believe me, you don't want my mother to have words with you."

Beth changed the playlist to Madness, and hit the song 'It Must Be Love'. Terry looked at Beth and both chuckled loudly.

Chapter 24

It was Mary Du Pont's day off, a day when she could indulge her passion for cooking. She was an avid watcher of all television cookery programmes, and snapped up new books as soon as they were released.

Today, she was having an Indian day. It would be street food for lunch; a pav bhaji with some bread rolls, and for dinner, it would be a Keralan Irachi Ishtu, all homemade of course.

Selwyn appeared at the kitchen door at one p.m. on the dot, as instructed. He loved home-cooking days almost as much as he loved Mary.

"Something smells wonderful," he said, as he walked into the kitchen and kissed his wife.

"Street food for lunch," she said, as she started to dish up. "How was your morning?"

"Not too bad," he replied. "The police have agreed that we can reopen the cathedral tomorrow morning as normal, though whether anything will be normal there again is another matter. We've been sent some marketing material from Chapman and Burke to review, and I've had a phone call from Fiona, my link person on the investigation team, arranging a catchup meeting this afternoon. I'm afraid my parish commitments have taken a bit of a back seat these past few days, but we must prioritise according to need."

"So Fiona has arranged a meeting with you? Just for a catchup you say?" asked Mary.

"Yes, just a catch up. I presume she wants to update me on progress, and she might have a few questions about parish protocol. Nothing to worry about, my dear. Now, street food, you say," he replied, as a plate full of bhaji was placed in front of him. "If it tastes as good as it smells, I think we're in for a treat!"

***

Julian Jefferson-Briggs was packing a small bag in preparation for his return to their pied-à-terre in London. He was aware that many of his constituents were worried by the discovery of the body in the cathedral, and there were a number of tasks he could complete by working at home or in his constituency office, but he felt he needed to be back in his ministry HQ to steer through his big announcement. He also wanted to be closer to the home secretary who was, allegedly, on manoeuvres with a view to becoming the country's next prime minister. He calculated that working closely with her on a Canterbury Crime-Reduction strategy would be a very good career move, as he had tried to explain to his wife the previous evening.

"But why are you going back to London so soon," she'd asked. "There is a very high-profile murder in your constituency, and your voters are very worried that there's a madman running around this city. Surely, an MP's place at a time like this is in the heart of his constituency, showing his constituents that he understands their concerns and cares about them and is there for them, should they need anything."

"Oh darling, we've been through this already. I've got a lot of media work lined up to discuss the new suicide prevention initiative, and I need to see the home secretary in person to try to get this crime reduction strategy off the ground. Both of these are very important, but also, getting close to the probable next prime minister will do my career no harm. And anyway, Harry has been an excellent bridge between my constituents and me since I was first voted in as their MP, and I have every confidence that he will continue to provide the support they need, but of course, I can be home in under two hours if anything significant happens or if anyone desperately needs to see me."

"And what about me?" Elizabeth asked. "You're leaving me alone in a large house in the middle of the countryside. Our nearest neighbours are three miles away. What guarantees do we have for my safety when you're back in London?"

"Come with me," Julian replied. "You'll be available via telephone, Zoom, and email if anyone needs you, but being in London will provide a distraction from these awful events."

"I can't leave now, Julian. I've been allocated a direct link with a senior member of the investigation team, and someone needs to provide support to both Harry and Freya, and to junior staff at the cathedral. I'm needed here, so here I'll stay. Just make sure the burglar alarm is set up correctly before you leave," barked Elizabeth, as she walked out of the room.

Chapter 25

It took just over forty minutes to get from Ashford to Sittingbourne, plenty of time for Beth and Terry to discuss tactics for the interview ahead. On arrival, they parked on the road outside the bookies and waited for the Tanners to arrive. At 1.05 p.m., their patience was rewarded when both brothers pulled up outside the shop in Frankie's car.

"Ooh, get him driving a Rolls Royce Ghost," said Terry.

"One of Dave's sources told me that Frankie had insisted on being gifted the Ghost instead of the money that some young lad with a very well-off dad owed him," said Beth. "Well, instead of the money, and in exchange for a promise not to cut off three of the lad's fingers on each of his hands. It's shocking how easy it is to build up gambling debts, especially with so many online sites available these days. I'm glad my only vice is wine. Well, wine and the odd kebab!"

They waited until Frankie and Billy and their two associates entered the shop before they got out of Terry's Dacia and followed in their footsteps.

Beth and Terry showed the assistant working behind the counter their warrant cards, and asked to see the owner.

"You're out of luck," replied the assistant. "It's only me here today."

"Oh really," said Terry. "Then who did we just watch park up a Rolls Royce Ghost and walk in here just a minute ago?"

Frankie Tanner filled the doorway between the shop and the office. He looked and sounded a lot like Boycie, a favourite character in Only Fools and Horses. "It's okay, William, we've just arrived. I'll deal with our guests," he said, and stepped to one side to allow them to enter his office. Inside, they found an angry looking Billy Tanner sitting in the corner, and noticed that the two associates from the car were now in the kitchen making themselves a brew. Frankie saw them looking towards the kitchen and said, "I'd offer you both a cuppa, but you won't be staying that long. Unfortunately, Billy and I have got a meeting at two p.m. so we'll have to leave here in twenty minutes, but in the meantime, how can we help you, officers?" asked Frankie.

Beth smiled and launched straight into the interview. "I'm DCI Bethany Harper, and I'm leading the investigation into the murder of Jimmy Wheeler. Can you tell us how well you knew the victim?"

"I barely knew him at all," replied Frankie. "We know he used to live on The Cox, and I think he came into my shop once to put a few bob on the Grand National, but we were only on nodding terms, we never spoke."

"Oh come off it, Frankie," said Terry. "You and Jimmy were both conducting business on The Cox – you with your betting shop, and him with his loan sharking. Don't tell us you two never met."

"Officers, please, we run a legitimate business," said Frankie. "My shop on the estate is our only involvement with The Cox, and it's the only involvement we want so we mind our own business. We get on with our business and let others get on with theirs. I sincerely hope no one has said anything different to you?"

"The way I hear it, Billy here is a money man too, and usually sets up a loans business on the estates where you've just opened a new betting shop. That would make The Cox his next target, but Jimmy Wheeler was in the way, eh Billy? How well did you know him?" Terry asked Billy.

Billy looked at Frankie, who nodded, then said, "Same as Frankie. Barely knew him."

"Okay, so neither of you had ever spoken with Mr Wheeler? No business discussions, nothing? And he never said anything to upset you in any way?" asked Beth.

"Like I said, we run a legitimate business officers," said Frankie. "We had nothing to do with Mr Wheeler, god rest his soul, and again, I can only express my most sincere hope that no one has said anything different to you?"

Beth decided to stop wasting time and get straight to the point. "Let me tell you what I think, Billy," turning to the sullen presence in the corner of the room. "Jimmy Wheeler was loan sharking on The Cox, and you and your brother wanted to muscle in. It's your form, Billy, everyone knows that. You wanted a piece of the action but he wouldn't let you anywhere near, so you killed him."

"What the fuck is this?" asked Billy, as Frankie laughed out loud. Billy jumped up from his chair and demanded "Where's your evidence?" only to shrink back, when Frankie glared at him.

"Officers, my brother makes a very good point. You can't stroll in here accusing one of us of murder without any evidence. So, if you have any evidence, please arrest us but if not, and you would like to speak with either of us again, please let us know in advance, and we will ensure that we have legal representation with us when you call. In the meantime, we have a meeting to get to so..." said Frankie, as he opened the door to escort them out.

"Thank you very much," said Beth. "Here are our contact cards. If either of you can think of anything that would help our investigation do, please, get in touch." And with that, she and Terry left the bookies and made their way back to his car.

"Fucking cheek," said Billy, when he was alone with Frankie. "What do you think they know?"

"Nothing, Billy, they know nothing," Frankie replied as he watched Beth and Terry through the office window.

"Fucking cheek," said Terry, when he was alone with Beth. "We need to find Kevin Carter urgently, and get him to talk. With a bit of luck we can persuade Jackie to give him the nod to do that, and then, as soon as we have anything on either of the Tanners, we can bring them in."

"Absolutely," said Beth. "Let me give Ki a ring to find out where we are with tracking Kevin Carter. He's like Lord Lucan, isn't he?" The joke fell as flat as the mood in the car. "In the meantime," said Beth, "Chill your beans please, and concentrate on the drive back to base. Everyone will get their comeuppance, I promise you."

Chapter 26

When Ki and Dave got back to their desks after interviewing Philip Crossfield, they gave Fiona and Clarissa an update on the altercation between two men, who looked like Jimmy Wheeler and Selwyn Du Pont. Fiona got goosebumps at the thought of a breakthrough, and was glad that she'd already called Selwyn to arrange an introductory meeting at two p.m. that afternoon.

When Fiona and Clarissa arrived at the cathedral, they went to the Constables' Lodge and asked to see Selwyn Du Pont. Selwyn had already told the administrator that he was expecting a visit, and she showed them to the meeting room she'd booked for them. After asking them if they'd like a tea or a coffee, she retreated to the Lodge just as Selwyn marched into the room.

"Good afternoon, ladies," he said jovially. "Thank you very much for taking time out of your busy schedules to meet with me to update me on progress with the investigation. I am, as I'm sure you've gathered, Selwyn Du Pont, Canon Missioner at the cathedral."

"I'm Detective Inspector Fiona Richardson, and this is my colleague, Detective Constable Clarissa Griswold."

"I was at Cambridge with a Griswold," said Selwyn, extending a hand to Clarissa, much to Fiona's irritation.

"I'm sure you'll understand," interrupted Fiona "That there isn't a great deal that we can share with you about the investigation itself, other than to confirm that we are all working very hard to find the perpetrator of this horrendous crime."

"Yes, of course, I completely understand that you're bound by the rules of confidentiality. In that case, is there anything I can help you with from the cathedral's perspective?" asked Selwyn.

"Well, we do have a question for you, but it's more to do with any extra-curricular activities you might have. Do you carry out any work with Canterbury Cares, the local homeless charity?" asked Fiona.

"Why yes, I've been volunteering with homeless charities since leaving university, and that was a long, long time ago," he smiled, a little less brightly than when he arrived. "I've been involved with Canterbury Cares since I arrived at the cathedral ten years ago. Why do you ask?"

"We've been told that there was an altercation at the charity's office one evening towards the end of September. It involved the man we believe to be Jimmy Wheeler, and a member of the clergy, who we believe to be you. We have requested copies of the charity's CCTV footage to confirm who was there that night, but it would be much easier if you could confirm whether or not you were at the shelter on the evening that a man who resembled Jimmy Wheeler was there," said Fiona.

"An altercation, you say?" Selwyn appeared to think for a moment before replying, "Ah yes, I think I know what you're referring to. Yes, I was at the shelter that evening and yes, a man who, now you come to mention it, looked a lot like Jimmy Wheeler did come to the shelter. He said he was looking for one of his clients who owed him some money – quite a lot of money, he said. He told me that if I didn't tell him where to find this individual, he would conduct a search himself, and then he'd burn the shelter to the ground. Well as you can imagine, I was horrified at this threat, and it is with much regret that I have to admit, I did release my anger in a physical way."

"You thumped him," said Clarissa.

"Yes, I am embarrassed and disappointed to admit that I did thump him," replied Selwyn.

"We've checked our records and we can't find a report on this incident. Did that surprise you at the time?" asked Fiona.

"Yes, very much so," replied Selwyn. "I physically assaulted a man in front of dozens of witnesses, including an associate of his, who looked as though he could be quite nasty and pretty handy with his fists, but nothing came of it. I didn't see the man again, or his associate, I wasn't visited by the police, which I deduced was the result of his not reporting the incident, so yes, I was surprised that the incident started and finished there that night."

"We hear that the man threatened you in a non-verbal way as you left. That must have been worrying for you?" asked Fiona.

"Let me think," said Selwyn. "Oh, do you mean the slash-your-throat action he did? I've worked with desperate people for most of my life, and I can assure you that did not disturb me in the slightest. I've had much worse said to me when people are angry or in despair."

"And to be clear, you had no contact at all with Jimmy Wheeler after that incident?" Fiona was nothing if not persistent.

"No, no contact at all," replied Selwyn.

"Why did you not mention the altercation to us as soon as Mr Wheeler's body was found in the cathedral?" asked Fiona.

"Well, it was only now that I made the connection between the incident at the shelter and the body found in the cathedral otherwise I would, of course, have contacted you immediately," replied Selwyn.

"And what happened to the individual that Jimmy had come to see? What was their name?" asked Clarissa.

"I don't know his full name, just his first name, Trevor. He was in the showers when the incident happened, and when he came out and heard about what had happened, he grabbed his bag and went out into the night, and I haven't seen him at the shelter since, I'm afraid," replied Selwyn.

"How often did Trevor visit the shelter?" asked Fiona.

"I'm afraid I can't answer that. I saw him there a few times myself, but he could have been there more often," replied Selwyn.

"Did he normally stay overnight?" asked Fiona.

"As far as I can recall he did, yes," replied Selwyn.

"But you haven't seen Trevor at all since that incident?" asked Fiona.

"No, I haven't," replied Selwyn.

"Okay, well thank you for your time," said Fiona. "If you can think of anything else relating to that incident, or anything relating to Jimmy Wheeler that could help us move the investigation forward, do, please get in touch with us."

"Yes of course. And thank you for support."

As they walked back to the station, Fiona asked Clarissa what she'd thought of the interview.

"Well, we had to drag the details from him, which is odd because I would have expected more openness and co-operation from a cleric, so I'd say he's hiding something from us."

"I agree," said Fiona. "I'm going over to Canterbury Cares as soon as the four p.m. debrief is over, to check out the CCTV footage and ask staff and volunteers for as much information as possible regarding the mysterious Trevor. Can you come along or have you got another engagement? We can take our own cars, and head home straight from the shelter."

"Unless there's an interesting development," said Clarissa.

"Indeed. Unless there's an interesting development," repeated Fiona.

Chapter 27

"Okay, can we all settle down please," said Beth. "I know we've all had a busy and productive day today, so let's get straight to it.

Terry and I went to the William Harvey this morning to see The Shank. He was as uncooperative and unsociable as you might expect – I'm not sure whether he said 'No comment' or 'Fuck off' most often, but we got absolutely nothing from him. We'd been asked not to put too much pressure on him when he was on the ward, so we've asked to be notified when he's discharged, then we can interview him under caution. See if that makes him a little more talkative.

We went from Ashford to Sittingbourne to interview the Tanner brothers. They were, as you can imagine, as uncooperative as The Shank. We really need someone to go on the record about these guys so we can talk to the CPS about getting them off the streets.

Ki, how are you getting on with UK Protected Persons Service?"

Ki and Dave were in Ickleford, executing the search warrant on Shirley and Jackie's house. They joined the team via a secure video link along with Jenny, all three of them huddled in Jenny's car.

"UKPPS are looking at Muhammad's request," he replied. "If it's not dismissed out of hand, they'll make an appointment to meet with him and discuss options, but his isn't the most pressing case in their inbox at the moment, and as we know, protection might not even be needed depending on Frankie's next move."

"Okay, thanks," replied Beth. "How are you getting on with tracking down Kevin Carter and Jeff Robinson?"

"Dave's been doing a morning call every day to the elderly couple we met in the greasy spoon, just checking in to make sure they're okay. According to them, Kevin and Jeff have both been spotted walking around The Cox and going into Jimmy's old flat, so they're still around. We're hoping to get the warrant to enter their flats first thing tomorrow," said Ki.

"Excellent work, Ki and Dave. How's the search of Shirley and Jackie's home going?" asked Beth.

"We haven't found anything useful yet. Did you say you wanted to interview Jackie yourself?" asked Ki.

"Yes, I do. I'll be coming to Ickleford as soon as I've given the Super his daily briefing. I should be with you by around six or six thirty p.m., depending on the Super's curiosity and the traffic on the roads," replied Beth.

"Just one more update from us," said Beth. "Digital Forensics have come up trumps on Jimmy's phone – familiar names and lots of messages, which Terry and I will review in the morning. Unfortunately, the same cannot be said of his laptop which, it would appear, was only used for watching American football. So, that means he must have kept paper records, which is why we need to search the homes of his nearest and dearest.

Ki and Dave, can you please check in with Michelle and Muhammad to see if they noticed any one of the Wheeler gang writing anything down, and if they did, what sort of book were they writing in? Large, small, purple cover etc. That will hopefully give our search a bit of focus.

Okay, can you please give us an update on your interview with Philip Crossfield?"

Ki started the update and told Beth about the altercation Philip had witnessed at Canterbury Care, and they'd passed it to Fiona and Clarissa to follow up with Selwyn Du Pont.

Dave cleared his throat and took over. "We're going to check the CCTV in McDonald's, and the CCTV on the number seventy-one bus to verify Philip's story."

"Great work. Thank you," said Beth. "What do you think of his story?"

"We both think he's trying too hard to be co-operative and open with us – you know the drill, 'I came here of my own volition to try to help you' and the ridiculous presentation of outstretched palms to show how open and truthful he was being; he shared some platitudes about life being too precious to even joke about taking another life. All textbook stuff. We'll check in with his old army buddies, but we'll also get in touch with some in his chain of command for a different perspective," replied Ki.

"Excellent. Thanks Ki. Okay, Fiona and Clarissa. How has your day been?" asked Beth.

As usual, Fiona took the lead. "Arthur Lloyd has sent us a more detailed list of staff and volunteers who had borrowed the keys during a working day over the last twelve months. It's not complete, but it's got more detail than his previous list, so we spent the morning running checks on those we know had borrowed the keys, and we'll pick that up in the morning, by which time Arthur should have sent us more names from some of the close constables, who weren't available yesterday. The head of housekeeping has confirmed that her Deputy has never shared her keys with anyone, so assuming no one is lying to us, that puts housekeeping in the clear.

Thanks to the intel from Ki and Dave's interview with Philip Crossfield, we went to the cathedral this afternoon," and she gave an update on their interview with Selwyn Du Pont.

"Once this debrief has ended, Clarissa and I will be heading to the Canterbury Cares shelter to check their CCTV, and interview some staff and volunteers to see if we can confirm Selwyn's story, and to find out who this Trevor is," said Fiona.

"Excellent work, Fiona and Clarissa," said Beth. "Okay, Terry and Dave – have we heard back from the medicines management people about the oramorph?"

"Not yet Guv," said Terry. "But Dave's been calling them every day for an update."

"Okay. Well done everyone. I feel we've really made progress today, and we're edging closer to having a few very plausible suspects.

Right. I'm off to see the Super, so I'll leave you to carry on with the next stages of your investigations. Thank you so much, guys."

Chapter 28

Beth followed Terry's car to Ickleford. The journey took just under an hour, and they arrived just as the uniformed team were packing up for the day.

Ki left the house to meet Beth and Terry at their cars. "Nothing," he said. "We've searched every nook and cranny, but there are no files or paperwork relating to the Wheeler business."

"That's not entirely surprising," said Beth. "Are they both in here?" Ki nodded. "Okay, let's go and speak with them. See you tomorrow, Ki."

They found Shirley and Jackie sitting in the kitchen. "Oh god, not another one. You gonna be long?" asked Shirley. "We've left poor Dawn on her own with that Jenny for most of the day, and we want to get back to her."

"Jackie was happy to leave Dawn for several hours last night to have a meeting in Jimmy's old flat at The Cox though, eh Jackie. We heard that you're the new boss of the Wheeler business. Now, how can someone step into that role when she knows nothing at all about the business, I wonder?" asked Beth, before reminding Jackie of her own words, "Home is home, business is business."

"I don't know what you're talking about," said Jackie. "I popped to The Cox yesterday to check that your lot hadn't left Jimmy's flat in a state. I don't know who's been filling your head with stories about me taking over from Jimmy, but they're wrong, or they're lying to you."

"Stop messing us about, Jackie. You were seen going into Jimmy's flat last night, and Kevin Carter, Jeff Robinson, Gary Nixon, and Mikey Curtis were also seen going in. We know that you must have been telling them about the new arrangements for the Wheeler business, because we know that Kevin and Jeff have been spreading that information around The Cox today, so just cut the crap and answer the questions," said Terry.

"You wanna watch your language," Shirley told Terry.

"So, Jackie, going back to my first question, how can someone who knows nothing about her brother's business take over that business after he's died?" asked Beth.

Jackie glared at Beth, then looked at her mother and shrugged. "Jimmy had a bit of a health scare last year. His doctor did loads of tests but in the end, it wasn't nothing serious. So, that's when he started talking to me about the business, saying that if anything happened to him, he wanted me to look after things so that we could look after Dawn for him. When you were asking us about the business the other day, we was still in shock about Jimmy's death, so I told you about the posh boys but didn't think about anything else at the time."

"Yes, we know who the posh boys are. And so does someone on The Cox, who gave their leader a good beating last night. Do your lads know anything about that?" asked Terry.

"No idea what you're talking about," Jackie replied.

"No? Strange coincidence, don't you think, that someone who, in your own words, scared your brother a few weeks before he was killed, suddenly ends up badly beaten on the estate your brother used to operate from," said Beth.

Jackie shrugged.

"What about the Tanners? What do you know about them?" asked Terry.

"There's a Tanners Bookies on The Cox, isn't there mum?" asked Jackie.

"Yeah, I think that's the name of the bookies, but I'm not sure. Haven't really mixed with them so don't really know much about them," replied Shirley.

"Yeah that's right," said Jackie.

"Okay, let's talk about Jimmy's loan shark activities," said Beth. "You know that lending money without a licence is illegal in this country, don't you? But you're going to continue to do so."

"I'm afraid you've been misinformed," said Jackie. "Jimmy used to give his friends a bit of a loan sometimes, but mainly he used to sell goods door to door on the estate. He got a pedlar's certificate so it's all legit. People would ask if he had something, like kids' shoes or clothes, and he'd sell it to them. Course, he had to put a little mark-up on the goods, higher for those who couldn't pay him outright, otherwise how would he make a living, but like I said, it's all legit. A bit like a catalogue. You know, Freemans and the like – the one that those ladies off Strictly Come Dancing advertise. Oh, and before you ask yes, I've applied for a pedlar's certificate myself."

This was news to Beth and Terry. They needed to get back to base to check it out, but in the meantime, they had one pressing question.

"Where are Jimmy's books, Jackie. We've checked his office and couldn't find them, and there's nothing on his laptop, so who's got the books?" asked Beth.

Jackie sat in her chair, and looked silently at Beth.

"Jackie, if we're going to catch the person who killed and mutilated your twin brother, we need to know who would have a motive to do that, and the best place to start is with his books. Who owes him money, Jackie?" asked Beth.

"Leave it with me," replied Jackie. "I'll have a look for them."

Beth nodded, then Terry asked, "Can you find them and get them to us tomorrow, Jackie? And get Kevin or Jeff, or preferably both, to deliver them to the station."

"I'll see what I can do," replied Jackie.

Beth and Terry made for the door. They both sat in Terry's car to digest the interview with the Wheeler women.

"A pedlar's certificate? How did I not know about this?" asked Beth. "I'm tamping, Terry, absolutely fucking tamping. And as for getting the books to us tomorrow, I look forward to seeing the abridged version of the books, listing only the clients she wants us to know about, and none of the others, one of whom could be our murderer. Fuck sake. They're running rings around us." Beth let out a long and loud yell, which made Terry jump, then said "Jesus, I need a drink. I'm going home. Time for you to go home too, Terry. If you get a wiggle on, you'll make Harry's bathtime," and with that, they went their separate ways.

In the year 580, the Frankish Princess Bertha agreed to marry the pagan King Æthelberht of Kent, on condition that she was allowed to continue to practice her Christian faith in pagan England. Æthelberht agreed and refurbished an area of what is now the old St Martin's church, just outside Canterbury's city walls, to support her worship.

When the Pope sent St Augustine to England in 596, on a mission to convert the English to Christianity, Bertha is reported to have been a significant support to him.

To honour this remarkable woman, the Bertha trail has been laid in Canterbury. A series of fourteen bronze plaques are embedded in the pavements to guide people from Canterbury Cathedral to St Martin's church, where Bertha used to pray. Over the years, many people have followed the trail and walked to the small church.

This morning, a woman walked alone.

Gloria Byrne had parked in the underground car park at Canterbury Cathedral, only available to staff and Chapter members, and walked to St Martin's church to start a day's work. She saw him as soon as she walked in – the man kneeling in front of Bertha's altar. 'Dear God, please, not another one.' Her instinct was to turn and run, but it was trumped by the need to check if he was okay, and if there was anything she could do to help him, so she approached the kneeling man with trepidation and put a hand on his shoulder. The man fell back as far as his hands, bound to the altar, would allow. It was then that Gloria saw that the kneeling man, soon to be identified as Frankie Tanner, was dead and his ears had been removed.

Gloria staggered backwards and stifled a scream.

Chapter 29

Superintendent Donald Campbell marched into the squad room and straight into Beth's office, closing the door behind him.

"They've found another body. It's in St Martin's church this time, and this time, they've cut the ears off the victim. As far as I'm aware, the eyes remain in situ.

One of the uniforms who was first on the scene has identified the victim due to previous engagements with him and his family. It's Frankie Tanner, Beth," he said.

Beth sat quietly for a moment, shocked by the latest development.

"This is going to increase the pressure on the team," Donald continued. "My main concern is that they will try to parachute someone from the National Crime Agency in to take control. I will, of course, strongly resist any such suggestions, as will the DCC, but we need to start seeing some results, Beth. I know it's been less than a week since we found the first body, but we haven't yet got any strong suspects."

"I have to disagree, Sir," replied Beth. "Philip Crossfield remains a strong suspect, and we're not yet convinced by Selwyn Du Pont's explanation for the altercation in the Canterbury Cares shelter, but as you are aware, investigating a member of the clergy at Canterbury Cathedral is a very delicate matter. Add to that the fact that the Wheelers and the Tanners were in the same business that the Peckham Posh Boys are in, and the Posh Boys have ambitions to include Kent, or at the very least East Kent, to their areas of operation, and we have more suspects."

"Is The Shank still in the care of Dickens Ward?" asked Donald. "If so, he'll have a pretty solid alibi."

"I received an email from the Nurse in Charge of Dickens Ward at 11.58 p.m. last night, to say that The Shank discharged himself from her ward at nine thirty p.m. so that puts him back in the frame," replied Beth.

"Right. We need to look into his activities after he left the hospital last night. We also need to know if Philip Crossfield has any connection with Frankie Tanner, and does Selwyn Du Pont have any connection, other than one altercation, with either of the victims? I need answers to these questions today, Beth."

Donald let out a long sigh, and shook his head. "I'll see you at St Martin's shortly," he said, and left for his car.

Beth followed Donald out of her office and stood at the front of the squad room. All eyes looked expectantly at her, as she reluctantly broke the news.

"There's another body. This time, they've cut the ears off. The victim is Frankie Tanner. We need to get over to St Martin's church immediately."

The team were as shocked as Beth had been by this development, and peeled off to go to the church.

"You okay Guv?" asked Terry, as soon as they sat in his car.

"God, Terry, this is bad. It's very bad. But it might prove helpful in narrowing the field of suspects, or introducing new, stronger suspects, so we need to get stuck in to the investigation immediately. I mean, there's one pretty obvious connection between Jimmy and Frankie, but one killing the other would make more sense than both being killed. It puts The Shank front and centre, I suppose, but we need more information about his movements, and we need more time which I hope we're going to get. And more resources would be very helpful too. I'll ask the Super how colleagues in other teams are fixed at the moment. I would imagine this case will take priority over most other cases, so we might be in luck," replied Beth.

St Martin's church sits just off the A257, a ten minute walk from the centre of Canterbury and its cathedral, and a four minute drive from Canterbury police station. The beautiful old building is a proud UNESCO World Heritage Site, and the history and heritage of the building sent a shiver down history-buff Beth's spine, as she and Terry joined the rest of the team at St Bertha's altar. Mac the Knife had, as ever, beaten everyone else to it, and had unshackled Frankie Tanner and laid him on his back.

"Hey Mac, how are you doing?" asked Beth warmly. "What have we got?"

"No obvious cause of death," said Mac. "We'll know more once we get him to the mortuary. There are post-mortem mutilations to the face; as you can see, the victim's ears have been removed. The technical name for the removal of the ears as an act of punishment is cropping." Beth was impressed by her friend's knowledge until Mac replied with a simple "I read it in *'The Hunchback of Notre Dame'*." Beth smiled at Mac's love of trivia, or general knowledge as she preferred to call it. She was a great friend to have in pub quizzes.

Beth knew that there was no point asking her next question, but did so nevertheless. "So, are we looking at the same murderer here, Mac?"

Mac rolled her eyes and said, "You know full well I can't answer that yet, but I can confirm what you have already seen – there are similarities between the murder of the victim found at the cathedral, and our victim here, insofar as there is a lack of blood at the scene, we've found no potential murder weapon, the victim has been stripped of all forms of ID, and the body has been mutilated. Now, if you'll let me get on, I can furnish you with facts rather than conjecture." She winked at Beth to acknowledge that she understood Beth had to try.

"We'll leave you to it. And thanks for everything, Mac," said Beth.

Beth turned to the team. "Ki, Dave, find Muhammad Khan and take him to the station for questioning. We are no longer viewing him as a witness, but as a suspect in both murders. Please make that very clear to him.

Clarissa, please take a statement from the member of staff who found the body and get hold of any CCTV they might have, then you and Fiona can head back to the squad room and start looking for connections, other than the obvious, between Jimmy Wheeler and Frankie Tanner, and between the victims and our current suspects. Does Philip Crossfield know Frankie Tanner? Can you find any link at all between Frankie and Selwyn Du Pont? And if, in the highly unlikely event that Kevin Carter and Jeff Robinson turn up bearing gifts, please interview them as witnesses in the murder investigation for Jimmy Wheeler. And find out if there's more of a connection than we already know between Kevin and Jeff, and Frankie Tanner. Terry, you and I will visit Frankie's wife to break the news to her and, if we can find him, we'll inform Billy as well. Thanks everyone. If anything urgent crops up, please let me know otherwise I'll see you all at the four p.m. debrief."

Beth spotted Emma Draper and Matthew Rye talking to the Super and the DCC when she walked into the building, and headed in their direction. The Super excused himself for a moment to catch up with her.

"Sir, we're pulling Muhammad Khan in for questioning as a suspect, and we're going to look into possible connections, other than the obvious, between our victims and between each of them, and each of our suspects. Terry and I are off to let the victim's wife know that his body has been found here, then we'll start looking at any interaction between Frankie and The Shank," said Beth.

"Thanks Beth. I assume the four p.m. debrief is going ahead as usual today? If so, I'll join you," asked Donald.

"Yes sir. We look forward to seeing you then," replied Beth, then made her way to the door to meet Terry and head to see Frankie's wife in Chatham.

Chapter 30

St Martin's Island is one of the most exclusive residential areas in Chatham and was, ironically, home to fifty-two-year-old Frankie Tanner and his thirty-two-year-old wife, Chantelle. "The boys would love this massive garden. Plenty of space to run around and play a bit of footy. Any chance of a pay rise, Guv?" he asked.

Beth laughed. "Oh Terry, we're in the wrong game, mate! Still, we all have to play the hands we're dealt, so let's see how Chantelle deals with this hand," she said, making her way to the couple's front door and ringing the bell.

The door was answered by a petite blonde woman, immaculately dressed and perfectly-presented, looking quite irritated. "What do you want?" asked Chantelle Tanner.

Beth and Terry showed her their warrant cards. "We're looking for Frankie Tanner's wife," said Beth.

"Yeah, that's me. What do you want?" she repeated.

"Can we come in?" asked Beth.

Chantelle let out an exaggerated sigh, rolled her eyes, then moved aside to let them in, and showed them into the main reception room.

"Well?" she said. "I've got a haircut booked in half an hour. I need to get ready and get over there, so get on with it."

"Chantelle, the body of a middle-aged man was found in St Martin's church in Canterbury this morning. I'm sorry to tell you we believe that it's Frankie," said Beth.

There was a long silence as Chantelle absorbed the news. "God. What happened to him?" she asked.

"It's too early for us to know how he died. We'll know that after the post-mortem, and as soon as we know, we'll tell you," said Terry.

Chantelle composed herself. "Right," she said to herself, then turned to Beth and said, "You'll need me to identify the body, won't you? And we need to tell the family. I need my mum. Let me call her and get to come over, then we can go and identify Frankie."

"Yes, of course," said Beth. "But we'd like to ask a few questions first. What was Frankie's schedule yesterday?"

"It was just a usual Thursday. He went to work and didn't come home."

"When did you first notice that Frankie hadn't come home?" continued Beth.

"He never does on a Thursday. He's got a flat in Canterbury and he stays over every Monday and Thursday. And some other nights, if he's really busy. He works very hard, and he's extending his business in East Kent now, so he needs to be able to stay locally to do that," replied Chantelle.

"Whereabouts is his Canterbury flat?" asked Terry.

"No idea. Never been there. Margaret will know. She's been his secretary for over twenty years, and she knows pretty much everything there is to know about his business dealings, and his personal arrangements. She's more like a second mum than a secretary." Chantelle explained, "His own mother died when he was fifteen, and there was no father figure in their house, so being the eldest, Frankie took his role as head of the family very seriously. Oh, hark at me going on. Sorry. This has all come as a bit of a shock to me."

"What's Margaret's surname, and where can we find her?" asked Terry.

"Margaret Foster. She works in Frankie's office on Chatham High Street. I'll write down the address for you."

"Chantelle, why haven't you ever been to Frankie's flat in Canterbury?" asked Beth.

"Never needed to – we never go out in Canterbury and Frankie told me the flat in Canterbury was very basic; just a place for him to have a kip a few nights a week. It was cheaper than grabbing a hotel every time he needed to stay over, he used to say, so it's not like a second home or anything," she replied defensively.

"I'm so sorry we have to go into this detail with you Chantelle. We know it can't be easy for you and we really appreciate your support," said Beth, then paused. "This is a really difficult question to ask you, but can you think of anyone who would want to hurt Frankie?"

"Yes. No. Oh god, I can't think straight. Let me identify him then I'll have a proper think about that."

Chantelle started to cry quietly, then clenched her hands and stared at the floor. Once she'd composed herself she said "Okay. Let's get on with this."

"Chantelle," said Terry gently. "If you're going to identify the body, you need to know that Frankie suffered some trauma before death. I'm sorry to tell you that Frankie's ears have been cut off."

There was another long silence as Chantelle absorbed the news then she asked quietly, "It's just like Jimmy Wheeler. We heard they'd cut his eyes out and his ears off. So, Jimmy's murderer killed Frankie?"

"Sorry Chantelle but it's too early to be able to confirm or deny that. All I can tell you is that as soon as we know, so will you. How well did you know Jimmy Wheeler?" asked Beth.

"I didn't know the man himself – never met him – I only know what I've read online, and what people have told me, but it must be the same killer. This cutting ears off and stuff is too weird for there to be more than one person doing it. You can see that, right?" asked Chantelle.

Beth looked at her in silence then said, "Okay. We'll leave you to call your mum, then we'll head off to the mortuary. Can I get you a cup of tea or something stronger?"

"No, I'm okay. I'll just make that call then we can go."

Beth went to Terry's car to call the Super and left Terry with Chantelle, listening to the conversation. Within fifteen minutes, Beth, Terry, Chantelle, and Mrs Smith, as Chantelle's mother insisted on being called, were heading to the mortuary where they made their way to the relatives viewing platform. Although he was new to the team, Terry was already feeling too familiar with this room.

Beth looked at Chantelle and asked, "Are you ready?"

Mrs Smith put an arm around her daughter's shoulder as Beth nodded to Mac, who removed the sheet from Frankie's face.

Chantelle sobbed loudly, and buried her head in her mother's shoulder. "Yes," said Mrs Smith. "That is my son-in-law, Frankie Tanner. Now I'd like to take my daughter home please."

Terry arranged for both women to have a cup of tea as they waited for the police car to take them home, then he and Beth returned to his car.

"Well I've spoken to the Super and the good news is that we've got three extra staff members joining the team for the foreseeable: DI Steve Robinson, DS Martha Kennedy, and DC Prisha Sharma. All three are from CID – their loss is our gain! I've spoken with Martha and asked her to take on the Family Liaison role for Chantelle, and all three are in the squad room as I speak, having an introduction to the case from Fiona and Clarissa. Although mainly Fiona, I would think.

The bad news is that the DCC is, apparently, spitting feathers. Not only do we have another murder, but it's less than a week since the last one, and we haven't got a prime suspect in place. He's asked the comms team to arrange a press conference at five p.m. tonight, and he wants me and the Super to present it. No family presence at this point. I think the main focus needs to be setting the record straight on the mutilations – some of the rumours are scaring people unnecessarily, when the truth is quite scary enough. I'm expecting Dawn and Chantelle to provide comms with some very respectable suit-and-tie photos of their men, so I think we need to be clear on the circles they moved in, and the business connections they had, within reason of course."

"God, that's a fine line. Good luck with it. Where to next?" asked Terry.

Beth handed him the scrap of paper with Jimmy's office address on. "I think it's time for us to meet Margaret Foster and break the sad news to her," sighed Beth, as the heavens opened and the rain started to fall.

Chapter 31

Elizabeth Jefferson-Briggs woke to the smell of bacon sizzling under the grill. The smell and sound confused her – Julian was at their flat in London, and only they and their cleaner had keys to their home, and since cooking was not in the cleaner's job description, who was in their kitchen and why was the air filled with the smell of bacon? The only logical answer was that Julian had, for some reason, come home early; but as a precaution, she picked up Matthew's old baseball bat before making her way downstairs. She smiled fondly as she remembered Matthew's excitement as a twelve-year-old, watching the Boston Red Sox play at Fenway Park, and one of his very rare requests for some money so that he could buy the full set of baseball memorabilia – a shirt, a hat, a ball, and that bat. Suddenly, her eyes welled with tears until she was brought back to the present, when the kitchen's fire alarm started shrieking.

Elizabeth walked cautiously down the stairs, and stood with her back to the wall next to the kitchen door.

"I can hear you, darling. You'll need to do better than that if a burglar breaks in," said Julian.

The tension left Elizabeth's body immediately.

"You were always a terrible cook," she replied. "Open the back door to let in some air to stop that awful noise," but Julian was already a step ahead of her and the fresh air was rushing in.

Once calm and quiet had been restored to the house, they looked at each other, hugged and laughed. They both missed that physical contact terribly when they were apart.

"What are you doing here? And when did you get here?" she asked, slapping him on his shoulder. "I wasn't expecting you home until tonight. Aren't you supposed to be on the Today programme?"

"I was bumped late last night," he replied. "I found it difficult to sleep, thinking about you here alone, so I thought 'this is ridiculous! I'm getting in that car and driving to Canterbury to cook a full English breakfast for my beautiful wife,' and that's what I did. I think I arrived here at about three fifteen a.m. and I didn't want to disturb you so I slept in Matthew's room. Sorry. I should have messaged you to tell you about the change of plan but it was late," he said, kissing the top of her head.

"Oh darling, it's good to have you home. Now please, step aside and let me finish the breakfast before the police come and storm the house after getting reports of alarm bells ringing endlessly."

As she said that, Julian's mobile phone rang. He took the call and responded to the caller in a subdued and sober manner.

"That was the chief constable," he told his wife. "There's been another murder."

***

Selwyn Du Pont was not hungry. That was unusual on an ordinary day, but there was nothing ordinary about today. There had been another murder and he needed to break the news to Mary. He knew it was much better for her to hear it from him, but he was struggling to find the words.

"Your overnight oats are ready, and your tea and toast will be ready soon," said Mary, as he approached the kitchen. Selwyn stood fixed in the doorway. "Is everything okay, darling?" his wife asked.

"There's been another murder," said Selwyn, unable to think of any other way to share the news.

Mary buckled and cried, "No. No, no, no, Selwyn, please, tell me there's been a mistake?"

"There's no mistake my darling," he said, pulling her into a protective bear hug and holding her tight until she stopped shaking.

"Who is it? What happened? Who's doing this, Selwyn?"

Selwyn again tried to find the words to share the news with her but again, he struggled so he chose the direct route. "I've heard that the victim is Frankie Tanner. He was killed and his body was left in St Martin's church. I don't know who's doing this my love. I wish I did." Mary started shaking again, and drew away from her husband.

"Frankie Tanner," she whispered. "Oh Selwyn, first Jimmy Wheeler now him. That's awful. This whole thing is getting closer and closer to home. I'm scared, Selwyn, I'm really scared."

"I'm here my love. I will look after you. No harm will come to you, I can promise you that."

Chapter 32

The Cox looked as grim as its residents' prospects. As Ki and Dave approached the greasy spoon, Dave spotted Malcolm and Jean Dixon, the elderly couple they'd met on their first visit to the caff. Dave waved at them and popped his head around the door. "Good morning, you two. How's the all-day breakfast?" he asked.

"Very nice thank you," replied Malcolm.

"You could do with some yourself to put a bit of meat on your old sparrow legs," Jean told him with a laugh.

"You cheeky monkey," replied Dave, with a smile and a wink.

A natural people person, there was never any doubt that Dave Roberts would become a policeman as soon as he left school. His mum had a very successful career in East Kent Police, having started her service with the Met Police in London, where she had followed her dad and grandad into the force. Dave himself had trained at Hendon, before joining the Met to cut his teeth, then moving back to Kent to be closer to his family.

Dave was excellent at interacting with, and nurturing, the victims of crime, getting them to relax and remember more detail than some of his colleagues could draw out. He was also very good at managing most criminals, particularly the younger ones, and had one of East Kent Police's most prolific collection of sources and informants.

At thirty-two years old, the fact that Dave was still single was a source of amusement or false jealousy to most of his friends, and a source of disquiet to most of his family. He'd love to settle down, he just hadn't met the right woman yet. "Not everyone can meet someone like you," he'd once told his dad over a pint before the Sunday roast. In reality, the hours he worked tended to rule out a good social life; he was not an ambitious man, much preferring to have a hands-on role in a team than a management role, sorting budgets and dealing with HR, but he liked a job well done, and was always more than happy to work the hours needed to deliver that. The truth was, Dave Roberts loved his job. He must do. He'd married it.

Ki and Dave made their way to Muhammad Khan's flat and knocked. Then knocked again. The door was opened after several minutes by a dishevelled-looking Muhammad in his vest and pants, with one eye open and the other opening slowly. He'd clearly just tumbled out of bed, but invited both officers in.

"We'd like you to accompany us to the station, Mr Khan," said Dave.

"What's this about? Is it about my protection? Why can't we talk about that here?" asked Muhammad, looking quizzically at Ki.

"We'd like you to accompany us to the station on another matter," replied Dave. "Could you please grab whatever you will need for the next few hours and come with us?"

"A few hours? Down the station? What's going on lads?" asked Muhammad.

"We're investigating the murder of Frankie Tanner," said Dave, and waited for the news to sink in. "We will be interviewing you as a suspect in this investigation, and we will also be interviewing you as a suspect in the death of Jimmy Wheeler."

"What? Frankie Tanner's dead? And he was murdered. When did this happen? What happened? It wasn't me. You can't pin this one on me. I told you already. I haven't got it in me to harm anyone," said Muhammad hysterically.

Ki and Dave remained silent and watched Muhammad's shoulders slump as he realised there would be no alternative but to collect his essentials, arrange cover for his cab that night, leave a note for his wife, then follow them to Ki's car.

At the station, Dave arranged for Muhammad to have a cup of tea as they waited for his appointed solicitor to arrive, after which he did the formalities for the interview tape.

Then Ki took the reins.

"Mr Khan, we are investigating the murder of Frankie Tanner, a bookmaker with a shop on the Coxhall estate.

Can you please tell us about your interactions with Mr Tanner?"

"You know what my interactions have been. I'm on your books waiting for protection," sighed Muhammad.

"For the tape please," asked Ki, and waited as Muhammad recounted the meetings he'd had with Frankie Tanner and why Frankie had offered him a role in his organisation.

"So, you told Mr Tanner that you were not prepared to accept his offer, and you were not able or interested in beating Jimmy Wheeler, or anyone else, to within an inch of their lives?"

"Well, I never actually told him that. I knew the consequences would be bad if I did, and I've got a wife and three kids at home."

"So, Frankie thought you were one of his boys?" asked Ki.

"No. Well, I don't know. I definitely didn't tell him I was, but then I didn't tell him I wasn't, so I suppose he probably assumed that I was, but of course, I wasn't." Muhammad stopped talking when his solicitor put his hand on his arm.

"Can you tell us where you were between the hours of five p.m. last night and eight a.m. this morning?"

"I was at home between five p.m. and a quarter to eight, having dinner with my kids and helping them with their homework. Well, not that I'm much help, especially with maths, but you know what I mean." The solicitor's hand once again rested on Muhammad's arm, helping him to regain some focus. "Then, I was working from eight p.m. to eight a.m. The graveyard shift they call it. It's rubbish, especially if you don't like cleaning up puke, but the company pays a good bonus for drivers to cover it, so it's a good shift for someone like me, who needs the money."

"Is that why you changed your regular working hours a few weeks ago?" asked Ki. "The controller we spoke to earlier said you used to work the eight a.m. to six p.m. shift, but asked to be moved to the graveyard shift, no reasons given."

"Yeah, well, y'know, times is hard," shrugged Muhammad.

Ki paused before asking "Can anyone confirm that you were working between eight p.m. and eight a.m. last night?"

"The controllers keep records of which jobs are given to which cabbies, when the jobs start and when they finish, and there are CCTV cameras in the waiting area at the cab office so when I wasn't on a job, you'll be able to see me sitting in the cab office with a cup of tea."

"Our forensics team is currently impounding your car, Mr Khan. We'll be checking your dashcam footage, as well as conducting other forensic tests. Your dashcam is working okay, isn't it? It's just you didn't mention it earlier. I know there'll be a copy of your dashcam activities on the cab office server, but we need to check that there were no obvious problems with your kit," said Ki.

Muhammad suddenly had a face like thunder. He slammed a hand on the table in front of him, jumped up and grabbed Ki by his shirt collar, dragging him from his chair and shouting, "You can't take my car. I need that car. It's how I make a living. How am I going to pay the rent and the bills and put food on the table if you've taken my car? My bab's already going on about money, and what else the kids need. When she hears I can't work because you've taken my car, she'll flip."

Dave grabbed Muhammad's wrist and said, very calmly, "Sit down, Muhammad. Come on, calm yourself."

Muhammad's solicitor stood, put his arm on Muhammad's shoulder and said quietly "Mr Khan, this isn't helping. Please sit down and calm down." Muhammad's temper receded and he took his seat.

"Sorry," he said, running a hand through his hair but not looking at Ki. "I'm really sorry."

Ki continued, unflustered. "We're aware of the position you're in, Mr Khan, and we will ensure that your car is returned to you as quickly as possible. Now, just to save time – when we look at the CCTV footage from your cab and from the waiting room at the cab office, we are going to find evidence that you were not in the company of Frankie Tanner at any point from seven forty-five p.m. last night to eight a.m. this morning. Is that right? No unexpected gaps in your cab's CCTV or from the waiting room?"

There was a brief silence from Muhammad.

"Well, I obviously had to go for a slash a couple of times and they're not allowed to film us in there," was his reply.

"So apart from your visits to the lavatory, we will be able to watch you on CCTV for the whole twelve hours and fifteen minutes. Is that right?"

The question was met with another brief silence, then a whispered exchange with his solicitor, then "Well, there was my break time. I popped out to have my dinner at about midnight. I usually switch off my cab CCTV then, so my bab won't find out how much I eat on shift," he said and attempted a laugh to lighten the mood, which had dipped after his earlier outburst. The exchange fell flat.

"What did you eat last night, Muhammad?" asked Ki.

Again, there was a brief pause followed by a whispered exchange with his solicitor before Muhammad volunteered "No comment."

"Oh, come on Muhammad, this is your chance to give us a proper alibi. Where did you go when your cab's CCTV was switched off last night?" tried Ki.

"No comment," replied Muhammad.

"Okay, let's move on to the murder of Jimmy Wheeler. You've told us about your interactions with Mr Wheeler. Where were you on the night Mr Wheeler was murdered?"

Muhammad looked at his solicitor, who shook his head, then replied "No comment."

"Muhammad, if you're going to need our protection in the future, I would urge you to consider very carefully the way that you respond to the questions in this investigation. Where were you on the night Jimmy Wheeler was murdered?" asked Ki, a little more loudly than for previous questions.

Muhammad again looked at his solicitor, who shook his head, and replied "No comment."

At this point, Muhammad's solicitor stepped in. "This sounds like a fishing expedition to me, so if there's nothing else, gentlemen, I suggest we draw this interview to a close. If you find any evidence that links my client to either of these crimes, we will co-operate fully with you at that time."

It was clear to both Ki and Dave that they weren't going to get any further with Muhammad that morning, so Ki nodded his agreement to the end of the interview.

Dave switched the recording machine off and Ki opened the door to allow Muhammad and his solicitor to leave the building, escorted by a uniformed colleague.

"Well," said Dave. "There's a turnaround. From a pathetic 'please look after me' to almost assaulting a police officer in a matter of days! What do you think?"

"I think there are a number of reasons why Muhammad was off grid for however long last night – maybe he's got a girlfriend – but at least forensics have got his car and have already started working on it, so maybe that will answer the questions which Mr Khan will not," Ki sighed. "I don't know yet, Dave. My gut says he really hasn't got it in him to kill anyone, let alone mutilate a dead body, but then, I've seen some bloody good actors in my time in these interview rooms, so I'm not yet confident that he's not our guy, especially after that dramatic change in demeanour earlier. Some forensic evidence from anywhere, including the body dump sites, would be very nice at this stage. Every little helps…"

Chapter 33

Margaret Foster was sitting at her desk when Beth and Terry walked in. She welcomed them with a cheery "Good morning," and asked how she could help. They both showed her their warrant cards before Beth said "I'm afraid we've got some bad news for you, Margaret. The body of a middle-aged man was found in St Martin's church in Canterbury this morning. We're treating his death as suspicious. I'm sorry to tell you that man is Frankie Tanner."

Margaret sat in stunned silence for several minutes until Beth asked if they could get her a drink. "No. No, I'm fine thank you. Are you sure it's Frankie?" she asked.

"Yes, I'm afraid so. His body has been formally identified. Margaret, we need your help. We need to catch Frankie's killer pretty quickly, so anything you can tell us to help us do that will be really appreciated," said Beth.

Margaret stared at her with a mixture of disbelief and anger, but quickly nodded her consent before adding, "Okay. I'll help you in any way I can to make sure that whoever the bastard is that killed Frankie is caught and put behind bars for the rest of his miserable life."

"Thank you, Margaret. Can I start by asking you about his living arrangements. Chantelle told us that

Frankie stayed overnight in Canterbury at least twice a week. Do you have an address for his Canterbury flat?"

Margaret nodded and wrote an address on a post-it note.

"Is he alone when he's in that flat, Margaret?" asked Beth.

Margaret paused before replying. "No. He's got a girlfriend at the flat. Her name is Tracey Jarvis."

Beth and Terry exchanged glances. "Does Chantelle know about Tracey?" asked Terry.

"No," came the reply. "And I'd like to keep it that way if possible."

"We'll only discuss this with Chantelle if we absolutely need to," said Beth, before moving on. "Can you tell us about Frankie's relationship with Jimmy Wheeler?"

"Jimmy Wheeler had some business dealings on The Coxhall estate in Canterbury. Frankie and Billy wanted a part of it. Jimmy wouldn't let go of any of it, so they had a few run-ins. Frankie wouldn't have killed Jimmy though. Not his style."

"Was it just Jimmy that Frankie had an argument with, or were others involved?" asked Terry.

"No. Just Frankie and Jimmy. Billy had his own argument with one of Jimmy's lads, but I can't see that escalating to Frankie," she replied.

"What about the other estates that Frankie's got a shop in. Was there anyone on any of those estates who might have wanted to hurt Frankie?" asked Terry.

"There have been a few issues in the past but no one's taken things further, and I can't think of anyone who would or could go this far. In Frankie's world, it was all about flexing muscles, not flashing knives or guns. Did anything else happen to Frankie? We heard Jimmy's eyes were cut out and his ears were cut off. Was Frankie harmed after he was killed?"

"The killer cut Frankie's ears off," said Terry, and waited for a response. When none came, Beth asked "Does that make a difference? Can you think of anyone who would mutilate someone after death?"

Margaret sat at her desk and contemplated the question and an appropriate response.

"Frankie heard about a guy in Canterbury who will, for a fee, look after your problems for you. He's ex-forces and he'll take all jobs, from a bit of roughing up through a proper beating to actual murder, or at least that was what Frankie was told. The rumour was that he did a couple of tours of duty and wouldn't let the enemy rest in peace – if he found the body of an insurgent, he used to get handy with a knife. Frankie heard that this guy had been mutilating their faces. Sounding like your man?" asked Margaret. "Frankie was told about him because apparently, this guy had a proper gripe against Jimmy. I don't know what it was about. Anyway, whoever told Frankie about him did so because he thought he was doing him a favour by helping him get Jimmy out of his way, but like I said, murder wasn't something that Frankie would consider. He was more likely to give Jimmy a bloody good beating, or get one of his lads to do it for him, than he was to kill or ask someone to kill for him."

"What do you know about this man?" asked Beth. "Do you have a name for him? Or a way to contact him?"

"I think Frankie called him something like the 'The Sword', or 'The Bow', no – it's 'The Crossbow'. That's what he's known as. The Crossbow. I don't know if Frankie could contact him directly or only through the guy who told him about it, and I don't know who that was, so I can't help you with that, but I'll check with Billy – he won't talk to you – because that Crossbow is just a gun for hire, so there's no reason why he wouldn't be hired to clear the way for someone who wanted in on Frankie and Jimmy's businesses."

"That is really helpful, Margaret. Thank you so much. Is there anyone you can think of who would want to harm Frankie, or employ someone like The Crossbow to do that for them?" asked Beth.

"I can honestly tell you that no one comes to mind. Not for murder and cutting off ears. I can think of three or four people who would want to give him a bloody good hiding, but no one who would want to kill him," replied Margaret.

"Have you heard of the Peckham Posh Boys?" asked Terry.

"Frankie told me that someone from Peckham was trying to muscle in on Jimmy's business in Canterbury, and he was keeping an eye on them to make sure they didn't start trying to muscle in on any of Frankie's businesses, but as far as I'm aware, they didn't bother Frankie at all. You want me to check that with Billy?" she asked.

"Yes please, Margaret. So, is there any one you can think of in his personal life who would want to hurt him?" asked Terry.

Margaret stared at him, debating whether or not to reply. Eventually, she said "You didn't hear this from me but his youngest sister, Mandy, married a proper wrong 'un. He was too handy with his fists, was Mehmet; she was always telling Frankie she'd 'walked into door' or 'slipped in the kitchen and hit her face on one of the cabinets' but we all knew it was him, the little shit. Frankie kept telling her she'd have a home with him if there were any problems in her own home, but she wouldn't ever admit to it, until the time Mehmet put her in hospital. It was not long after that when he ended up in hospital himself. Someone had given him a right good beating after he left the pub one night. Frankie went to visit him to explain that what happened was awful, and he was sure that Mehmet wouldn't want it to happen again, so perhaps it would be safer for him to move back to Peckham, where he was born and raised. He agreed with Frankie and moved away that weekend. We haven't seen him in these parts since."

"Do you know where in Peckham he lives? And what his surname is?" asked Terry.

"It's Mehmet Akan. I know he lives on one of the estates in Peckham, but I'm not sure which one. I can ask Mandy if she knows. Do you want me to do that?"

"Yes please, Margaret. That would be really helpful. And thank you for being so helpful today," said Beth. "Is there anything else you can think of that might help us find Frankie's killer?"

"I can't think of anything at the moment," she replied. "Leave me your numbers, and I'll call you after I've spoken to Billy and Mandy, or if anything else comes to mind. Frankie was a good man. I loved him like a son and I will miss him so much," and then the tears started to flow. Beth tried to comfort her but was waved away, so she and Terry left Margaret to start grieving in peace.

As Terry started driving back to Canterbury, Beth said "The Crossbow, eh. Let me email the organised crime team to see if he's on their radar, because it sounds like he's got form for this kind of killing. It's an interesting name for a hired gun. Any thoughts on that?"

"Crossbow. Crossfield. You can see how that could evolve," said Terry. "I reckon we should get in touch with his army superiors as soon as we get back to the office, but surely the cathedral would have done a Disclosure and Barring Service check on him before employing him, and anything like a disciplinary would appear there?"

"Only if he was disciplined," replied Beth. "And what about Mehmet?"

"I can see why he might want to kill Frankie but what's his motive for killing Jimmy? I know we haven't officially linked the two murders but as Chantelle said earlier, the mutilations are so unusual they must have been done by the same killer. And I think she's right. We're looking for one killer. Or we're looking for a double-act. And if he, she or they have already killed two people, removing the eyes from one and the ears from another, then we need to move very quickly before they kill again and cut the tongue out. 'See no evil, hear no evil, speak no evil' don't you think?"

"Yes Terry. I really do think that." replied Beth, uneasily.

Chapter 34

It took Beth and Terry forty-five minutes to drive from Chatham to Canterbury, and a further twenty minutes to find the flat which Frankie Tanner shared with Tracey Jarvis. "There's off the beaten track and then there's Captain's Corner," said Terry. "Good job I did the Duke of Edinburgh award."

The flat itself was in a beautiful old detached house, and Terry was the first to spot the swimming pool in the garden. "Blimey, bookmaking pays well these days. He owns two amazing properties, and that's just as far as we know," he said.

"We need to check his books. Does he own these properties outright or are they mortgaged. If they're mortgaged, is he doing well enough to afford both homes?" said Beth. "I'll get on to his solicitor when we get back to base. Let me just email Martha and ask her to get the details from Chantelle or Margaret."

They made their way to the grand front door and rang the bell for the address Margaret had given them. A few minutes later, the door was answered by a woman whose eyes were red and puffy from crying.

"Yes?" she asked.

"We're looking for Tracey Jarvis," said Beth, as she and Terry showed her their warrant cards.

"I'm Tracey. Come in," she replied.

Tracey Jarvis was about the same age as Chantelle, but there the similarity ended. Tracey was tall and stocky to Chantelle's petite frame, and looked as though she'd dressed in the dark that morning, as opposed to Chantelle's perfectly-presented appearance. But the main difference was that Tracey Jarvis was at least six months pregnant.

"Would you like a cup of tea or something?" Tracey asked.

"No thank you, we're good. Do you live here alone, Tracey?" asked Terry.

"No, my boyfriend spends half the week here and half the week at his other home," she replied.

"And your boyfriend is?" asked Terry.

"Frankie Tanner," she replied, and broke down in tears.

Beth moved closer to comfort her. "We were coming here to tell you the sad news that we'd found a body this morning, which has been officially identified as Frankie Tanner, but it looks as though you already know," she said.

Tracey had managed to compose herself a little. "Yes, I manage his shop on Canterbury High Street, and I'm quite close to Margaret. She phoned me because she didn't want me to hear it from you – nothing personal I'm sure. I can't believe he's gone."

"When did you notice that he was missing?" asked Beth.

"He normally gets here at about six thirty p.m. but if he's busy, he'll text to let me know he'll be a bit later. I wasn't expecting him home until after the pubs closed last night, because he told me he was meeting up with an old mate, Michael Haines. I know what these catchups can be like, so I went to bed at ten p.m. and I was out like a light until eight a.m. this morning," she said, stroking her baby bump. "There was no sign of Frankie when I woke up, but I just assumed he gone to work early so I was shocked, really shocked, when Margaret phoned with the news. What happened to him?" asked Tracey. "Did he suffer?"

"We're waiting for the post-mortem to take place before we can confirm those details, but as soon as we know, we'll let you know," replied Terry.

"Tracey, I'm sorry to have to ask you these questions at such a difficult time for you, but did Frankie mention any threats he'd had? Was he scared of anyone?" asked Beth.

"He talked to me a lot and I'm sure he wouldn't mind me sharing some stuff with you two, so that you can catch whoever did this to him. He was pretty shaken up by a young lad from London who came down here, waving a knife around and threatening anyone who didn't give him what he wanted," replied Tracey.

"Have you heard of the Posh Boys? Or The Shank?" asked Terry.

"Yes, that's it, the Posh Boys. That's the gang who came to Chatham, and The Shank is the guy Frankie said was mental and shouldn't be allowed to carry any weapons because he couldn't control his temper and one day he'd end up killing someone."

"Was there anyone else he was worried about? Anyone who'd threatened him in any way?" asked Beth.

"A man in his position will get threats from people who owe him money and the like, but he didn't tell me about anything he took seriously apart from Jimmy Wheeler and his gang."

Beth's ears pricked up. "So Frankie and Jimmy knew each other?" she asked.

"Yes. They'd known each other for a few years. They met on a stag night in Margate for a mutual friend, Martin Haines – Michael's brother. Lovely bloke. I only met him once before he was killed in a motorbike accident. Frankie and Jimmy were both crushed when that happened."

"Was Frankie crushed when Jimmy was murdered?" asked Terry.

"It freaked him out a bit. It was the eyes and ears thing that really got to him. He thought there must be a psycho out there. Margaret told me that Frankie's ears had been cut off so I guess Frankie was right all along. Are you looking for the same murderer for both Frankie and Jimmy?" asked Tracey.

"Like I said, we're waiting for the post-mortem before we can comment on that, but as soon as we know, we'll let you know," replied Terry.

"So what were the threats that Jimmy and his gang made towards Frankie?" asked Beth.

"Jimmy told Frankie to eff off his patch or he'd get someone to sort him out good and proper. Frankie knew that Jimmy was handy with his fists, so he thought it was odd that he'd get someone else to do his dirty work for him, which is what I think made him a bit worried. Then, he told me that he'd heard Jimmy had hired some ex-army bloke to give him a massive going over but he only knew him by his nickname. God. I can't remember what he said that name was. Sorry."

"You're being really helpful, Tracey, Thank you. Does The Crossbow mean anything to you?" asked Beth.

"Yes. That's the one. The Crossbow. Frankie said it was funny because someone had offered to put him in touch with The Crossbow to sort out Jimmy for him, because they said he had a grudge against Jimmy, but I guess anyone who pays the fees calls the shots. Business is business, Frankie used to say," replied Tracey, before the tears took over.

Once Tracey had composed herself, Beth asked "Do you know if Frankie and Jimmy ever did any business together?"

Tracey looked uncomfortable for a moment, then answered. "I guess it's okay for me to tell you this now, seeing as both Frankie and Jimmy are dead. After meeting at Martin's stag do, Jimmy used a few of Frankie's shops to clean some money for some of his associates. It worked well for both of them for a while, with the cut they were taking on the money."

"So, what stopped that arrangement?" asked Terry.

Again, Tracey looked uncomfortable before answering. "Jimmy told Frankie that he wouldn't be needing his shops any more because he was using another business to clean the money. Frankie didn't like that and tried to find out what that other business was, but Jimmy wouldn't say, so Frankie did some asking around and he was told that Jimmy part-owned an art gallery. Frankie laughed hard at that, and thought that the person who told him that was taking the mickey, but someone else said the same thing so Frankie thought it could be true. Frankie knew that Jimmy was cleaning much bigger amounts than he used to through Frankie's shops, so he asked Jimmy for a piece of the action but Jimmy wasn't having it – said his business partner wouldn't take on any new partners – so Frankie decided to take Jimmy's loans business off him and give it to Billy."

"What happened next?" asked Beth.

"Frankie opened a shop on Canterbury High Street, then opened another on The Cox, making friends in the right places along the way, then a couple of months ago, he told Jimmy that he should stick with his money cleaning business and hand over the loans business to his brother Billy. Jimmy said no, obviously. So, Frankie said that he would make it happen."

"Frankie was planning on making Jimmy hand over the loans business to Billy. How was he going to do that?" asked Terry.

"It started the day Frankie opened his business on The Cox. Frankie and Billy worked the counter for the first few weeks and when the punters came into the shop, they'd strike up a conversation to find out if anyone had a loan with Jimmy Wheeler. If they did, they'd offer them better rates and more time to repay so they weren't so squeezed. Jimmy went mental. Frankie heard that he'd beaten up some of the customers he'd lost to Billy. It all got really nasty and then Jimmy was killed."

"Did that make Frankie think that he was in danger too?" asked Beth.

"He never said as much to me, but I think it must have been on his mind because he started taking Simon and Big Ben with him pretty much everywhere he went."

Beth guessed that Simon and Big Ben were the two men busy making themselves a brew when she and Terry visited Frankie's shop in Sittingbourne just a few days ago.

"Okay, thanks Tracey. You've been a huge help to us today. I just wanted to check one more thing and again, I'm sorry to have to ask this, but you said that Frankie spent half his week here and the other half at his other home. What can you tell us about his other home?"

"I know that he's married to Chantelle and I know that he did love her but she was a proper trophy wife, y'know. Loved spending time getting her hair and nails done, loved spending Frankie's money on new clothes and bags, and all sorts. She was good at throwing parties, by all accounts. Quiet dinner parties, as well as big garden party-type things. Not my scene. And not really Frankie's scene either, but he said he needed to schmooze the right people – coppers, councillors and the like – to make his life easier, otherwise he wouldn't do it. I guess you could say he had the best of both worlds; he had the business social life with Chantelle, and the quiet family life with me." Tracey could sense that Beth and Terry found this situation a little curious so she explained, "Chantelle doesn't know about me, but I'm not jealous of Chantelle, and I wouldn't have wanted my life any other way. I couldn't do that schmoozing stuff, and I enjoy having a bit of time on my own – have you tried reading a book when a bloke's wanting his dinner, or his feet massaged? So, I guess you could say that Frankie and I had the perfect life until this morning," and then the tears came back.

"Is there anything we can get you?" asked Beth. "Is there anyone we can call to come and be with you?"

"Margaret's coming over this afternoon, thanks. She'll look after me. I'll be okay."

"Okay. We'll head off but here are our contact details. If there's anything you need, or if any detail, no matter how small, comes to you at any point, please give us a call," said Beth, and she and Terry made their way back to their car.

"God that was interesting," said Terry. "So the Peckham Posh Boys have been threatening Frankie too, but he didn't tell Margaret, or she didn't tell us. What do you think? Is The Shank following up on his threats? Is there a psycho out there targeting loan sharks and bookies in general? Or is this more specific? Someone else knew Jimmy and Frankie and, for whatever reason, wanted them both dead and in a pretty horrific way?"

"Well. I wonder how much Margaret hasn't told us, because no one has mentioned that Jimmy and Frankie knew each other and used to do business together. I did think a helpful Margaret was too much to ask for."

"What do you make of the whole Chantelle thing? I think if I had a pregnant girlfriend in a flat a few miles away, Leah would, if you'll excuse my language, have my balls as earrings."

Beth chuckled at the use of language, but refused to allow herself to go any further with the imagery. "I think I can understand Tracey's position, and I think that Chantelle is probably very happy with her life and lifestyle, and so wouldn't want to know about anything that might threaten that, but even if she did know, I can't see her resorting to murder and mutilation, and anyway, what motive would she have for killing Jimmy Wheeler? No, I think we need to leave both women to grieve for their loss in their own ways, and we need to focus on Jimmy and Frankie's business matters. If I had a quid, Terry, I'd bet you that's where we'll solve this case. Right, back to base and don't spare the horses. I'm dying for a cuppa!"

Chapter 35

When Beth and Terry walked into the squad room, they were surprised to be told that both Kevin Carter and Jeff Robinson had appeared in Reception a few minutes earlier, bearing the gift of Jimmy's loans books.

"That's great news. Fiona. Clarissa. What did you find out at the homeless shelter yesterday?" asked Beth.

Fiona took the floor.

"We viewed the CCTV footage from the night of the altercation and saw Jimmy Wheeler walk into the communal area at Canterbury Cares, accompanied by Kevin Carter. Selwyn Du Pont was in that room along with several other staff, volunteers, and clients. We spoke with one of them yesterday – Malcolm Turner, the night manager on the evening of the assault. He confirmed Selwyn's version of events, including the part where Jimmy looked directly at Selwyn then did that finger-across-the-neck movement.

We asked Malcolm if Selwyn had told him what the altercation was about, and he said no, he wouldn't speak about the detail; Selwyn just said that Jimmy was a very unpleasant man who had made threats against the shelter, but that there was no need to worry because they wouldn't be seeing him again.

We asked Malcolm if he knew a Trevor who used the shelter, but he couldn't think of one. They ask their overnight residents to sign a register, so that they have records of the numbers of people sleeping in the shelter, in case there's a fire and they need to check that everyone's been evacuated, but Mickey Mouse stays there most nights so Malcolm isn't confident of finding a Trevor in their records. He did, however, say he'd ask other staff and volunteers if they knew of a Trevor and he'll let us know if he hears of one."

"Great work. Many thanks, Fiona and Clarissa. Okay, Terry and I will interview Kevin. Ki and Dave, I'd like you to interview Jeff. Let's go to my office for a quick strategy meeting."

As soon as they'd agreed on the questions to be asked, Beth, Terry, Ki and Dave set off for the interview rooms to find Kevin and Jeff.

"Ah, the elusive Kevin Carter," said Beth. "Thank you for coming in today and bringing Jimmy's loan books with you. Shirley Wheeler suggested we speak to you in connection with her son's murder, so any help you can give us today will be appreciated."

Kevin stared at Beth and Terry but didn't speak.

"Let me start by asking you if anyone had threatened Jimmy in the weeks leading up to his death?"

"You know about the Posh Boys?" asked Kevin. "Their leader is called The Shank and he came to Canterbury to try to get a piece of the action on The Cox, but Jimmy wasn't having it, so The Shank got a bit gobby and started flashing his blade. You should have a word with him for a start."

"Like you did?" asked Terry. "When you gave him a good beating and tied him to a kid's roundabout on The Cox?"

Kevin shrugged. "I don't know nothing about that," he replied.

Beth decided not to pursue that incident in this interview and instead asked, "Who else threatened Jimmy?"

"Lots of people threaten people like Jimmy but it's all bollocks," replied Kevin. "People say things when they're pissed off, but they don't do things afterwards. People like Muhammad Khan. I know you know about him. So we never took those threats seriously."

"Tell us about Selwyn Du Pont," said Beth.

"Who?" asked Kevin.

"Selwyn Du Pont. He's one of the clergy at the cathedral, and he volunteers at the Canterbury Cares homeless shelter."

Kevin stared at Beth but said nothing.

"We know that at the end of September, Jimmy went to the shelter and was knocked to the floor by Selwyn Du Pont. But you know this. You were there. So what was it all about?" asked Terry.

"I didn't hear what Jimmy said to him, so I can't help you with that. You'll have to ask that clergy bloke."

"Jimmy must have been angry with such a public humiliation. Thumped and floored by a clergyman. Did he go to the cathedral to have another 'word' with Selwyn?" asked Terry.

"Not when I was with him," replied Kevin. "Do you think this bloke killed Jimmy?"

"We're still investigating all leads but let me be clear," said Beth. "If Mr Du Pont, or anyone else involved in this investigation, is harmed in any way, we will go in hard to find and prosecute the perpetrators. Is that clear?"

Kevin shrugged but didn't say anything.

Beth paused to allow her promise to sink in, then changed subject. "What about the people on the loans books. Did any of them threaten Jimmy?" she asked.

"Not that I know of," replied Kevin.

"And what about the old loans books. The one that had the clients that Billy Tanner took. We hear that Jimmy dished out a few beatings to them. Did any of them threaten him in return?" asked Beth.

"Not that I know of," replied Kevin. "And who told you that Jimmy had beaten anyone up? You want to be careful who you believe. Some people are just jealous of other people's success."

"People like Frankie Tanner?" asked Beth. "What was the relationship between Jimmy and Frankie?"

Again, Kevin stared at Beth but said nothing.

She persisted. "Did they do some business together back in the day?"

"I worked with Jimmy on the loans business. That's all I know about. I know that he had other stuff going on but he didn't tell me much about it. You'd need to ask Frankie Tanner," said Kevin.

"We would," said Terry. "But Frankie Tanner was murdered last night."

Kevin looked shocked at the news. Beth gave him a minute to compose himself then asked, "Where were you last night, Kevin?"

"No way," he replied quickly. "This ain't on me. I was with my girlfriend in her flat all night last night. I'll give you her mobile number and she can tell you that herself but I didn't kill Frankie Tanner. No way."

"Okay, give us your girlfriend's name, address and her mobile number and we'll contact her," said Terry. "Do it now, please," he asked, passing Kevin a pen and some paper. Once he had the details, he asked the uniformed officer in the room to take them through to the squad room and ask Clarissa to contact her before Kevin had a chance to speak with her.

They moved on.

"We know that you're taking on the loans work so who's taking over his other business interests?" asked Beth.

Kevin shrugged.

"Is it Jackie?" asked Beth.

"You'll have to talk to her about that," replied Kevin. "I don't know anything about any business other than the loans."

"Do you know who Jimmy's solicitor was?" asked Terry.

Kevin gave them a name. "Yes, we know about her. Did he have another solicitor?" asked Beth.

"Not that I know of," replied Kevin.

"Considering you were his best mate and his right-hand man, there seems to be a lot that you didn't know about Jimmy's life," said Terry.

Kevin glowered. "That's not true. Just some business stuff that's all," he replied.

"So if you know all about his personal life, you'll know if he was happy living in Ickleford or if he missed living in the city," asked Beth.

Kevin looked puzzled. "Eh? Who's been filling your head with that shit? Dawn loves living in that village and Jimmy loved Dawn, so he was happy living anywhere as long as she was in the house, and if anyone's told you any different, they're lying."

"That's the thing we keep hearing when we talk to people about Jimmy. How much he loved his Dawn and how much she loved him. So there was no room for anyone else in that relationship? No girlfriend in Canterbury waiting for Jimmy when he was back in the city?" asked Beth.

"No. There fucking wasn't. He only ever had eyes for Dawn and she's going through hell at the moment, so don't you go upsetting her more with bollocks about what Jimmy might have been up to when he was working. Because there was no girlfriend in his life. Just his wife," shouted Kevin.

"Okay, okay. Thanks Kevin. Let's calm this down a little," said Terry, and gave him a moment to cool. "Can we just ask you about the night that Jimmy was killed. What time did he finish work that night?"

"We got back to The Cox at about six p.m. that night, and Jimmy got behind the wheel to drive himself home," replied Kevin.

"Was he going straight home, or had he arranged to meet someone on the way?" asked Terry.

"As far as I know, he was going straight home," came the reply.

"So he wasn't meeting with anyone in the loans books? Or other business clients?"

"No. He can't have been. He never had a meeting without one of us being around, even if it was only that dick, Gary."

"So the meeting with Selwyn Du Pont was business, if he took you along?" asked Beth.

Kevin shrugged.

"Kevin, help us out here. We need to know who had a motive to kill Jimmy if we're going to have any chance of catching them. So, he either wanted to see Selwyn about the loans business, or about his other business interests. Which one was it?" asked Beth.

Kevin paused before replying. "It wasn't always that clear cut. Sometimes, one business crossed over with his other businesses. Like this one. I don't know the detail but I think it had something to do with clearing a loan," he said.

"Selwyn Du Pont had a loan with Jimmy?" asked Beth.

"No. But I think he knew someone who did, and I think he was using Jimmy's other business to help, but that's all I know," replied Kevin.

"What's the name of the art gallery that Jimmy part-owned?" asked Terry.

Kevin shrugged.

"But that was one of his other business interests?" continued Terry.

"Jimmy told me once that putting money in banks was a mug's game, and there was better ways to look after your cash. He told me that there was big money in old paintings and it was a good game to get into. That's all I know about it," replied Kevin.

With that, Kevin crossed his arms and looked away. Beth felt she'd had all the information she could for now, so decided to draw the interview to a close.

"Okay, thanks for coming in, Kevin. We'll probably have more questions for you once we've had a look through the loans books so don't leave Canterbury," said Beth, and gave him more paper to write the names of the clients who'd moved from Jimmy to Billy.

Beth and Terry made their way back to the squad room where they found Ki and Dave, who offered no new information. The answers they gave were so similar, it was almost as though Kevin and Jeff had rehearsed for their interviews.

"Clarissa, did you get in touch with Kevin's girlfriend?" asked Beth.

"I did. She said," and Clarissa read directly from her pocket notebook. *"He rocked up here at about half ten last night, honking of beer and carrying a takeaway, and he was here until about half nine this morning."*

"Okay. What time did Gloria, was it Gloria?" asked Beth. Clarissa nodded. "What time did Gloria leave the church yesterday? Did she lock up or was someone else around?"

Clarissa checked her pocket notebook again. "She left just after three thirty p.m. and locked the doors behind her."

"So, the church was locked up at three thirty p.m. and Kevin Carter turned up at his girlfriend's flat at ten thirty p.m. last night. We need Mac to confirm the time of death," said Beth. "We might have ourselves a new suspect."

"But Kevin was Jimmy's best friend," said Fiona. "I can see he has a motive to kill Frankie, but why would he kill Jimmy?"

"Maybe he wanted to take over the business and no one knows the loans business better than him. Bit of a miscalculation with the gallery side of the business, but he is at least head of the loans work now," replied Dave.

"I want him viewed as a potential suspect rather than a witness until he can prove otherwise," said Beth. "Something doesn't feel quite right with his story."

Chapter 36

Donald Campbell walked into the squad room just as Beth was informing the team that all leave had been cancelled, and they'd all be working this weekend. His timing couldn't have been better; Beth was grateful that the appearance of the Super had suppressed the impending tsunami of groans and swearing.

Beth nodded at the Super then went on to introduce the new members of the team, the three detectives on loan from CID – Steve, Martha and Prisha – and the two ambitious uniformed officers who'd volunteered for a temporary transfer – PC Jane Unwin and PC Chris Trent. All five confirmed that they'd received a full briefing from Fiona and felt ready to hit the ground running.

"Okay," said Beth. "Today's been quite the day. The Super and I have a press conference in just under an hour so we need to be focused."

She shared details of hers and Terry's interviews from earlier that day, then each member of the team updated their colleagues on their day's activities.

"Great work everyone, and thank you. Okay. Mac has advised that in her opinion, we have one killer. Frankie Tanner has a needle mark on his back, between both shoulder blades, so Mac's sent a sample of blood and hair off to toxicology." Beth turned to Donald. "Sir, if you could apply any pressure to get the tox results as quickly as we did in Jimmy Wheeler's murder, that would be very helpful."

Beth grabbed a black marker pen and moved to the white board.

"So, let's start with motive. Who knew both Jimmy Wheeler and Frankie Tanner and wanted them dead?

The most obvious suspect is The Shank, but who else has connections to both victims? We have Muhammad Khan and also Kevin Carter," Beth looked at Donald and explained "We think Kevin might have had ambitions to take over Jimmy's loans business and for that, he'd need to get rid of Jimmy and Billy Tanner, via Frankie Tanner.

Who else has a motive?

Jenny and Martha, have either the Wheeler women or Chantelle come up with any suggestions on who might have wanted Jimmy and Frankie dead?"

Jenny was the first to speak but had nothing to say. Neither Dawn, Jackie or Shirley could think of, or were prepared to share, any possible suspects with her.

Martha's contribution was more productive. "Chantelle has spent the afternoon telling as many friends and family members as she can about Frankie's murder, and occasionally speculating about who might be responsible for it. To date, she's put his brother-in-law Mehmet in the frame, because she'd 'never trusted that wife-beating bastard'; she said we 'want to look at some of his customers who put money they ain't got on horses that can't run' and who, as a result, build up debts they can't repay; and also his brother Billy – apparently, Frankie and Billy fell out over something several months ago, but Frankie didn't share the reason with her, and although Billy didn't really get on with Frankie anymore, he needed him to earn a living."

"That's very interesting about Chantelle's list of possible suspects, especially the new insight into Frankie's relationship with his brother Billy. Good work, Martha," said Beth.

"Okay, Dave, get in touch with your source to get the name and contact details of the guy who gave Frankie Tanner his Rolls Royce Ghost, and find out where he and his son were last night. We also need to know if either of them has any connection to Jimmy Wheeler. And ask them if The Crossbow means anything to them. Also, do your sources know of anyone else who paid a high price to Frankie Tanner and, or, Jimmy Wheeler. If so, we need to know who they are.

Fiona and Clarissa, keep looking for a link between Philip Crossfield and Frankie Tanner, and between Selwyn Du Pont and Frankie."

"Guv," said Clarissa, "Arthur finally sent the external CCTV from the cathedral precincts over to us, and on the night of Jimmy's murder, Philip Crossfield can be seen walking the security rounds between six p.m. and ten p.m., so if Jimmy went straight home after work, and left The Cox at six p.m., that would put him in the layby in which his car was found at some point between 6.35 p.m. and seven p.m., depending on traffic. So Philip can't be involved in Jimmy's abduction and murder, unless he had an accomplice or unless Jimmy didn't go straight home that night. Dave, I checked the CCTV and Philip's story of his dinner and journey home that night checks out, but that doesn't mean he didn't leave again."

There was a brief silence as the team absorbed the latest information, before Beth said "That's great work. Very well done, Clarissa.

Steve and Prisha – we need to look into who Philip's accomplice is, if he has one. You can start by looking into where his sister Michelle was on the night of Jimmy's murder. No matter how implausible we find the idea that she could in some way be involved in an abduction or a murder, she is the most obvious person linked to Philip who has a motive to kill Jimmy Wheeler. If we draw a blank with her, start looking at his friends and any old army contacts he has who could have helped him.

Okay. What about opportunity? As soon as Mac gives us an estimated time of death, we need to know where all our suspects were. In the meantime,

Chris, get hold of the CCTV footage from the William Harvey and the surrounding roads from about nine p.m. last night until eight a.m. this morning. The Shank discharged himself at nine thirty p.m. last night. Where did he go? We need that information urgently.

Dave, we need to know where Muhammad Khan went when he was off grid last night. Send Muhammad's car registration number to traffic and ask them to check CCTV from wherever he was the moment he shut down his dashcam to the moment he switched it back on again. And ask them to track Jimmy's car from The Cox from five p.m. on Sunday as far as they can go; we know that the smaller roads leading to Ickleford haven't got CCTV cover, but the main roads that feed those smaller roads do – we need to know if Jimmy went straight home or if he went elsewhere, and if so, where was that.

Jane, we need to know how the bodies were taken to the churches. We know that St Martin's has no CCTV, and that the CCTV inside the cathedral wasn't working on the night Jimmy's body was left there, convenient when you think about it, but Canterbury Council must have CCTV footage from the areas surrounding both buildings on the night both bodies were left there, so have them send it over for you to review.

Martha, we need someone in Frankie's life – Chantelle, Tracey, Margaret – to send us his car registration number, because we need to find that car. Once you have that information, please send it on to traffic and ask them to let us know as soon as it's found.

Fiona and Clarissa, we need to know who had access to the cathedral keys but also the keys to St Martin's church. Once you have the full list, check them against the database, then start cross-referencing the names with the suspects to see if we can find a connection.

Jenny, we need to know who Jimmy's business solicitor is. Ask Dawn to see if she knows, but if not, ask

Jackie and Shirley; I don't expect either to be helpful, it shouldn't stop us trying.

Terry, get in touch with Philip Crossfield's old army bosses to get their view on whether he was a peacemaker or an instigator for trouble, on and off base. Also, throw the name 'The Crossbow' at them to see if anyone reacts. And follow up with organised crime to see if that name is known to them.

And finally, we need to look at the means. Why have our victims had their eyes and ears removed? See no evil, hear no evil, and speak no evil come to mind and if that's the case, it suggests there will be a third murder so we need to find our killer or killers quickly before that has a chance to take place. And why have the bodies been left in places of worship? If the Christian faith had no significance for the victims, then does it have any for our killer, or is it just a way to get more attention for the murders? Jenny and Martha, follow up on this angle with the Wheeler women and Chantelle, and Terry and I will follow up with Tracey."

The white board was, by now, full of suspect names and action points.

"Right, before the Super and I head off, does anyone else have anything they need to discuss or they'd like us to raise in the press conference?" There were no takers so Beth said, "Okay, we're off. Thank you all very much for all your hard work so far. I'll see you all here tomorrow morning and the coffees will be on me."

Chapter 37

The conference room was buzzing when Donald and Beth walked in with Kathryn Fleetwood, East Kent Police's head of comms. Unusually for an East Kent Police press conference, journalists from the local and national news outlets had to battle with international journalists for the best spot in the room.

Donald stood behind the lectern at the front of the room and the journalists fell silent.

"Thank you all for coming today. I'm Superintendent Donald Campbell and I'll shortly be making a statement on the horrific events of the last week here in Canterbury. Joining me today are Detective Chief Inspector Bethany Harper, who is leading the team investigating the murders, and will take your operational questions after my statement. Also joining us is Kathryn Fleetwood, our Head of Communications, and she will be available to answer any press-related queries at the end of this press conference.

The purpose of this press conference is to share as much information as we can at this stage without compromising the investigation, but the hope is that we can put to bed some of the rumours surrounding the deaths, and give the residents of Canterbury some peace of mind.

On Monday morning, the body of a forty-eight-year-old man was discovered in Canterbury Cathedral. The victim's eyes and eyelids had been removed. This man has been identified as Jimmy Wheeler, a former Canterbury resident and local salesman.

This morning, the body of a fifty-two-year-old man was discovered in St Martin's Church, just outside the Canterbury city walls. The victim's ears had been removed. This man has been identified as Frankie Tanner, a Chatham resident who also owned a property in Canterbury. Mr Tanner owned a number of betting shops in East Kent.

These crimes are abhorrent and we are supporting the victims' families at this very difficult time.

We are appealing today for your support to help us catch the killer or killers. Do you know either of these men? Do you know anyone who would want to harm either of them? Any detail, large or small, could be significant and could help us solve these crimes, so please get in touch with us as quickly as possible. You may think that the information you have is not relevant, but please let us make that decision.

To the people of Canterbury, I say this; DCI Harper's talented team are working extremely hard to bring this matter to a close, and the broader East Kent Police Force is giving the team all the support it needs. We ask you to remain calm but vigilant. If you see anything unusual or suspicious, please call our dedicated helpline on the numbers shown on the boards behind me, and speak to one of our team.

Thank you for your time. I'll now hand over to DCI Harper to take your questions."

Donald sat down and Beth replaced him at the lectern.

"Thank you very much, Superintendent Campbell. Okay. I'm not familiar with all journalists in the room today, so I'll just point and ask the microphone operator to move to you. Please state your name, your news outlet, then ask your question. Let's start with you in the blue shirt in the front row."

"Paul John, South East London Press. Are you looking for one killer of both men, or two killers?"

"At this time, we are unable to confirm whether both men were killed by the same person."

Beth continued to point and move the microphone operator across the room.

"Sarah Baldwin. South Wales Western Mail. How were the victims killed?"

"I'm sure you'll understand that at this time, there are some details that we are unable to confirm, and others that we are unable to share, due to the ongoing nature of the investigation. I'm afraid I can't answer that question at the moment."

"Noah Barker. The Kentish Reporter. Given the mutilations to the bodies, are you looking for someone with a medical background?"

"That's one possibility, but if you do a quick search on YouTube for eyeball removal, you'll get a number of results to help you do that, so we can't restrict the search to anyone with a medical background or exposure to surgical practices."

"Harry Wilcox. Kent Online Daily. Both men lived outside Canterbury. Why were they murdered and dumped in Canterbury?"

"That's a line of enquiry that we're following up on, but both men had a very clear link to Canterbury."

"Isabella Rossi. la Repubblica in Rome. The bodies of both men were found in religious settings. What is the significance of that?"

"That's a very good question. I would ask anyone who knew either of the victims to get in touch if they can think of a reason why their bodies might have been left in the cathedral or a church."

"Martin McMurray. The Sun. We have been told that Jimmy Wheeler was a loan shark who used to beat up his clients. Could this be a motive for his murder?"

"We are looking into the background of both victims, and I would ask that if any of you have received any information relating to this case, you share that with us at the end of this press conference."

"Jennifer Richards. The Mail. Removing eyes and ears says 'See no evil, hear no evil' to me. Who will be 'speak no evil'?"

"Of course, we are investigating this as a line of inquiry, but it is very important not to jump to conclusions or other motives may be missed. And can I please ask you not to sensationalise these crimes or to attempt to predict future events. The people of Canterbury are rightly concerned about this week's developments and they deserve responsible reporting, not predictions or conjecture."

"Jeremy Johnson. Kentish Times. We understand that Frankie Tanner, the bookie, was known to encourage the build up of debts which he would then recover both financially or in other ways, for example by demanding goods from his debtors. We also understand that he was also known to follow up these demands with physical violence. Another motive?"

"As I said earlier, we are considering all possible motives, if you have any information relating to this case, please share it with us at the end of this press conference."

"Andie Jamieson. South East Times. How would a loan shark from a poor council estate in Canterbury become a dealer for artwork worth tens of thousands of pounds?"

Beth paused briefly. This information was not yet in the public domain, and it was the subject of an investigation by another team. Conscious of how important it was not to compromise another inquiry, Beth decided it was time to end the questions.

"I can only repeat, we are looking into everything about the background of both victims, so if you have any information relating to this case, please share it with us at the end of this press conference.

Okay. I'm drawing this press conference to a close now, but I would again appeal to the public, if you know either of the victims and might have information which could help our investigation, or you saw anything suspicious either on Sunday night or Thursday night, please share that information with us confidentially using the numbers on the boards behind us.

Thank you all for coming today."

Chapter 38

After leaving the station, Beth called Kate on her mobile. "How are you, my lovely?" she asked.

"I'm fine, darling, thank you. A bit tired as usual, but I've just had a very tasty spinach and spring onion omelette, and I'm about to settle down to watch a repeat of Marple so everything's okay over here. I saw you on the news earlier. I'm very proud of you, Beth. And I have every confidence that you will solve these crimes very quickly."

Sometimes, you just need the confidence boost that comes with the lifelong love and support of someone like Kate, thought Beth.

"Thanks, Kate. I really needed to hear that. I'm just on my way to meet Mac for dinner. Do you need me to pick up anything on my way home?"

"No. I've got everything I need thank you. You go and have a lovely time. And say hello to Mac from me."

Beth told Kate that she loved her, then ended the call and walked through the underpass to meet her old friend Mac at the Italian restaurant they'd enjoyed eating at for over a dozen years. Giuseppe's was a family-owned restaurant with an excellent selection of red wine and some delicious food. It was the perfect place to unwind after a hard day at work.

"I've ordered a bottle of Montepulciano," said Mac, as Beth joined her at the table.

"Ladies, how lovely to see you both again," said Guiseppe as he poured their wine. "Are you ready to order food?"

"Oh yes, I think so," said Mac, knowing full well that Beth would order a lasagne with garlic bread.

"Yes thanks, Guiseppe. I'll have a lasagne with garlic bread, please. Mac?"

"I'll have a spaghetti bolognese please, Guiseppe."

The two women looked at each other and chuckled. "If it ain't broke, don't fix it," said Beth.

"I couldn't agree more," replied Mac. "So how's the new chap settling in? A baptism of fire, I think you'll agree!"

"I most certainly would," said Beth, taking a large gulp of wine. "He's a nice person, which fits well with the team, and he's very bright. We're lucky to have found him."

"And he's lucky to have found you and your team," replied Mac. "It's pretty rare for a team like yours to have such a low turnover of staff. I've said it before and I'll say it again – you're too nice! You need to stop watching Midsomer Murders and start watching reruns of Taggart."

Beth chuckled. She knew that, almost without exception, her team were an unusually content group of people, who genuinely got on with each other and with the job. "We few, we happy few, we band of brothers," she said with a broad smile. "Not everyone is happy in their role, of course."

"Fiona?" asked Mac.

"Fiona," replied Beth. "I know she's very ambitious, and is a great detective who will, I have no doubt, make it to the top of policing, but only if she keeps that ambition in check. I heard Clarissa telling Dave the other day that Fiona was too bossy, and isn't prepared to follow any of Clarissa's suggested lines of enquiry, which Clarissa's finding very frustrating and a little stifling. I think some of that comes from Fiona's insecurity when it comes to Clarissa's background – a Viscount's granddaughter and a Cambridge graduate will have that natural confidence that the rest of us have to work at – but some of it is just Fiona's need to demonstrate how very good a detective she is, which is completely unnecessary because we can all see that in her results. I don't know, Mac. Maybe I should have paired Clarissa with Ki and Dave with Fiona. And maybe I will if the situation doesn't improve."

"Staff management is, without question, the most difficult role for a manager, so you have my sympathies. But for what it's worth, I and many others think that you are an excellent manager so just go with your instincts."

"Thank you so much, Mac. I try to follow the ideas that generally, you get more from staff when you discuss things with them, rather than talk at them; a good work-life balance matters a lot, even to most coppers; and each individual has their own motivation for performing well in a role – for some it's salary, for others, career progression. Find out what everyone needs and help them to achieve it, then you get a happy team with a low turnover," said Beth. Her statement was met with a sceptical raised eyebrow from Mac. "I read a HR article in a magazine in a dentist's waiting room once," explained Beth.

"Ha! The very best way to learn," said Mac, with a warm smile. "How's the investigation going? I saw the press conference earlier. Good question about the medical background."

"Yes it was. What do you think? Would someone need medical knowledge to perform the mutilations we saw on both bodies, or would watching a YouTube video be enough? Are you able to tell anything from the bodies?" asked Beth.

"It would certainly be possible for someone to perform the mutilations after watching an instructional video and frankly, there are far too many of those available on the internet, but in this instance, I'd say the killer does demonstrate greater medical knowledge than the average man or woman on the street. Now, I'm not saying they've had surgical training, but they've certainly had exposure to dissection practices."

"Mac, I really need a time of death for both victims, but particularly Frankie Tanner. What can you give me?"

"I would estimate that Jimmy Wheeler died between six p.m. and eight p.m., and Frankie Tanner died between eleven thirty p.m. and two a.m., but those are estimates and come with the usual caveats."

"Do you have any way of giving me an estimate of when Frankie's body might have been taken to St Martin's?"

"No, I'm afraid not. You'll have to rely on their CCTV for that."

"Yes, I would if they had one. You'd think everyone would have functioning CCTV these days, but not the church, apparently. Why do you think the killer chose oramorph as their weapon? It's a curious choice, don't you think?"

"But not particularly unusual," replied Mac. "Harold Shipman used diamorphine as his murder weapon. The impact is quick – depending on the dose given, it might only take a few minutes for the victim to stop breathing."

"Yes, but isn't it difficult to get hold of? Wouldn't it be easier just to buy some arsenic off the internet?"

"I think, off the record of course, that the use of oramorph is quite instructive. I wouldn't want to order something like arsenic off the internet – how quickly could you catch me then? But you can get a prescription drug like oramorph on repeat, and what do you do if you don't use it in the quantities you request? You can build up quite a stockpile for later nefarious use, such as using it against, or selling it to, others. And, of course, oramorph as a quick-acting drug is useful if your victims are bigger or stronger than you, and you need a quick knock-out."

Beth paused to consider Mac's statement. "That's really helpful, Mac. Thanks very much. God, this is one of the fastest-moving cases I've ever worked on. Two victims in one week. Here's hoping the killer takes the weekend off to give us a chance to catch up."

"You know, as always, that if there's anything I can do to help, you've only to say. Now, on the subject of oramorph, how is Kate doing?"

"Well, she's a tough old bird so she's battling on, and the pain relief is certainly helping her get through the day and sleep well through the night, but she's sleeping a lot now, Mac. She's got a new consultant oncologist. We had our first appointment last week, and sleeping more is an indicator that the end of life is near, but no one can ever know how long anyone has left so we're just getting on with things as best we can at the moment." Beth's eyes suddenly filled with tears, and Mac reached out a comforting hand to her old friend.

"Still, we did have a bit of a laugh at our own unconscious bias. Dr Sam Freene is not the man we expected to see but, a woman. And a very attractive one to boot!" said Beth. "On the way home from the appointment, Kate was trying to suggest that Dr Freene could be the perfect match for me, but I haven't got the capacity to think about anything other than work and Kate's health at the moment."

"Nor would you be able to do anything about any attraction, as well you know. Even if this doctor's professional association is with Kate, as her niece, you're too close to the patient for a personal relationship to develop. Have you tried Tinder?"

"Mac!"

"What?" replied Mac, with a chuckle. "I found my new boyfriend on Tinder and he is gorgeous. He's also rolling in money. He took me to dinner in London last weekend and, booked us into the Savoy for the night!"

"Giovanni," said Beth, calling Guiseppi's youngest son. "Another bottle of Montepulciano please. This is going to be a very interesting evening!"

Chapter 39

At eight forty-five a.m. the following morning, Terry walked into Marge's Manor as agreed to help Beth carry the coffees back to the station.

"Morning Guv," he said, as he took the largest tray. "The press conference went well yesterday. It was good that a couple of journalists raised the points about Jimmy and Frankie being handy with their fists. Saved you having to find some appropriate words."

"Yes. That was a really lucky break," replied Beth and stared at him.

"Ah right. They were primed to ask the questions so that you didn't need to so it won't impact our relationship with the victims' families. Nice work! Did you also get that journalist to ask about Jimmy's Gallery business?"

"No, I bloody didn't, and I've got no idea how she found out about it. The Super and I had to placate the head of Organised Crime when we got back to the station. Luckily, his team had very nearly reached the point in their investigation where they were going to make some arrests, so they've brought that forward to this morning. Guy Fanshawe should be in our station by now, and we've been granted an interview slot with him this afternoon. Some more good news is that they were going to arrest Kevin

Carter, Jeff Robinson and two others for several unsolved burglaries in which some very nice pieces of artwork were stolen, so at least one of our suspects is off the streets."

The squad room was already a hive of activity by the time they walked in, and the coffees were picked off very quickly.

"How are we getting on?" asked Beth. "What's the situation with the CCTV footage we need?"

"The William Harvey security team came up trumps, and I've started watching their footage. I've spotted The Shank leaving the hospital at 9.37 p.m. and I'm just following the car's progress now," said Chris.

"Excellent. Let us know how you get on," said Beth. "Jane, has Canterbury Council responded to your request yet?"

"Yes, I've had an email to say that the footage we need will be with us by lunchtime today," replied Jane.

"Very good. Thanks Jane. Okay, has anyone worked through the notes of the phone calls received on the hotline after yesterday's press conference?"

"I have," said Dave, who'd been at his desk since six thirty a.m. that morning. "I've filed the ones that were easy to dismiss, like 'I was Jimmy Wheeler's secret lover and we were living together in Herne Bay. He told me he'd leave me everything in his will,' in the Green folder. Anything that doesn't sound quite right but needs to be checked out, like 'I saw Jimmy Wheeler in the Clacket Lane Services on the M25 at two a.m. on Monday morning' in the Amber folder, and the few really interesting calls, like 'You spoken with Frankie's brother Billy yet? No love lost there...' in the Red folder.

"Excellent. Thank you so much, Dave," said Beth, then moved to her desk to start working through the Red folder.

As well as some people who were already on the team's radar, there were some new names in some of the messages, including one man named Trevor Reed. Beth picked up her desk phone and dialled the number left by last night's caller. The other end of the phone was picked up after two rings. "Hi. Am I talking to Denise Ward?"

"Yes. This is Denise speaking," came a timid reply.

"Hi Denise. I'm Detective Chief Inspector Bethany Harper from East Kent Police. I'm leading the investigation into the deaths of Jimmy Wheeler and Frankie Tanner. Thank you for calling our hotline last night. You mentioned that we might like to speak with a Trevor Reed in relation to these murders. Can you tell me how you know Trevor?"

"He used to be my boyfriend but we split up a few months ago."

"What makes you think that Trevor might be involved in these murders?" asked Beth.

"He used to tell me he was a trained killer, and if I ever needed anyone sorting, he'd sort them for me."

"Why do you think he'd say that?"

"He said he used to be in the army and they'd given him proper training in killing the enemy, so whoever was my enemy, was his enemy, and he'd sort it."

"Why do you think he might be involved in the murders of Jimmy Wheeler and Frankie Tanner?"

"He's got a bit of an obsession with religion – he's got a massive tattoo of a cross on his back – and when I heard that those bodies had been found in the cathedral and in a church, it sounded like the sort of place he'd dump a body if he'd killed someone."

"Did Trevor know either victim?" asked Beth.

"I don't know, but he wouldn't need to. He said if you paid him the going rate, he'd 'eliminate' someone for you. He used to joke that I'd get a great discount off him cos I was his girlfriend. I was never sure that he was joking though."

"Okay. Whereabouts can we find Trevor, Denise?"

"I don't know. When he wasn't stopping overnight with me, he used to sleep on the streets, or sometimes in one of the homeless shelters. You could try them?"

"That's really useful information, Denise. Are you at home for the next few hours? If so, I'll send a couple of members of my team over to take a statement."

"Um yeah. That should be okay. They won't be wearing uniforms or arriving in a cop car, will they? I don't want my neighbours to know I'm talking to you."

"No that's fine. Our detectives wear their own clothes and drive unmarked cars. Okay, we'll have someone with you within the next fifteen minutes," said Beth. She left her office and updated the team on her conversation with Denise. "I'm not getting too excited yet, but that conversation ties together a number of possible leads.

Steve and Prisha, can you please get over to Denise's flat and take a full statement. If there's any legitimacy to her comments, we need to find Trevor Reed today."

Chapter 40

For the second time in a week, Emma Draper chaired an extraordinary meeting of Chapter. The second body had shaken the entire Cathedral team, and she knew she had to lead from the front.

"Thank you all very much for coming at such short notice," said Emma. "As you know, our team of staff and volunteers have been profoundly affected by the events of the past week. The Archbishop and I would like to thank all of you for the care and support you have shown our team; when this organisation most needed strong leadership, we found it at this table and we are very grateful for it.

The Archbishop will be arriving here tomorrow morning to speak directly to the team and offer them emotional support. We will also be arranging for those who need additional support to receive counselling from a local organisation.

I've been in touch with Chapman and Burke, and they have agreed that it's too soon to launch their communications strategy. We'll review the situation with them regularly, but the Archbishop is keen to walk the fine line between maintaining a respectful silence and returning to some form of normality, so quite when we will launch the strategy is unknown at this stage."

"I appreciate that there are sensitivities around this issue, but we should aim for a return to normality as quickly as possible," said Elizabeth Jefferson-Briggs. "I hope I don't sound mercenary, but we do rather need the injection of funds that the comms strategy could generate so…" Elizabeth paused and waited for a challenge, but none came. "Julian is, as always, available to make any calls or visits necessary to move things along. We will, of course, await your sanction," she said, with an icy nod towards Emma.

"I doubt that things will ever return to normal for our volunteers and staff," said Sophie Wilson, a former HR Director for a non-governmental organisation and a recently-appointed member of Chapter. "But a change to the new normal will at least help them begin to move on."

"Thank you both. I will share your comments with the archbishop.

Now, I've spoken with Superintendent Donald Campbell, who continues to be unable to share much detail with us, but those of you who watched the press conference yesterday evening will know that the victims were a loan shark and a bookie, who were known to be violent. Their bodies were left in religious settings. The Superintendent would appreciate any help that anyone can give as to why that might be. Does anyone know why the bodies were left at the cathedral or St Martin's? Does anyone here have a theory as to why that might have happened?" asked Emma.

The Chapter members did their best.

"Perhaps the killer has got a grudge against the cathedral or our Church?"

"Perhaps the killer is making the victims atone for their sins?"

"Perhaps the killer is asking God to forgive him for his sins?"

"We don't know, Emma. Isn't this within the police investigation's remit, not ours?" asked Elizabeth.

Emma clenched her right hand in an attempt to contain her exasperation. "I think it's incumbent on us all to give the police as much support as we can, whether it would appear to be within our remit or not," said Emma. "Well, if any of you can think of a reason why the bodies might have been left where they were, do please let Bethany Harper or one of her team know. Does anyone have anything else they would like to discuss before we finish?"

The silence and the shaking of heads drew the meeting to a close, and the members left the meeting room, one by one, apart from Elizabeth and Selwyn, who left together. Selwyn offered to walk Elizabeth to her car in the cathedral's underground car park, and suggested they use the ramp from the crypt rather than the external entrance, to avoid the torrential downpour which started as the chapter meeting ended.

"Well that was interesting," said Selwyn.

"Quite the opposite, wouldn't you say?" asked Elizabeth. "We heard nothing that we didn't already know after watching the press conference yesterday. We were asked to speculate on issues that are beyond our areas of expertise, and we were lectured on the need to support the police, as though we wouldn't do so if we were able. And that was delivered in a style better suited to a teacher talking to their pupils, than a Dean talking to Chapter. Honestly!"

Elizabeth tutted loudly, and Selwyn chuckled quietly.

"I cannot deny, although it is thoroughly unchristian of me, I find it difficult to mourn Mr Wheeler and Mr Tanner. Given their propensity for violence and their tendency to prey on the most vulnerable in society, I'm rather inclined to celebrate their passing," said Selwyn.

"I couldn't agree with you more," said Elizabeth. "The fewer such hateful creatures we have in the world, the better the world will be. But where will this end, Selwyn? Hopefully, the killings will stop or the investigation will conclude before much more damage is done to our church and our cathedral."

"I understand that the police have a number of suspects and they're confident of finding the killer soon; no matter what the Detective Chief Inspector said at the press conference, they are working on the basis that 'Speak No Evil' will be the next murder, and most likely before too long, and they're determined not to allow it to happen."

"Well, your contact point in the murder squad is clearly telling you more than mine is telling me! All Ki wants to discuss is why the CCTV wasn't working in the cathedral last Sunday night, and has it been fixed yet. Who are these suspects, do you know?"

"Fiona is as reticent to share operational details as your chap is; I get my information from a member of another team who is very close to a member of the murder squad. But no, no details have been shared regarding the identity of the suspects, I'm afraid. I will continue to ask and as soon as I know more, I will call you."

"Thank you Selwyn. You should have joined the police force. You are far more helpful than any police officer I've ever met!" said Elizabeth, as she kissed Selwyn on the cheek and climbed into her car.

"Here's hoping Bethany Harper and her colleagues resolve this situation sooner rather than later, before the victims become more worthy."

Chapter 41

Beth and Terry made their way to Interview Room four where they found Guy Fanshawe and his solicitor waiting for them.

"Good afternoon, Mr Fanshawe. I'm DCI Bethany Harper and I'm leading the investigation into the deaths of Jimmy Wheeler and Frankie Tanner. This is my colleague DS Terry Corfe," said Beth, then got straight to the point. "We know that Mr Wheeler was a friend of yours, but did you know the second victim, Frankie Tanner at all?"

"I'm not sure I'd call Jimmy a friend, as such, but I can tell you that I'd never heard of Frankie Tanner until yesterday."

"So you and Mr Wheeler weren't friends?" asked Terry. "How would you describe your relationship?"

"I'd say we were acquaintances," came the reply. "We'd sit and have a drink, and a chat about the snooker if we were both at a loose end in our local pub."

"How long have you known Mr Wheeler?" asked Terry.

"My wife and I moved to Ickleford shortly after Jimmy and Dawn moved there, so about six years," replied Guy.

"Where did you move from?" asked Terry.

"We used to live in Canterbury," he replied.

"Mr Wheeler and his wife also used to live in Canterbury. Did you and him meet there at all?" asked Beth.

"No. No we didn't," replied Guy.

"Do you know his sister Jackie?" asked Terry.

"We've seen each other a few times at the White Hart, but I can't say that I know her, per se," replied Guy.

Beth paused before moving on. "Did Mr Wheeler ever mention to you that he'd received any threats?" she asked.

"No, none. But as I explained earlier, we weren't friends, just acquaintances, so that's not something that I would expect him to share with me."

"Did he ever discuss any security concerns he might have had? For example, did he feel safe living in Ickleford?" asked Beth.

"He never suggested otherwise to me," replied Guy. "That's why we move from the cities to the villages, I suppose."

Beth nodded her understanding.

"Does the name 'The Crossbow' mean anything to you?"

There was a sharp intake of breath from Guy, but he quickly regained his composure. He coughed to try to cover his reaction, then out came the entirely expected response, "The Crossbow? No, I'm afraid not."

Beth nodded and moved on.

"Did Mr Wheeler ever discuss religion with you? It's the sort of thing we can all start talking about after a few drinks, wouldn't you say?" asked Beth, with a smile.

"I'm sure that would be the case for many, but not, I'm afraid, for us," replied Guy.

"Did he ever mention Canterbury Cathedral's Canon Missioner, Selwyn Du Pont, to you?" asked Beth.

Guy made a facial gesture to indicate that he was thinking about the name before replying "No. No, I haven't heard that name before."

Terry stared at Guy then asked "So, you and Mr Wheeler would sit at the bar in the White Hart and discuss nothing other than snooker?"

"Yes. That about sums it up," replied Guy.

"But you didn't always sit at the bar, did you Mr Fanshawe?" asked Beth. "There were times when you and Mr Wheeler would take your drinks to a quiet table away from prying eyes and ears. What did you discuss when you were at those tables?"

Guy gave Beth a stony glare. "Gosh. I'm not sure I can remember those conversations," he replied icily.

"Let me see if I can help you," said Beth. "Here's what I think. You and Jimmy Wheeler met some time ago and realised that you could have a mutually beneficial relationship. He could supply you with paintings that weren't on the open market, which you could sell on to your clients for significant sums of money. He could also clean a lot of money through your gallery, for which you'd receive a healthy sum of money. And if anyone got a little antsy with you, Jimmy and his associates could take care of them for you. But a few months ago, things started to get difficult. Jimmy decided that it was time to part company with Frankie Tanner, whose betting shops he'd been using to launder smaller sums of money. Jimmy had decided to consolidate his money laundering under one roof – yours. But Frankie didn't like it. He was losing his cut and it was going to hurt, so he wanted to become part of your business. You wouldn't let that happen, so Frankie got angry. What happened next, Mr Fanshawe? Did Frankie threaten you? Did he threaten Jimmy? Did you and Jimmy decide that the only way to sort the Frankie problem was to kill him? Jimmy was good with his fists but killing someone? That was a step too far for him so he looked for someone who could help you. And he found 'The Crossbow'. But something went wrong with the arrangement. Did The Crossbow take your money but fail to fulfil his side of the deal? Or did you find The Crossbow and pay him to remove both men from your life? You didn't need Jimmy when you could continue to have the business through his sister, Jackie, so why put up with the aggro from two men with reputations for violence. Get rid of them before they turned on you?"

There was a brief silence, before Guy forced a laugh and said "Fantasy. Absolute fantasy."

"Two of Mr Wheeler's closest associates, Kevin Carter and Jeff Robinson, have just been arrested in connection with breaking and entering, and the theft of paintings. That's not fantasy, Mr Fanshawe, that's fact. So how would a couple of lads from a council estate in Canterbury sell expensive stolen paintings, do you think?" asked Beth.

Guy glared at her, but didn't respond.

"You might not be inclined to talk, Mr Fanshawe, but I fully expect others to sing like canaries. Co-operating with the authorities can bring rewards. Please think about that," said Beth. She waited to see if her statement would get Guy to talk but he continued to stare silently at her. "We have no further questions for now," said Beth, as she and Terry left the interview room and made their way back to the squad room.

"Well, his answers were short and sweet, and very few of those were truthful," said Terry.

"Agreed. He only stalled when we asked about The Crossbow," said Beth. "We need to do more digging about how and when Jimmy and Guy met. And we need to look into Guy's relationship with Jackie – with Jimmy gone, he would need to know Jackie pretty well to trust her enough to carry on a business-as-usual, with her in Jimmy's place. There's a lot more going on here than he's prepared to discuss. Well, if he won't help us answer these questions, Terry, we'll just have to find someone who will…"

Chapter 42

The team gradually returned to the squad room from three thirty p.m. onwards. On a Saturday afternoon at work, each and every one of them was being sustained by coffees of various types, from the smallest espresso to the largest caramel latte.

At four p.m., Beth started the debrief with an overview of her activities that day, before working her way around the room asking everyone to update the team on their progress. She started with Steve and Prisha, asking specifically about the visit to see Denise Ward.

"She didn't really have much more to tell us than she told you on the phone, Guv," said Steve. "She did, however, hand over several photographs of Trevor which we have circulated to our colleagues in uniform, asking them to keep an eye out for him when they're on patrol."

"Did you get the feeling that her comments were genuine, or that she's a bitter ex-girlfriend trying to get revenge by setting him up?" asked Beth.

"We both felt that she honestly believed Trevor could have committed these murders, didn't we," Steve asked Prisha.

"We did," she replied. "We also got the feeling that she wasn't so much worried about her neighbours spotting the police calling at her flat, more that Trevor might be keeping a jealous eye on her. That in itself could, of course, be the reason behind her call to the helpline, but Steve and I both believe she's being genuine."

"Okay, thanks Prisha. Have you had any joy with finding a possible accomplice for Philip Crossfield?" asked Beth.

"We started looking at Michelle as the accomplice, so we stopped at The Cox on our way back from Denise's flat and caught Michelle as she was getting back from the shops," said Steve. "She was very impatient but she laughed out loud when we asked her where she was on the evening of Jimmy Wheeler's murder. She said that she took her kids to a birthday party for one of her son's friends that afternoon, that lasted from three thirty p.m. to five thirty p.m., then she called in with a friend of hers, whose kids are the same age as her kids, and that was from about five forty-five p.m. until seven thirty p.m. then she took the kids straight home, gave them their bath and put them to bed just before eight p.m. We've contacted both sets of friends and both mums confirm that Michelle and her kids were with them when she said they were, so we'll start looking at the army connection tomorrow."

"Great work. Thanks both," said Beth. "Terry, can you work with Steve when he's working with the army to see if we can find a link between Philip Crossfield and Trevor Reed, as well as to find out if Philip was known to calm situations or if he was handy with his fists?

Okay. Jenny – do any of the Wheeler women know who Jimmy's business solicitor is?"

"Guv, prepare to be shocked," replied Jenny. "Dawn, who knows nothing about Jimmy's business dealings, actually knows who his business solicitor is. Apparently, he was in primary school with them all before he parted company and went to the grammar school in Faversham. They all kept in touch and when Jimmy needed someone he could trust to look after his business dealings, he chose him. I've emailed his contact details over to you."

"Wow. There's a result!" said Beth. "Ki. Tell me Gary's helped us move the case forward as well?"

"Yes, he has," replied Ki. "We caught up with Gary at The Cox earlier, and asked him specifically about Jackie. He said she owns a very distinctive sports car, a second-hand silver Mazda MX-5, and he saw it parked up near the building Jimmy was in more than once over the past year, when he was waiting in the car for Jimmy to finish his meetings, so unless Jackie coincidentally happened to be in the vicinity, then it looks like she would have been in a number of Jimmy's meetings.

I also asked Andrea if Jackie was on her radar, and she said that she was, but the way she'd heard it, Jackie was more of an apprentice to Jimmy than a boss in her own right, although they weren't overly surprised to hear she'd stepped into that role after Jimmy was murdered. Andrea's hoping to get some more information from her interviews with Kevin and Jeff, and she'll keep us updated on progress. She also asked me to let you know that they've released the Canterbury Gallery sales and purchase transaction books if you need to have a look for anything related to our investigation."

"Excellent progress," said Beth. "Thanks Ki. Okay. Fiona and Clarissa, what do we know about the keys for St Martin's?"

Fiona answered. "We've spoken with Gloria and there are only two sets of keys for St Martin's. Both are kept in a key safe in the Constables' Lodge, and have to be signed for by whoever's working in the church that day. We asked Gloria if anyone had asked if they could borrow the keys from her; the answer was no, but she puts them in the top drawer of the back office when she's in the church, so anyone with access to the office could, technically, have borrowed them to make a copy. She's having a think about who went into the back office over the past few months, and she's going to ask Marina – who covers St Martin's when Gloria isn't working – to do the same, and she'll get back to us tomorrow or Monday morning."

"Very good. Thanks Fiona," said Beth, then asked "Okay, any updates on the CCTV footage? Chris?"

"I tracked the car The Shank got into after he'd discharged himself from the William Harvey down the A251 to Faversham, then the M2, and the A2 down to London, then round the south circular to Peckham. It looks as though he just went straight home from hospital and stayed there, because the car he was travelling in went onto the Alan Turing estate at eleven fifteen p.m. and didn't leave again before eight a.m. yesterday morning. I've asked Southwark staff to send over the CCTV footage from the estate to see if I can confirm that he went into his flat and didn't leave again within the timeframe we're checking. I'm hoping to receive that either today or tomorrow morning at the latest."

"Thanks Chris. Keep us posted on what Southwark's CCTV shows," said Beth. "Okay Jane, did Canterbury get you the footage you need?"

"Yes, the files arrived here just after two p.m. and I've started working through the footage. I'll send you a full report as soon as I've finished watching it," replied Jane.

"Great, thanks. Dave – have traffic got back to you on the movements of Muhammad and Jimmy's cars?"

"Not yet Guv, no. And I haven't had an opportunity to chase them because Ki and I have been out of the office all afternoon having a very interesting conversation with Felix Cavendish. He used to own a Rolls Royce Ghost until Frankie Tanner took a shine to it, and he surrendered the car to him in exchange for his son Barnaby's debts and, allegedly, to protect several of his son's fingers. Felix predictably denied any knowledge of The Crossbow, and both he and Barnaby have an alibi for the estimated time of Frankie's death – they were at Felix's parents' Diamond wedding celebration, and Ki and I viewed the venue's CCTV which puts them in the hotel until one a.m., after which they got a cab home because they were too drunk to drive – but the most interesting fact to emerge was the name of his best friend from his university days, the man who is godfather to his son Barnaby. That man is Selwyn Du Pont."

Chapter 43

There was a collective gasp in the squad room when a connection between Selwyn Du Pont and Frankie Tanner emerged, albeit at that stage a tenuous one.

"I know I don't need to tell you how very sensitive it is to view Selwyn Du Pont as a suspect rather than a witness, so keep digging for more evidence of a link to the murders, and I'll discuss this with the Super before we bring him in for interview. I'll keep you all posted on developments," said Beth. "Right. We've made great progress today, team. Well done to you all. Finish off what you're doing, then head off for some rest, and we'll all catch up tomorrow morning."

Beth went to her office and grabbed Jimmy's loan books. She had to work back through six books before she found the first name she'd been looking for. Barnaby Cavendish. He'd managed to rack up a debt of fifteen thousand pounds to Jimmy Wheeler just over a year ago; this was after he'd built up what must have been a considerably larger debt with Frankie Tanner, which the Rolls Royce Ghost was used to clear. The amount surprised Beth. Perhaps loan sharking was a more lucrative business than she'd originally thought. Jimmy's net was certainly spread more widely than just The Cox.

Beth continued to check the loans books to see if Selwyn had borrowed any money from Jimmy but there was no evidence of this. Next, she logged on to check the newly-released Canterbury Gallery transactions books. She searched for Selwyn's name and found it appeared just over a year ago, selling a painting called "Sunset Through The Clouds" to the gallery for twenty thousand pounds, which the gallery later sold on for thirty five thousand pounds. The sale to the gallery was completed four days before Barnaby's debt to Jimmy Wheeler was cleared in full. Beth had seen all she needed to, and took the information to Donald.

"I was worried that this would happen. Can you imagine how the press will handle the news that one of our main suspects is a member of the clergy at Canterbury Cathedral? But you're right, of course. The evidence is beginning to stack up against him, and we can't ignore that. Please leave this with me for now. I need to discuss it with the chief constable and the DCC. As soon as I've done that, you can bring Du Pont into the station for a formal interview."

"Thank you, Sir. The team know that this is a very sensitive situation and will treat all requests for information with that in mind."

"Right. As soon as I've spoken with everyone I need to, and I rather suspect that will include our comms team, we can move on with the interview.

Great work, Beth. I'm very pleased with your progress in such a short space of time. Here's hoping we can close this case before we get another victim."

Beth left Donald's office a little deflated after the reminder that there would very likely be another victim unless the murderer was stopped soon. She went back to the squad room to log off and pick up her rucksack. Dave was there, working his way through some CCTV footage.

"Dave. I know you love your job but you do need to have a break," said Beth. "Come on. I'll buy you a pint of Shepherd Neame's finest lager and, if you behave yourself, I'll also buy you a bag of your favourite pork scratchings."

Dave smiled. "How could anyone refuse that offer," he replied, and logged off quick sharp.

Chapter 44

Jackie Wheeler ended her call and threw her mobile to the other end of the sofa with a frustrated "Fuck sake."

"What's up?" asked Shirley.

"They've arrested Kevin and Jeff," replied Jackie.

"What? For the murders?" asked Shirley.

"Nah. For the burglaries," replied Jackie. "If they charge them and keep them on remand, we're fucked."

Shirley considered the options. "It's early doors, love. We have to wait until we find out what the cops are planning. At least we haven't got any more burglaries on the cards for Fanshawe so that takes a bit of pressure off."

"He's been arrested too," said Jackie.

"What? They've arrested Guy Fanshawe? Christ. I wasn't expecting that," said Shirley.

"Yeah, exactly. That whole business is gone now. So where do we go next? We've still got the loans, but that's going to be tough without Kevin and Jeff. Gary told me he's got a few mates looking for some work so I'll have a word with them, but someone needs to look after the loans, and without Kevin, it'll have to be me.

And we need to find somewhere to clean some money pretty quick. A couple of Jimmy's associates won't wait. If we can't sort them out, they'll find someone who can, then that's another business gone," said Jackie. She worked through a few options in her head before saying "Maybe I should have a word with Billy?"

"Tanner? You want to ask Billy Tanner to clean our money through Frankie's shops? Have you lost your marbles?" asked Shirley.

"Mum, we're desperate. We've lost our biggest earner with the paintings so we've got to keep cleaning money otherwise things will start getting tight. Frankie was pissed off with Jimmy. Billy isn't pissed off with me. It's got to be worth a go, hasn't it?" asked Jackie.

Shirley poured them both a large gin. She was working through the options but knew that Jackie was right. The only way to patch up the business quickly was to use the tried and tested route through the Tanners. "Alright, love," she said. "Give it a go."

Chapter 45

Terry had a new travelling companion – he was just getting used to having Beth in the passenger seat when Steve appeared. Beth has better taste in music, he thought.

They were on their way to the army barracks in Thanet to meet Captain Andrew Saunders. A quick call yesterday to Army headquarters confirmed that both Philip Crossfield and Trevor Reed finished their service at the Thanet base at much the same time, and Captain Saunders was in the line management chain for both men.

The journey was brief and full of football chatter and before long, Terry was parking in the visitors' spot outside the main building.

They were met in Reception by a tall, handsome, uniformed man in his late thirties, who steered them into a meeting room where teas and coffees had already been laid out.

"Thank you for seeing us today," said Steve.

"Always happy to support colleagues in the police force," replied Andrew. "How can I help you gentlemen?"

"Can you confirm that both Philip Crossfield and Trevor Reed served under your command until they left the army eighteen months ago?" asked Steve.

"Yes. Both men were based here at the end of their service."

"Were they friends?" asked Terry.

"Yes, I would say so," replied Andrew.

"We'd like to find out a little more about both men. Can we start with Philip Crossfield. How would you describe his temperament?" asked Steve.

"I would say that Crossfield was the calming voice in his platoon; always the first to step in and try to deescalate a fractious situation. He was a bit of a father figure for some of our younger recruits, but he took an interest in the welfare of all his colleagues, not just the younger ones. I know that a number of his colleagues went to him during difficult times, and he would always try to help them."

"Would it surprise you to be told that he had committed a serious criminal act?" asked Steve.

"To some extent yes, it would," replied Andrew. "He was a great believer in the power of words more than actions. But that's not to say that he wouldn't be prepared to protect himself and others if the situation demanded."

"So, for example, if someone threatened a close family member, what sort of action would he take?" asked Terry.

"Well that would depend on an assessment of the threat itself, so that's a very difficult hypothetical question to answer."

"You seem to know Philip well. What do you think he would do if he was jumped from behind and badly beaten?" asked Steve.

"I think he would take steps to ensure that such an attack wouldn't happen again and, depending on the individuals concerned, I think Crossfield would make attempts to talk to them to find a solution to the conflict."

"But if the only way to protect himself or a close family member was to resort to physical violence, do you think that he would take that path?" asked Steve.

Andrew paused to consider the question then replied, "I think we are all capable of taking any actions needed to protect ourselves and our loved ones."

"Thank you," said Steve. "Moving on now to Trevor Reed, how would you describe his temperament?"

"Trevor Reed is an altogether more complex character," replied Andrew slowly. "In many ways, he was the polar opposite of Philip Crossfield – Reed was more of a thump first, ask questions later kind of chap."

"Would it surprise you to be told that he had committed a serious criminal act?" asked Steve.

"I would be less surprised to hear that news about Reed," replied Andrew.

"Did either man face any disciplinary action for any reason?" asked Terry.

"No, neither man received disciplinary action," replied Andrew.

"Was there ever any chat about un-soldier like behaviour that could have given rise to a disciplinary?" asked Steve.

"I'm sure you will understand that I cannot speculate on such matters."

"Off the record?" asked Steve.

Andrew remained silent.

"We're investigating two murders, Sir," said Terry. "Your co-operation would be very gratefully received. Were there ever any rumours about the behaviour of either man that gave you cause for concern?"

"Off the record," said Andrew. "Yes, there were rumours about Reed's behaviour when we were on active duty. Some said that his behaviour towards the enemy after death was inappropriate and wholly contrary to the expectations of the British Army, but there was never any evidence. We came close to having a case once, but the eyewitness retracted his evidence before we could start proceedings. We were unable to confirm why he had his change of heart but of course, we had our suspicions."

"Can you give us an example of this inappropriate behaviour?" asked Steve.

"Again, and this must remain strictly off the record due to a lack of evidence, there was talk of mutilations on the bodies of insurgents. Eyes, ears, noses, lips, tongues – there were allegations that these were removed after death, but I repeat, we have no evidence to support these allegations."

"That's extremely helpful. Thank you. Just one last question; did either man have a nickname?" asked Steve.

"I'm afraid I don't know the answer to that, but if you come with me, I'll introduce you to our newly-appointed Sergeant. He served with both men and will know if they had a nickname or not," said Andrew, and walked to the door. Steve and Terry followed him into a room at the end of the corridor and were introduced to George Cooper.

"Cooper, these gentlemen have asked if Philip Crossfield and Trevor Reed had nicknames. Can you assist?" asked Andrew.

"Yes of course, Sir," replied George. "Crossfield was *'Papa Johns'*, because he was a fatherly figure to the young ones and he loved a slice of pizza. Reed was called the *'Crossbow'*, because he had a tattoo of a cross running the length of his back, and he was very good at handling a bow and arrow – he used to show us photos of the trophies he'd won at school archery competitions."

"Thank you, Cooper," said Andrew, and turned to Steve and Terry. "If there's nothing else, gentlemen, I'll walk you to your car."

"There's nothing else. Thank you for your co-operation, Sir," said Steve, and the three men walked to the visitors' car park.

"What did you make of that?" Terry asked Steve as they headed back to the station.

"I think we've had confirmation, albeit unofficial, of the information Margaret gave you and Beth, and I think that makes Mr Reed a very strong suspect. Now, all we have to do is find him…"

Chapter 46

Beth sat at her desk and picked up her phone. She dialled a mobile number and Tracey Jarvis answered the call shortly before her voicemail would have kicked in.

"Hi Tracey it's Beth Harper. How are you bearing up?"

"I'm okay, thank you. Slowly adjusting to the news about Frankie. How's the investigation going?"

"The post-mortem has been held and in the pathologist's opinion, the same person killed both Frankie and Jimmy Wheeler. We're also following up on some new leads so hopefully, we'll be able to move the investigation on soon."

"God, it's scary to think there's a psycho on the loose in a place like Canterbury. Do you think that I'm in any danger?"

"At this stage, we can't be sure what the killer's motive is, so I can't say with certainty that you're not in danger, but if you're worried, I can put a uniformed officer on your door."

"No, it's okay. The security in this building is very good, and I won't be going out and about in the dark, so I think I'll be okay but if something happens to change that, can I have a copper with me then?"

"Yes of course. Just let me know if you feel you need someone with you and I'll arrange it."

"Thank you. I was going to phone you this morning to let you know that Margaret said she'd seen Frankie's car on the access road to our home. Did she phone your office to tell you that?"

"No, I haven't heard anything about that, so I'll get someone over there today to secure it. Do you know if Frankie would have had his laptop with him in the car? We've looked in the Canterbury shops and at his other home, but we can't find it," said Beth, as she typed an email to traffic to get them over to Captain's Corner to collect the car and secure the scene until that was done.

"You should find it in the boot of his car. Check underneath the spare tyre; he was always careful to keep things like phones and laptops out of sight."

"That's great – thanks Tracey. I don't suppose you know his password? Our tech guys can break it but this would save time."

"Yes, I do," said Tracey, and shared the detail with Beth.

"Tracey, I've got a few questions I need to ask you. Are you okay to do that now?"

"Yeah, that's okay."

"Firstly, we heard that Frankie and Billy had an argument a few months ago, and their relationship hadn't really recovered from it. Do you know what that argument was about?"

"Billy's got a new girlfriend. I don't know who she is – Frankie wouldn't give me a name – but I know that he was really angry about it."

"Angry? Can you think of who, or what type of person, would make Frankie angry?"

"No, but I haven't really thought about it. I've never been a big fan of Billy's, so I've never spent much time thinking about him, but I'll have a think today and I'll let you know if I can come up with anything."

Beth sent a quick email to Dave to ask him to check with his sources to see if anyone knows who Billy's girlfriend was. "Great, thanks Tracey. I've just got one other question. We found Frankie's body in St Martin's church. Can you think of a reason why his body was left there? Either at St Martin's or at any religious setting?"

"No I can't. I haven't stopped thinking about it since I heard about St Martin's. It can't be anything to do with Frankie. He didn't have a religious bone in his body. I think it must be something to do with the killer."

"Okay. Thanks Tracey. Is there anything else you can share with us?"

"Yes, but I can't tell you this on the record."

Beth was silent.

"Please, promise me that you won't use this in court or anything, and that you won't tell anyone where the information came from."

"I can't promise the first, but I will certainly protect you as best I can if I'm unable to keep your details confidential."

It was Tracey's turn to be silent.

"If I have to reveal my source, and I think you're in any danger at all, I will pull out all the stops to get you proper protection quickly. I promise."

There was another brief silence, then Tracey said, "Okay, but I won't say this in court. Billy's had contact from Jackie Wheeler. She wants to start cleaning money through Frankie's shops again, and Billy's said yes. I run a legit shop on Canterbury High Street, and I don't want anything to do with that sort of thing, but I can't say no to Billy. I don't know if there's anything you can do to stop him using my shop, but if you can, I would be grateful."

"That's very interesting, Tracey. Thank you for sharing it. Leave this with me and I'll see what we can do. Now, you take it easy and don't forget to let me know if you need someone posted on your door. And if you can think of anything else, anything that can help us catch this killer, you've got my number. Take care," and with that, Beth ended the call to Tracey and typed an email to Andrea Walker, asking her to come and see her in Beth's office the following day.

Chapter 47

Beth could sense that her team were getting tired as they gathered for the four p.m. debrief. The usual jokes and ribbings were replaced with 'I just want a long soak in a hot bath,' and 'So, I told her I think a bottle of wine and a takeaway will be as much as I'm up for tonight.'

"Okay, let's get started and keep it focused so that we can head off and chill out a bit," said Beth. "Where's Dave?"

"He took a call from one of his sources," said Ki. "I think he's in one of the interview rooms."

"Well, let's start and you can fill him in on the detail after the debrief," said Beth, who went on to update the team on her activities. Next, she went round the team asking each one for updates on their day.

Ki had been reviewing the messages on Jimmy Wheeler's phone. There were a few exchanges which he'd sent on to Andrea Walker, but thus far, there was nothing of particular interest to their investigation.

"And finally," said Ki, "Dave caught up with traffic. When Muhammad's car went off grid last night, traffic followed his progress from outside the taxi office to the docks in Chatham. They said he was there for twelve minutes then went straight back to base. Dave got in touch with the Chatham CCTV team who sent us footage immediately. It showed that Muhammad walked towards one of the ships and met someone at the bottom of the gangplank, who gave him a large sportsbag. Dave watched Muhammad put the bag in his boot then drive off. Dave then asked traffic to trace Muhammad's movements after he clocked off, and he was seen driving to The Cox. When he was there, local CCTV shows him taking the sports bag out of his boot, carrying it to Tanners Bookies, where he stayed for three minutes and left without the bag. Dave's shared this information with forensics, and they'll let us know when they've checked the boot. Traffic said they'll be checking on Jimmy Wheeler's movements last Sunday evening soon."

"Excellent. Keep us posted on what forensics and traffic say next," said Beth.

There were updates from other team members, largely explaining why there was nothing more to report just yet. As Beth was getting ready to bring the debrief to a close, the squad room doors flew open and Dave entered quickly. Everyone knew that Dave was not given to histrionics, so stared at him expectantly.

"Guv, Billy Tanner has got a girlfriend and they've been together for nearly a year. His girlfriend is Jackie Wheeler."

During Jesus's crucifixion, Roman centurion Longinus pierced his side with a lance. Drops of the blood that flowed from the wound fell into the eyes of the nearly-blind Longinus and his eyesight was fully restored. "Truly, this man was the son of God," he declared.

Longinus later left the army and became a monk in Cappadocia. He preached to, and converted, many people. Soon, the governor ordered that his tongue be removed.

Shortly afterwards, the governor ordered that Longinus be beheaded; martyred for his faith. Saint Longinus's relics now lie in the church of St Augustine, in Rome.

Over two millennia later, in the early hours of a cold Monday morning, a man walking his dog found the body of a young woman on the steps of St Augustine's Abbey in Canterbury. Her tongue had been cut out.

Chapter 48

Beth was in the shower when Donald called to let her know about the latest victim. She shivered when she heard his voicemail – exactly one week after the first body was found, a third body had been dumped in Canterbury. She pushed feelings of guilt to the back of her mind as she tapped in a message to the team WhatsApp group, telling them all to meet her at St Augustine's Abbey asap, and why.

Dave was the first member of the team to arrive at the scene. He'd been at his desk since six thirty a.m. and enjoyed the ten-minute walk in the fresh air. He took in the scene and started looking for clues, any clues that could help them move this blessed case forward.

Beth and Ki arrived at the crime scene at much the same time, and gave each other a silent nod. Both knew how serious this new development was, and both felt sick to their stomachs.

They put on their crime scene suits and joined Mac in the hastily-erected tent that covered the body and some of the crime scene. As soon as they saw the victim, there was a sharp intake of breath from Ki. "It's Muhammad Khan's wife," he said. Beth looked at him, stunned. This was a development they couldn't have anticipated, and it didn't fit with the profile of the other victims.

"What have we got, Mac?" asked Beth.

"I'll know more when I get the body back to the mortuary. All I can say with confidence at this stage is that there are post-mortem mutilations to the body – the tongue has been removed, and it's been left on the victim's right shoulder. We'll prioritise this body this morning," replied Mac, indicating that she too understood the gravity of this new development.

"That's great. Many thanks Mac. We need to get her husband to identify her body first, and we should be able to get that done very quickly, so if you could please hold off on the post-mortem until that's done, I'd be very grateful," replied Beth.

"Yes of course. As always, please let me know if there's anything more I can do to support you," said Mac, who turned to her team to arrange a swift transfer of the body to the mortuary.

Once again, Superintendent Donald Campbell and Deputy Chief Constable Ian Merryweather were in a huddle with Emma Draper and Matthew Rye. When Beth caught his eye, Donald made his apologies to the group and moved to her side.

"This is quite the development, Beth," he said. "There are similarities between this and the previous killings, but this victim doesn't appear to fit the profile of the other victims – female not male, young not middle-aged. What do you make of the situation so far?"

"We've identified the victim as the wife of Muhammad Khan," replied Beth.

"What? Khan is one of our strong suspects and now his wife is our latest victim. Get a handle on this one quickly, please Beth."

"Khan was one of our strong suspects, Sir, but CCTV footage appears to put him in the clear for Frankie Tanner's murder," said Beth. "But yes, we will get a handle on this one quickly. As soon as the rest of the team have arrived and have got their instructions, Ki and I will visit Mr Khan to break the news to him. Mac is going to prioritise the post-mortem as soon as Mr Khan has identified the victim, so hopefully we'll have some answers, or some indications of where this new development is taking us, before close of play today."

"Good. Let me know as soon as we've had formal identification, then I'll work with comms to release the information to the public, although given the prominent location of the crime scene, I suspect we won't be able to keep this quiet for too long."

"We're on it, Sir," said Beth, and moved back to the crime scene, where the team had all assembled.

"Okay," said Beth. "We know that the victim is Muhammad Khan's wife. Ki, you know Muhammad better than most of the team, so you're with me this morning. Clarissa, please get a statement from the man who found the body, then you and Fiona need to look for any connections between our suspects and Muhammad, and his wife. I would like the rest of you to take a good look at the crime scene to get a feel for what happened here last night, then head back to the squad room to carry on with the investigation. Ki and I will join you as soon as we've finished speaking with Muhammad."

The team nodded, and started to move away. "We'll take your car," Beth told Ki.

As soon as they started their drive to The Cox, Ki checked in with his boss. "How you doing, Guv?"

"I'm stunned at this latest victim," replied Beth. "God. They've got three young children, haven't they?"

"Yes, they have."

"This case isn't getting any easier, Ki. How are you doing?"

"I'm shocked that Mrs Khan's been murdered, but I would say that the link must be through Muhammad. Y'know, a sort of punishment beating by proxy. Not that anything makes this death any harder or easier to understand."

They soon arrived at The Cox, and parked outside Block three before walking to the Khan's flat.

As soon as they knocked on the door, it flew open.

"That was quick," said Muhammad. "I only phoned your station fifteen minutes ago. Have you found her?"

"Mr Khan. Can we please come in?" asked Beth.

"What? What's happened? Have you found her?" asked Muhammad, as he was joined at the door by a young woman, bearing an uncanny resemblance to his wife.

"I'm Aasma's sister, Zaynab. Please. Come in," and she gently moved Muhammad aside to guide Beth and Ki into the living room. "Would you like a cup of tea?" she asked.

"No, thank you," replied Beth. "Mr Khan, why did you phone the police station earlier?"

"What? Why don't you know that? Aasma's missing. We had a bit of an argument last night, and she said she was going to spend the night at Zaynab's, but when I called Zaynab this morning, she told me Aasma hadn't been there, so Zaynab came over straight away and I called you. Have you found her?"

"Mr Khan. The body of a young woman was found at St Augustine's Abbey this morning. We believe that it may be the body of your wife, Aasma. I'm so sorry, Muhammad," said Beth.

Zaynab started crying, and rocking gently in her chair. Muhammad fell silent then asked, "Does she still have her tongue?"

"Why would you ask that?" asked Beth.

"It's 'speak no evil' next, isn't it. Everybody's talking about it. The next victim will have their tongue cut out. So does she still have her tongue?" replied Muhammad.

"I can confirm that the tongue had been removed from the victim's mouth," replied Beth.

Muhammad heard this news then roared like a lion. He jumped up and threw the small coffee table at the wall. "You bastards. You incompetent bastards. If you'd caught this maniac, my Aasma would still be alive."

Ki moved to Muhammad's side, and laid a calming hand on his arm. "Muhammad, I know this news is very difficult but please, think of the others," and nodded towards Zaynab. Muhammad looked at his sobbing sister-in-law and felt the anger drain away.

"Muhammad, we need you to accompany us to identify her body," said Beth.

Muhammad nodded his head. "Zaynab, please look after the kids while I go to identify the body," he asked, as he grabbed his keys and coat.

On the way to the car, Beth called Mac to let her know they were on the way for the identification.

"Thanks for the update," replied Mac. "You might want to stay behind for the post-mortem after the identification. There are a few things I need to discuss with you."

"Yes of course," said Beth. "We'll see you soon."

They arrived at the mortuary in no time. Beth could scarcely believe she was in the relatives viewing platform for the third time within a week. This type of escalation was rare and extremely worrying.

Mac and her team were ready for them. "Muhammad, are you ready?" asked Ki.

Muhammad nodded his consent and steeled himself for the removal of the shroud from Aasma's face, but nothing he had seen before could prepare him for the reveal, and he let out a guttural scream.

"Muhammad, can you confirm that the body we've just shown you is that of your wife, Aasma Khan?" asked Beth.

Between sobs, Muhammad said that yes, the body was that of his wife, and Ki took him to another room to wait for a lift home.

Beth remained in the viewing platform until Ki returned, then Mac began the post-mortem.

Chapter 49

Within an hour, Beth and Ki were on their way back to the squad room, trying to absorb the information that had been revealed at the post-mortem.

"I need to go and brief the Super, then I'll update the team," said Beth, and headed straight to Donald's office.

"Beth, come in. This new body is causing great concern upstairs. What have you got for me?" he asked.

"The tox results are back and show that Frankie Tanner died as the result of a very large dose of oramorph, which Mac says was administered through a puncture wound in his back," replied Beth. "Forensics have confirmed that the rope used to tie Jimmy to the altar in the cathedral is the same as the rope used to tie Frankie to the altar in St Martin's. It's a common rope which anyone can pick up in any DIY store in the country. Both victims were tied using a clove hitch knot, which is also common, so there are no obvious clues here, but in Mac's professional opinion, this confirms that Jimmy and Frankie were killed by the same person or people.

This is a very difficult situation, Sir," said Beth. "I've come straight from the post-mortem and in Mac's opinion, Aasma Khan's killer is not the same individual or individuals as the killer or killers of Jimmy Wheeler and

Frankie Tanner. There are similarities, of course – the body was left at a religious site, and there was post-mortem mutilation, whereby the victim's tongue was removed, but unlike the previous murders, in which the eyes and ears were not left with the body, Aasma's tongue was placed on her body, specifically on her shoulder. Unlike Jimmy and Frankie, who both had puncture marks and were pumped full of oramorph, Mac found no puncture marks on Aasma's body, but there was blunt force trauma on the back of her head, initially hidden from view under her hijab which, due to the lack of blood, suggests that her hijab was replaced after her death. Mac's sent a sample of Aasma's blood and hair off to toxicology as a belt and braces, but doesn't expect to find any traces of the drug. And finally, the body was dumped on the steps of the Abbey, not tied to an altar within the Abbey. Of course, this might be because the Abbey is in ruins, and the killer wasn't sure where the altar was, but it's not something we should ignore."

"A copycat, do you think?" asked Donald.

"Possibly. Or possibly a message for her husband, made to look like a speak-no-evil killing in an attempt to throw us off the scent. But, of course, most murders are committed by someone known to the victim so we can't rule Muhammad out at this stage.

I need to get the team to start looking at this murder in parallel with the existing cases. If there's nothing else, Sir?"

"There's nothing else at this stage, Beth," replied Donald. "Carry on."

The whole team had assembled to wait for Beth's update, and further instructions on the day's priorities.

"Okay guys, in Mac's professional opinion, Aasma Khan's death is not the work of the same killer as Jimmy and Frankie who, Mac believes, were both killed by the same individual or individuals," said Beth, and went on to explain the detail to the team. "Ki and Dave, you've worked closely with Muhammad on the other murders, I'd like you to take a lead in looking into who would have a motive to kill his wife. Is this a copycat murder or did someone specifically target Aasma? Find out what you can about the argument the couple had last night, including what time Aasma left home to go to Zaynab's home, then let Jane and Chris know.

Jane and Chris, once you have that information, speak with Muhammad's neighbours in Block three. Did anyone hear or see anything around the time of the argument? Did anyone see Aasma leave?

Mac put the estimated time of death between nine p.m. and twelve midnight. Clarissa, we need the CCTV from The Cox and St Augustine's between those hours.

For the rest of you, please continue to work on the murders of Jimmy Wheeler and Frankie Tanner.

Okay. Any questions?" asked Beth.

"Shouldn't we move the family out and move forensics in to their flat, given that most murders are committed by someone known to the victim?" asked Fiona.

"At this stage, we have no evidence to suggest that this is a domestic incident, so we need to tread carefully," replied Beth. "If anything indicates any involvement by Muhammad in his wife's death, we will of course turn the flat into a possible crime scene, but as things stand, we will only perform the same checks as we did in the homes of Jimmy Wheeler and Frankie Tanner."

Fiona sighed her disapproval with Beth's decision, which Beth ignored.

"Okay team, let's get to it. Upstairs are anxious to get some answers quickly, so we need a speedy resolution to this murder," said Beth.

Chapter 50

At nine a.m. on the dot, Elizabeth Jefferson-Briggs arrived at the cathedral to meet with the Managing Director of the CCTV company, who had been summoned to explain why the issue with recording at night had not yet been resolved. The meeting was brief but productive, and the MD assured Elizabeth that the parts needed to fix the problem had been ordered and would be delivered by the end of that week, therefore the cathedral's internal CCTV would be up and running before the weekend. "Fact," he said.

Elizabeth raised a sceptical eyebrow and reminded him of his contractual obligations, before saying goodbye and heading to the main admin office to check on how everyone was getting on. It was there that she learned of latest murder. She was shocked. Visibly shocked. She picked up her phone to call Ki for an update, but her call wasn't answered, so she called Selwyn, feeling confident that his contacts at the police station would be able to supply the information they need.

"Elizabeth, good morning. Have you heard the news?" asked Selwyn.

"Yes. I'm in the admin office now. Shocking – the third body in a week. I've tried to speak with my contact in the murder squad, but keep getting through to his voicemail. Do you know any more about the victim or the suspects?"

"I have no further information at this stage," said Selwyn. "I've been getting through to voicemails as well. I would imagine they're all very busy at the moment, and as soon as the dust settles, we'll be updated. As soon as I know anything, I'll call you, but I need to go and break the latest news to Mary now. Wish me luck."

***

Selwyn stood at the kitchen door and braced himself. "I know, Selwyn. I've heard," said Mary. "When will this horror end?" she asked, wringing her hands.

"I don't know, my love. I don't know who the latest victim is, or whether this is indeed connected to the other murders," and with that, his phone rang. "Thank you so much for returning my call. As you can imagine, we're all hugely concerned about this latest development. What do you know about the victim?" Selwyn was silent as his contact in the police station updated him on the morning's news. "No … Good heavens … Really …Gosh … Well, thank you so much for your call. I will, of course, be discrete and if there's anything I can do to assist in this case, do please let me know."

"Who was that?" asked Mary.

"Do you remember Catherine Dowler? We were at Cambridge together. Her younger brother Roger is a Detective Chief Inspector in the Organised Crime unit at

Canterbury Police Station, and he's very close to a member of the murder squad, who told him this morning that the body is that of a young woman. At this stage, it looks as though she might be the wife of one of their earlier suspects. Now, that's quite a departure from the type of people Jimmy Wheeler and Frankie Tanner were. Doesn't move in any of the same circles. How extraordinary," said Selwyn, looking puzzled.

"Oh my goodness this is awful. Just awful. Do you remember when the Yorkshire Ripper used to kill prostitutes, then moved on to kill those not involved in that business? That's what's happening here, isn't it? The murderer has got a taste for blood, and is now going around killing innocents. Oh Selwyn, this is such a dangerous escalation. We must move. We really must," she pleaded.

Once again, Selwyn pulled his wife into a bear hug and stroked her hair. "My darling, you will be safe, I can assure you. You will be safe and this nightmare will soon be over, I'm sure of it. But for now, we must be strong. The younger members of the team need support, and we oldies are the best ones to provide that support, so come along. Stiff upper lip. Let's get over to the admin office to see what we can do to help."

***

Selwyn quickly spotted Elizabeth when he and Mary arrived at the admin office, and excused himself to go and update her on the situation.

"A young woman married to one of their suspects?" asked Elizabeth, incredulously. "What on earth is going on here? Do the police think it's the same killer?"

"Apparently not," replied Selwyn. "There are similarities in the murders, but there are significant differences as well, so the current thinking in the murder squad is that these are different perpetrators, and the hunt for Wheeler and Tanner's killer continues to run alongside the investigation into this morning murder. I'm sure I don't need to ask you to be discrete with this information."

"Of course, of course," said Elizabeth. "Discretion assured but I must go and update Julian on today's events. He'll want to be here, I'm sure."

"Yes, I'm sure he will. Now, let me go and check on how our team is bearing up under this latest strain. If I hear any more, I'll contact you," said Selwyn, and made his way to Mary's side.

Elizabeth made her way to an empty office for some privacy to call her husband. After giving him as full an update as she could, she asked when he would be coming home. He'd left home at nine p.m. the previous evening to make his way back to London, so that he could be at his departmental desk first thing. The suicide prevention initiative was proving to be of great interest to a great many people so between that, and his attempts to support the home secretary in her political manoeuvrings, Westminster was keeping him very busy.

"Oh darling, I can't see me being able to get home before lunchtime on Friday, at the earliest. Let me call Harry and Freya to see how they are, and if they need extra support, I'll ask one of my advisors to pop to Canterbury to hold the fort until I can get there."

Elizabeth did her best to hide her frustrations at her husband's inability to see the importance of local issues. "As you see fit, darling," she said through gritted teeth. "I'm currently looking after the team at the cathedral, but I'll make my way over to the constituency office as soon as I can to lend my support there. Goodbye." She ended the call with a grimace, rolled her eyes, and whispered "God, give me strength…"

Chapter 51

Beth said "Thank you so much," and put her phone down hurriedly. She went into the squad room to update the team.

"The Metropolitan Police arrested the Shank yesterday morning. One of the less-enthusiastic members of his gang is going to be a dad in a few months, and doesn't want his child growing up on the Alan Turing estate. He hasn't got the means or the contacts to move away, but also, he doesn't think the Shank would stand by and watch him do that. They call this guy Roady, short for Roadman, because of his sartorial style, and he's been working with the UK Protected Persons Service for a few weeks to get to this point. We've been offered an interview with Roady as soon as we can make it to Peckham, so I'm off. Terry – you're with me. We'll be back before the four p.m. debrief, but if you need us, we're on our mobiles."

They set off in Terry's car for the M2 to London. "Well that's the Shank off the hook for last night's murder, but he's still in the frame for Jimmy's death. We should know soon if he's personally in the frame for Frankie's death, but if Mac says it was the same killer for both, then the Southwark CCTV could get him off the hook for both those murders as well, don't you think?" he asked.

"Yes, the Shank is starting to look much less promising as a suspect in our investigation," replied Beth, running her hand roughly through her hair as she did when she was becoming irritated. "To be honest, I'm just glad he's off the streets for a while. By all accounts, it's only a matter of time before his behaviour escalates from physical assault to killing so maybe, just maybe, he'll get the help he needs when he's inside to calm him down, and make the streets safer for all of us," she said, putting Gangsters by The Specials on at a high volume as they joined the motorway.

Once they'd arrived in Peckham Police Station, they were led to an interview room and within five minutes, came face to face with the Roadman. It had already been explained to him that his co-operation with other police forces would be viewed favourably in his request for protection, so Roady arrived ready to talk.

Beth began the interview in a formal but friendly style. "Mr Walker, thank you for seeing us," she said. "We understand that you've been a member of The Posh Boys for a number of years. How close would you say your relationship with the Shank was?"

"He's my bruv," replied Roady. "We was in school together since year three, innit."

"So you'd know all about his plans? And his actions?" asked Beth.

"Yeah, he's my bruv. He tells me everything," came the reply.

"Why did he start moving in on East Kent?" asked Terry.

"Someone on the estate used to work for one of the geezers in Chatham, and said there was good money down Kent way, so the Shank said he'd have a bit and we went chasin' it," replied Roady.

"Who was the guy who used to work in Chatham? And who did he work for?" asked Beth.

"It was that twat Mehmet, innit. Got 'imself kicked off his manor by his fam, so came home with beef in his heart. It was him that sent the Shank to Frankie Tanner's place to get a piece of the action."

"What happened when Frankie met the Shank?" asked Terry.

"Frankie told the Shank to fuck off. Well you can't disrespect a man like the Shank, innit, so the Shank was vexed and showed him his blade."

"Vexed?" asked Beth.

"Yeah, vexed. Angry, innit," said Roady.

Beth nodded. "So what did Frankie do when the Shank showed him his knife?" she asked.

"Grabbed the arm holding the knife, gave him a hard kick in the balls, and told him to fuck off again," replied Roady. "Then he said he should move up the coast. He said there was a geezer called Jimmy Wheeler who was running a good racket in the Canterbury manor, so the Shank took us up there to do a deal."

"And how did Jimmy Wheeler react when the Shank arrived?" asked Beth.

"Ha! He was well scared. The Shank went in blade first and Jimmy was all like 'let's talk about this' but the Shank was all 'nothin' to talk about, just give me the loans and fuck off'. Jimmy said "My loans book won't mean nothin' to you, so gimme some time and I'll see what I can sort out so we can come to an arrangement," but a few weeks after there was still no noise from Jimmy, so the Shank said he was going down to sort him out, but when he got there he heard that he'd been murked."

"Murked?" asked Beth.

"Murdered." Roady sucked his teeth to indicate his disappointment at Beth's lack of knowledge of contemporary vocabulary. He moved on. "Then, some of Jimmy's crew got gobby and gave the Shank a few slaps. They tied him to a kids roundabout. Fuck sake. They're lucky the Shank's been arrested, or there'd be some serious shanking on The Cox."

"Did the Shank kill Jimmy Wheeler?" asked Terry.

"No. But he could've. And I reckon he would've if Jimmy didn't give him the loans next time he saw him, but someone else got in there first, innit."

"What about Frankie Tanner? Did the Shank kill him?" asked Beth.

"Nah. Shank's not fit enough after his beating, but he would've gone in and hoovered up along the whole East coast if he hadn't been roughed."

"Isn't there anyone who could kill for him? Or go and hoover up for him?" asked Beth.

"Shit no," replied Roady. "Shank's the bossman, innit. He does the work. It's pride, innit."

Terry paused before asking "Who is Muhammad Khan?"

Roady frowned and shrugged.

"Okay. Is there anything you can think of that can help our investigation into the murders of Jimmy Wheeler and Frankie Tanner?" asked Beth.

"Nah man. They was nothin' to do with the Posh Boys. Truth."

Beth nodded. "Okay. Thanks Roady," she said, as she and Terry left the room.

As they started their journey back to Canterbury, Terry asked Beth what she thought of the interview.

"I think he's most likely telling us the truth about the murders. I'm not inclined to look at the Shank as a suspect any longer, unless we get some new evidence to the contrary. Now, Billy Tanner and Jackie Wheeler make an interesting couple. Romeo and Juliet. Were they looking to take over their brothers' businesses and create one big business? That would be quite the motive for murder."

"Yes, theirs is one of the strongest possible motives we've seen on this case. Don't fret, Guv. You'll put this case to bed before they try to parachute the NCA in," replied Terry.

"And before there are any more deaths," prayed Beth.

Chapter 52

Terry and Beth arrived back at the squad room shortly before four p.m., and Beth called the debrief immediately but before they could start, Steve had information to share.

"Trevor Reed is dead," he told them.

"What?" asked Beth. "What happened?"

"A hit-and-run, apparently. One of our uniformed colleagues was at the scene last night, and recognised the victim from one of the photos Denise Ward gave us," replied Steve.

"Suspicious?" asked Beth.

"No, a drunk driver. She was picked up this morning with a minging hangover, and couldn't remember a thing. When uniforms showed her the CCTV, she broke down and is now in custody," said Steve.

"God almighty, we're haemorrhaging suspects," said Beth. "The Shank was almost certainly tucked up in his bed when Frankie was killed. Muhammad was off doing something that looks dodgy when Frankie was murdered. Philip Crossfield was on CCTV walking around the cathedral grounds when Jimmy was murdered, but we might yet find an accomplice for him. We have no evidence linking Guy Fanshawe to Trevor Reed, who has gone to meet his maker, so that leaves us with Selwyn Du Pont, man of God."

"Aye, but we have a new lead to follow," said Terry. "The Billy Tanner and Jackie Wheeler angle looks promising."

"Yes, yes it does," said Beth. "We need to bring them both in together to prevent them having any discussions, and we need to do that tomorrow morning. I'll speak to the Super about this, then I'll liaise with the head of the Police Support Unit to get it done first thing. Is anyone unable to assist them?" asked Beth.

The team shook their heads so Beth replied "Okay. As soon as I've got a start time from the PSU, I'll WhatsApp you."

"Right, let's get the debrief underway," and she updated the team on the interview in Peckham station. "Ki and Dave, any progress on finding a motive for Aasma's murder?"

Ki started their feedback. "We've asked both Muhammad and Zaynab if they could think of anyone who would want to hurt Aasma, but both said that everyone who met her loved her, so they couldn't think of a motive. Muhammad's blaming himself, saying this has to be because of him, but can't articulate why or who might be responsible."

"What did they argue about last night?" asked Beth.

"Money," replied Dave. "The fact that they haven't got any and Muhammad hasn't got a car to start earning some. Aasma thought he should go and get any job he could find, but Muhammad wanted to wait until we returned the car; he kept telling her it would only be a couple of days but Jackie Wheeler sent Gary Nixon and Mikey Curtis across The Cox yesterday, to tell their debtors that just because Kevin Carter and Jeff Robinson had been arrested, there would be no change to the collections schedules so Aasma was, understandably, bricking it."

Ki took the floor again. "Once Aasma had put the kids to bed and got them settled, she and Muhammad started arguing, and after about half an hour, Aasma stormed out so she left home between nine p.m. and nine thirty p.m."

"Thanks Ki. Jane, Chris, what did the neighbours say?" asked Beth.

"The neighbours directly to their left and right heard them having a proper barney. Neighbours on the left put it at a few minutes after nine p.m., when the new BBC drama was starting. They reckon it had all gone quiet by nine thirty p.m. because 'at least we could hear the last half of the bloody thing'. They said there was a lot of shouting and it ended with 'a big bang', which they presumed was the front door being slammed," said Chris.

"Bit of a weird story from the neighbour in Flat six on the next floor up, Guv. Apparently, at around ten thirty p.m. last night, Muhammad knocked on their door and asked if he could borrow their wheelchair again. Not unusual, apparently – Muhammad's gran visits a few times a year, and she needs the support – but he normally popped up during the daytime and gave them a few days' notice, but he said he needed to borrow it there and then, so they gave it to him," said Jane.

Beth looked at Clarissa who shook her head and said "Still waiting for the CCTV to arrive."

"Okay," said Beth. "That's a very interesting development. We need that CCTV tomorrow. I'm happy to make a few calls if that will help move the request along. Do we have any more on any CCTV footage?"

Dave cleared his throat. "Traffic have confirmed that they followed Jimmy's car from The Cox on the night of his murder. He left there at 6.06 p.m. and took the most direct route to the turnoff for the road where his car was found. He turned off the main road at 6.38 p.m. and that was the last sighting of him on CCTV."

"So, it sounds as though he was heading straight home. Okay, thanks Dave," said Beth. "Steve, Terry, did your Army contact suggest anyone else who could have been an accomplice to Philip Crossfield?"

"No Guv. He was seen as a bit of a father figure to most of the lads, but according to the Sargeant who used to serve alongside him, he didn't have a particularly close friend in his platoon," said Steve. "He was the sort of guy who would go out and look for a former veteran who might have fallen on hard times, like sleeping on the streets, so that he could offer him his spare room until he got on his feet, but otherwise he was not someone who formed a close friendship with another veteran, apparently."

"Okay, well, we'll keep Philip on the radar for now, because he knew Trevor Reed well and Trevor had, albeit it off the record, a history of performing physical mutilations on corpses. Terry and I will have a little dig into Philip's personal friendships to see if there's anyone else who might be working with him, or who might step in now that Trevor's dead. Right. Any more updates today?" asked Beth, but the team shook their heads. There was always a dip in progress during an investigation, as the detectives worked the evidence to find the links that would ultimately take them towards a conviction. Everyone knew this, but it was always very frustrating.

"Head off now," said Beth. "You're all working the clues systematically, and we will close this case but now, it's time for some R&R."

Chapter 53

The following morning, Beth split her team into two groups. One, led by Ki, would support the PSU team going to Billy Tanner's flat, the other, led by Fiona, would support the team going to Dawn Wheeler's house to find Jackie. Beth and Terry would be at Billy Tanner's home.

At 5.10 a.m., on the dot, the PSU teams used their battering rams on the doors of both properties and entered the buildings. They found Billy Tanner fully clothed and fast asleep on his sofa, with some cartoons running on the telly in the background. Jackie Wheeler was in a pair of satin M&S pyjamas, fast asleep in one of Dawn's spare rooms.

The officers shouted "Police!" as they entered both properties, but it took more than that to wake Billy. On arrival in his living room, the officers shouted the same in his ear. That worked, and Billy's return to consciousness was matched with the increase in the volume of his swearing. He was arrested, and taken to a waiting police car.

As he was being driven to Canterbury police station, the PSU in Ickleford were being introduced to each of the Wheeler women in turn – Jackie was confused and kept repeating "What's going on? What the fuck is going on?"

as she was arrested, told to get dressed and taken to the police car waiting outside the house. Dawn was terrified and curled up into a ball on the floor, sobbing. Shirley was livid. Absolutely furious. She shouted "Leave her alone you bastards. She's got nothing to do with any murders, you twats," and hurled the first thing that came to hand at the policeman who'd read Jackie her caution. Luckily for her, her leopard-skin hot water bottle did not harm the officer, so she was merely warned to 'pack it in' and not arrested for assault.

At the station, Billy and Jackie caught sight of each other briefly, as they were being booked in. They each had their own solicitors, and were shown to holding cells to await their arrival.

Beth had allocated Billy's interview to Ki and Dave. She and Terry interviewed Jackie.

"Good morning, Ms Wheeler," said Beth. "Can I start by asking you where you were between six p.m. and eight p.m. on the evening your brother was killed?"

"Jesus Christ, you must be mental if you think I killed Jimmy. My twin brother. It's mental," replied Jackie.

"Can you please answer the question," said Beth.

"I was in Canterbury with a friend."

"Who is the friend?" asked Beth.

Jackie consulted with her solicitor before saying "Billy Tanner."

"What did you and Billy do that evening?" asked Beth.

"We grabbed a takeaway and watched a DVD."

"In Canterbury? Where did you do that? Billy lives in Chatham and you live in Ickleford."

"Me and mum kept our flat on The Cox when we moved to Ickleford."

"Which flat is yours?" asked Beth.

"Block four. Flat twelve."

"And how long were you together that night?"

"We met up at Shanghai House about six-ish and we both went home at about midnight."

"What about the night of Frankie Tanner's murder. Where were you between eleven thirty p.m. and two a.m. last Thursday night?"

"I was in the flat on The Cox. With Billy. We got there at about eight-ish and left just after midnight. I went straight back to Dawn's and got there at about half twelve."

"That was quick. Been thinking about your alibi, have you?" asked Terry.

"Course I've been thinking about those nights. Who can forget where they were when their brother was killed? And I was thinking about the night Frankie was killed when I was dragged into your station under bleedin' caution."

"Was anyone awake when you arrived back at Dawn's?"

"Mum shouted goodnight when I went to bed, but Dawn was out of it."

"Tell us about your relationship with Billy," asked Beth.

"He's my boyfriend."

"How long have you been together?"

"About a year."

"What did Jimmy and Shirley think about that?"

Jackie paused and stared at Beth.

"They don't know."

"No? Why's that?"

Jackie sighed in frustration at this intrusion into her personal life. She, like Beth, was an intensely private person.

"Because we wanted to keep it between us. It was private."

"What did Frankie Tanner think about your relationship with Billy?"

Jackie paused and considered her response.

"I didn't ever talk to him so I don't really know."

"Come on, Jackie. Billy must have told you what Frankie thought?"

"You need to ask Billy about that. I don't really know."

"We heard Frankie wasn't happy about it. Him and Billy fell out. Did he tell Billy to finish the relationship? Is that why you kept it quiet?"

"You need to ask Billy what happened between him and his brother."

"You can see why we think you and Billy have got a motive to get Jimmy and Frankie out of the picture," said Terry. "You two can be together, openly. No need to hide any more. And you can join the Wheeler and Tanner businesses. That would make you both a lot of money. Is that why you did it? Is that why you and Billy killed Jimmy and Frankie?"

"Don't be so bloody stupid," replied Jackie. "Haven't you got a brother or a sister? If you have, you'd know that you can't kill your own. You just can't."

"People do, Jackie," said Beth. "People kill siblings and sometimes the motive is money. Sometimes, the motive is more personal. But people do kill their siblings, Jackie."

"Well, me and Billy never did. I loved my Jimmy so much. He was my twin. I know it's only been a week but I miss him loads already. I'm sure Billy will tell you the same about Frankie. They went through a lot together – growing up was tough for them, but they got through it. Billy wouldn't kill his brother. He just wouldn't. Your lot need to stop asking us these stupid bloody questions and get out there to look for the real killer."

Beth paused, before moving the interview on. "Tell us about Guy Fanshawe," she said.

Jackie shrugged. "He lives in Ickleford," she said.

"He used to live in Canterbury," said Terry. "He lived quite near The Cox. Did you know him when you both lived in the city?"

"I met him in Club Canterbury about fifteen years ago. We went out together for a couple of months but it was nothing serious."

"Did Jimmy meet him when you were going out with him?" asked Beth.

"We all met up in the pub a couple of times, yeah," replied Jackie.

"All?"

"Me, Jimmy, Kevin and Guy. Jeff and Mikey was there sometimes."

"Where was Dawn?"

"Dawn doesn't like socialising much. And she really didn't like some of the pubs in Canterbury, so she'd usually wait for Jimmy at home."

"Did you continue to meet up in the pub when you all moved to Ickleford?"

"No. We only met up a couple of times when me and Guy was seeing each other. I think Jimmy used to chat to him in the White Hart sometimes."

"Did you know that Guy and Jimmy were in business together?" asked Beth.

"For Christ's sake. I've been really helpful because I want you to catch whoever killed my brother and my boyfriend's brother, but enough is enough!"

"Did you know that Guy and Jimmy were in business together?" repeated Beth.

Jackie and her solicitor conferred. "No comment," she replied.

"Did you know that Frankie and Jimmy were in business together?

Again, Jackie and her solicitor conferred. "No comment," she replied.

"Who's taking Jimmy's place with Guy – is it you, Jackie?"

"No comment."

"Who's taking Jimmy's place with Billy now that Frankie's gone – is it you, Jackie?"

"No comment."

"What about Trevor Reed? Did you know him?" asked Terry.

"No comment."

"What about the Crossbow? Does that mean anything to you?"

"No comment."

"Okay, Jackie. We need to go and check out your statement. Before we take you back to the holding cell, is there anything you'd like to add?" asked Beth.

"It wasn't us. It really wasn't us, and the longer you think it was, the more likely it is that the real killer will kill again, and god knows what he'll cut off next time."

Beth and Terry headed out of the interview room. When they walked into the squad room they saw that Ki and Dave were settled at their desks.

"How did you get on with Billy?" asked Beth.

"No comment," replied Dave.

"Not unexpected," sighed Beth. "God, I hate it when suspects say "No comment." Hopefully, the search of his flat will give us something. Anything. We really need a break here. Urgh. Right. I'm off to Marge's for a coffee. Does anyone want anything?"

Chapter 54

Beth took the long route to Marge's to clear her head. Jackie was right – they had no evidence to link her and Billy to any of the murders, and the killer or killers could strike again at any time. In fact, they had very little evidence to link anyone to the crimes. Does that make the killer forensically aware or lucky?

"What can I get you love?" asked Marge.

"A filter coffee and I'll have one of those energy shots – espresso, is it? – in it please. Actually, make that two energy shots," replied Beth

Beth took a more direct route back to her desk to find the squad room nearly full. "Super's looking for you Guv," said Dave.

Donald was in his office and waved Beth in. "I've spoken with the chief constable and the Deputy Chief Constable about Selwyn Du Pont. You can bring him in for questioning, but make sure you've got all your ducks in a row before you interview him. We'll only have one shot at this, Beth. I'll be in the room next door, watching." And with a brief nod of the head, Beth was dismissed.

When she got back to the squad room, it was almost full. "Okay, let's get started with today's debrief. Where's Clarissa?"

"She's had to go over to the council offices to get hold of the CCTV from The Cox and St Augustine's on the night of Aasma's murder. Why they couldn't just ping it over electronically as they normally do, I have no idea. She messaged me a few minutes ago to say that she was on her way back so she should be here before the debrief finishes," said Fiona.

"Well, let's get started and you can update Clarissa on what she's missed later," said Beth, before telling the team about her instructions from Donald. "Fiona, please get in touch with Selwyn to arrange a time for him to come here tomorrow. You'll be with me in the interview. Right. Chris – what's happening with the CCTV from Southwark?"

"Received and checked, Guv. It shows The Shank going in to the flat when he got back from hospital and not leaving again before Frankie Tanner's body was found."

"So that gets him off the hook for Frankie's murder and, by extension, for Jimmy's murder. If the Posh Boys were involved in the murders, then The Shank would have been the one to carry them out – he's the bossman, as I was told, and he's very hands-on. So, for now, I'm taking The Shank and the Posh Boys off the suspects list. Okay. Thanks Chris. Fiona, any progress on who had access to keys for both buildings?" asked Beth.

"Gloria has sent us a brief list of the people both she and Marina can remember heading into the back office over the last few months, but was at pains to point out that if they were busy, they wouldn't necessarily have noticed everyone who went into that room. She did say, though, that only substantive staff, clergy, and Chapter members knew the code to the back office keypad, so that takes the volunteers off the list. Unless, of course, the code was shared with someone else. We're cross-checking Gloria's list with Arthur's list, and running checks to see if anyone has any previous convictions or if anyone had an obvious motive to kill Jimmy and Frankie."

"Thanks Fiona," said Beth. "On the subject of motives, have we established a link between Philip Crossfield and Frankie Tanner yet?"

"Nothing at all just yet," replied Fiona.

"I called Margaret this morning for a catchup and asked her if the name meant anything to her, but she said no," said Terry.

"Thanks Terry. Have you found anyone in Philip Crossfield's life who might be an accomplice to these crimes?" asked Beth.

"Not yet, Guv, no," replied Terry.

"Okay. On the basis that we have no link between Philip Crossfield and Frankie Tanner, and there are no obvious accomplices in his life apart from possibly Trevor Reed, I'm going to park Philip Crossfield as a suspect for now. At least if Trevor Reed was our murderer, there should be no other killings from now on. Did Margaret have any other updates for us?"

"Nothing we haven't already found out, Guv," replied Terry.

"Right. Dave – any update from forensics on the boot of Muhammad's car?"

Dave cleared his throat "Yes Guv," he replied. "The sniffer dogs went crazy in the boot of his car, and forensics found tiny traces of a Class A drug in the area where the spare tyre is normally stored. Tests on the tyre identified the drug as cocaine. So, it looks as though Muhammad has been picking up drugs for the Tanners. That might be why he changed his shift pattern a few weeks ago?"

"Ach, that's tricky, under the current circumstances. You need to handover the information to the organised crime team – give Andrea a ring after this meeting, and explain to her about Aasma, then it's up to them how they move forward with the evidence. We'll put him on the sidelines for Jimmy and Frankie's murders," said Beth.

"But not for Aasma's," said Clarissa, who'd joined the meeting during Dave's update. "Have a look at this CCTV clip. On the night of Aasma's murder, the only movement from the Khan's flat between nine p.m. and midnight, Mac's estimated time of death, was Muhammad going to visit his neighbours at 10.32 p.m. and returning with what looks like the wheelchair for his gran. So, there's no sign of Aasma leaving the flat during that time. Now look at the CCTV from St Augustine's. There's nothing to see near the doorway where the body was dumped until 3.18 a.m. when this appears."

The team looked at the CCTV and saw a figure in dark clothing pushing someone in a wheelchair towards the entrance to St Augustine's. Once there, the body was unceremoniously tipped out of the wheelchair and onto the steps of the church. Then, the wheelchair pusher arranged the body, which must have included putting Aasma's tongue on her shoulder, before rushing off with the wheelchair.

"Muhammad?" asked Clarissa.

"Same build, for sure," said Beth. "Can you zoom in on the face?"

"I tried that but it's covered. A scarf, I think, but could be a balaclava. If we go back to the CCTV from The Cox, at 3.03 a.m. we can see the same figure leaving the Khan's flat pushing the same wheelchair and at 3.35 a.m., that figure lets himself into the flat with his own key," said Clarissa.

"So, unless there was someone of the same build as Muhammad already in their flat before nine p.m. that night, it puts Muhammad at the very top of our list of suspects for Aasma's murder. Great work. Thanks Clarissa," said Beth. "Oh, and can you ask the council to send us the CCTV footage from The Cox on the evening of Jimmy and Frankie's murders – we need to see the footage for Block four in particular. Jackie Wheeler said that she and Billy Tanner were in her old flat when Jimmy was murdered, and around the time when Frankie was being attacked, so we need confirmation of that, if it exists."

"Ki. Dave. Arrest Muhammad in connection with the murder of his wife, and bring him in for questioning. Also, ask Zaynab to pack a bag for the children and take them to her home. I'll arrange for forensics to start working on the flat asap," said Beth, choosing to ignore Fiona's smug smile.

"Ki. You and I will interview Muhammad," said Beth. *And bang goes the early finish,* she thought with a sigh.

Chapter 55

Terry and Dave were in the viewing room next to the interview room when Beth and Ki arrived.

"Mr Khan," said Beth. "You have been arrested in connection with the murder of your wife, Aasma. Can you tell us what happened at your home after eight p.m. on Sunday night?"

"This is wrong. It's just wrong. I didn't kill my wife. I loved her. We've got three kids together. They love their mom and this is breaking their little hearts. Why are you asking me about her murder instead of finding the real killer?"

"Please answer the question, Mr Khan," replied Beth. "What happened at your home after eight p.m. on Sunday night?"

Muhammad sighed and looked at his solicitor, who nodded.

"I gave the kids their bath at about eight-ish then I put them to bed, like I always do when I'm not working. I read the littlest one a story, then the two oldest wanted me to make up a story for them, so I was with the kids until about nine-ish. When I got back to the living room, Aasma had turned the volume down on the telly. That always means she wants to talk about something serious. She started going on about money. We're skint, but that doesn't stop the rent or the food bills, or the leccy bill or those bastard Wheelers sending their men to my home to scare the crap out of my bab. We argued. It happens in a marriage. Aasma said she was proper fed up with living like we do – hand to mouth, she called it. I don't know who'd said that to her. Anyway, I said that I'd have my car back soon, and could go back to work and earn some money, but she was just proper pissed off and said she was going to sleep at Zaynab's, then she slammed the door and left."

"What time was that?" asked Ki.

"About half nine I think."

"Did Aasma often spend the night with her sister?"

"Not really. Just when she was pissed off with me. It's surprising it wasn't more often," replied Muhammad, with a wry smile.

"Can you tell us who was in the flat that night?" asked Beth.

"Just me, Aasma and the kids," replied Muhammad.

"And what happened after Aasma left?"

"I watched a bit of telly then went to bed."

"What was on telly that night?" asked Ki.

"Oh god, I don't know. I wasn't really watching it. I just had the box on in the background."

"What time did you go to bed?"

"About eleven-ish I think. You know what it's like when you have an argument. It takes a bit to settle down."

"And were you in the flat the whole time that you were settling down? Just you and the children?"

"Yeah. Course I was. You can't leave little kids like them on their own."

"So who went to pick up a wheelchair from the flat upstairs at about half ten?" asked Beth.

This question took the wind out of Muhammad. He was silent for a while before saying quietly, "I don't know what you're talking about."

Beth turned her laptop so that Muhammad and his solicitor could see the screen, then played the clip showing a man fitting Muhammad's description leaving his flat, going up the stairs, speaking with a neighbour, then carrying a wheelchair downstairs.

"Is that you, Muhammad?" she asked.

Muhammad sat and stared at the screen, then he stared at Beth.

"Why did you go upstairs to borrow a wheelchair, Muhammad?"

Muhammad was silent. Stunned, as though he hadn't realised that the CCTV cameras on The Cox worked.

Beth moved the CCTV footage forward. "This is the CCTV from outside your home at three a.m. on the night Aasma was murdered. What do you think we're going to see, Muhammad?"

Muhammad looked as though he was about to faint. Or vomit. Ki stood and poured him a cup of water.

Getting no response, Beth hit play on her laptop. In the time it had taken Ki and Dave to arrest Muhammad, and bring him to the station, Chris had helpfully put together one clip of the figure leaving the Khan's flat pushing a wheelchair and leaving The Cox, arriving at St Augustine's, arranging the body, then returning to The Cox and finally the Khan's flat.

"Is that you pushing the wheelchair, Muhammad?"

Silence.

"Is that Aasma in the wheelchair? We've watched the footage from eight p.m. onwards, and there's no sign of Aasma walking out of the flat to head to Zaynab's house, so there's only one way she could have got from your home to St Augustine's, and that's in that wheelchair."

At first, Muhammad was silent and stared at the image on the screen. Then, he started rocking back and forth in his chair; slowly at first, then increasingly quickly. And then the roar came, followed by long, racking sobs.

Beth knew there was no point asking anything else until Muhammad was calmer. It took ten minutes for the sobbing to stop.

"It's hard," said Muhammad. "When you're trying to raise a family on one cabbie's wage, it's really hard. I tried to be a good husband and father, to provide for my family, but I just couldn't do it. So, I borrowed money from Jimmy Wheeler. That was a big mistake. I couldn't afford to pay it back so he gave me a proper pasting, and he did it in front of my wife. My poor love. She was terrified, and every time she saw anyone from the Wheeler gang on the estate, she'd shake. She'd literally shake. And that was all my fault.

I felt so guilty. My kids little tummies rumbling, even with help from the foodbanks, and them running around in charity shop clothes. It all gets you down, y'know. Then, Aasma just lost it on Sunday night. She proper laid into me, shouting and screaming about not being able to take any more of this life. Then she threw a book at me. It hit me on me head and it really hurt. Then she ran at me with her fists up so I had one hand on my head and put the other one out in front of me and she ran into it. I held her by her collar, and then I pushed her back. Oh god. I pushed her and she fell and she hit her head on the edge of the coffee table. I ran over to her, but she wasn't saying anything, then I saw the blood. There was so much blood coming from the back of her head, and then she made this noise. The same noise that my grandad made, just before he died. I think my dad called it a death rattle or something like that. And then I tried to find a pulse on her arm but there was nothing. I put my fingers on my throat to find my pulse, then I tried the same spot on her throat, but there was nothing. My Aasma had died, right there in the living room. I couldn't believe it. I just sat there, holding her and rocking her backwards and forwards. She loved it when I did that when she was upset."

"Why didn't you call an ambulance?" asked Beth gently.

"I wasn't thinking straight. I had all these things rushing round in my head. How was I going to tell the kids their mom had died? How was I going to look after them and the flat on my own? And then, I thought that if your lot saw my wife had died, you'd put me in prison, then my little ones would lose their mom and their dad at the same

320

time, and I just couldn't bear that," said Muhammad, before the tears returned.

Once he'd settled, Muhammad continued. "So I thought about the murders in the cathedral and that church, and I thought, everyone's waiting for the speak no evil murder, so if I put her body outside another church and cut her tongue out, you'll think it was that other bloke not me. I can't believe I did that to my beautiful wife," and he started hitting his head, repeating, "I keep seeing it, I just keep seeing it," until his solicitor put his hand on his shoulder.

He took a few minutes before he continued his statement. "After that, I got changed – I was covered in her blood – and went upstairs to borrow the wheelchair. I put her hijab back on her and put her in the chair, then I wheeled the chair to the front door and cleaned up the blood. She would have thought that was really funny, me doing housework," and the tears welled in his eyes again. "The blood came off the coffee table okay but it took ages to get the blood off the carpet. I did my best but I'm not sure I got it all. We had a small rug on the floor in the boys bedroom, so I went in and got that, then put the coffee table on top of it. I waited a few hours for everyone to go to bed, then I took her to the nearest church. I didn't know exactly what the 'see no evil' killer had done, so I reckon it was different to what I'd done, and that's why you've arrested me.

I didn't kill her, like in murders. I just stopped her from hitting me, and she fell over and hit her head. I don't know how we'll live without her," and with that, the tears returned.

Beth turned to the uniformed police officer in the room and said "Please take Mr Khan to the custody sergeant and get him booked in to a holding cell," When the room had cleared, Beth told Terry that she was going to see Donald to update him on the interview. "With his statement, we've reached the threshold to charge him with manslaughter and prevention of a legal burial," she said.

When Beth shared the new with Donald, he smiled for the first time in days. "That's great work, Beth. Well done. I'll update the chief constable and the Deputy Chief Constable, then we'll get comms to update the public. Hopefully, that will be a reassurance of sorts for them. Well done!" he repeated, and picked up his phone to start updating his superiors.

Beth made her way back to the squad room with a strong sense of concern. If the speak no evil murder had not yet been committed, then how long did she have to find the killer before he struck again.

Chapter 56

At ten a.m. the following morning, Donald joined Terry and Clarissa in the viewing room to watch Beth and Fiona in action.

"Good morning, Mr Du Pont. Thank you for joining us today. I'm Detective Chief Inspector Bethany Harper and I'm leading the investigation into the deaths of Jimmy Wheeler and Frankie Tanner. You've met my colleague, Detective Inspector Fiona Richardson."

"Yes, Fiona and I have met a few times. Good morning to you both. I hope you're both well. This is my godson, Jasper. He's a solicitor, and insisted he come along with me this morning, even though I told him that I've done nothing wrong." Selwyn attempted a chuckle, but it turned into a cough.

"Jasper Montague," said the godson, handing over a business card. Beth immediately recognised the company name – Montague, Buckingham and Barclay; one of the UK's most notoriously fierce defence solicitors.

"Thank you, Mr Montague," said Beth, then turned her attention to Selwyn.

"Mr Du Pont, several weeks ago, you had an altercation with our first victim, Jimmy Wheeler, at the

Canterbury Cares homeless shelter. Can you please tell us what happened that night?"

"Yes, of course. I was chatting with some fellow volunteers in the communal room, when the man I now know to be Jimmy Wheeler came in. He asked me if there was a man called Trevor at the shelter; he said that Trevor owed him quite a lot of money and if I didn't tell him where he was, he would search for him, then he would set fire to the building. I'm afraid I did not conduct myself in a manner befitting that of a man of my calling, when faced with that threat. I regret to say that I struck him."

"What happened after you struck him?"

"I'm afraid he fell to the floor. When he stood up, he left the building, turning to look at me and draw a finger across his neck, in what I can only think was an attempt to intimidate me. It didn't work."

"Why do you think he approached you and not any of the other volunteers to ask that question?" asked Beth.

Selwyn shrugged. "The dog collar is a little Marmite – some will make a beeline for the wearer, others will avoid one like the plague."

"Was Trevor in the building at the time?"

"One of the clients was called Trevor, yes."

"How well did you know Trevor?"

"As well as I know any of the clients at the shelter, although Trevor was one of the more talkative clients. He had a deep interest in religion, so we would often spend an hour or so discussing Christianity over a coffee."

"Do you know if he had any distinguishing features?"

"I know that he had a tattoo of a cross on his back," replied Selwyn.

"Mr Du Pont, I'm sorry to have to tell you that Trevor Reed has been killed," said Beth.

"No," said Selwyn. "Killed? Not another victim of the serial killer? I thought you'd already arrested someone for the third murder?"

"That's an interesting statement, Mr Du Pont," said Beth. "What makes you think that we've arrested anyone?" knowing that the comms team weren't releasing the information about Muhammad's arrest until later that day.

"Oh. I thought I'd read that somewhere, but I must be mistaken. So sorry," replied Selwyn. "So, how was Trevor killed?"

"He was the victim of a drunk driver," said Fiona coldly.

"Poor chap. So young." Selwyn slowly shook his head.

"Going back to Jimmy Wheeler," said Beth. "Had you met him before that night?"

"No, that was the first time he and I had met."

"Did you know who he was?"

"No, I hadn't heard of him before that night."

"And what about Frankie Tanner? Had you ever met or heard of him?"

"No, I was not familiar with Mr Tanner before hearing his name at your press conference."

Time to move on, thought Beth.

"Can you tell us about your relationship with Felix Cavendish?"

Selwyn and Jasper conferred quietly.

"Felix is an old chum of mine. We were at Cambridge together. I was the best man at his wedding, and my wife and I are godparents to his only child, Barnaby."

"Tell us about your relationship with Barnaby," asked Beth.

"We're very close," replied Selwyn. "Barnaby was born a few months after our infant son died. It was a cot death, and it was a very difficult time for my wife and myself. I suppose in a way, we gave young Barnaby the love and care we would have given our own son, had he lived."

"So you would do anything for him, as any parent would?" asked Beth.

"Yes. Of course," replied Selwyn.

"Has Barnaby had any issues over which he turned to you for support?"

Again, Selwyn and Jasper conferred quietly. This time, Jasper responded.

"What is the relevance of this line of questioning?"

"We know that Barnaby Cavendish has had a financial connection with both Mr Wheeler and Mr Tanner. Mr Du Pont has just denied any knowledge of the victims. I'm questioning the validity of those comments," replied Beth.

Selwyn nodded. "Yes, of course. As an undergraduate, Barnaby had some issues with gambling. Both his father and I supported him during this time."

"Supported him how? Emotionally? Financially?" asked Beth.

"Both," replied Selwyn.

"In what way did you support Barnaby financially?"

"He needed some money to clear a debt. I gave him that money."

"Who was the debt with?"

"I didn't ask."

"The debt was owed to Jimmy Wheeler," said Beth, and Selwyn looked surprised. "How much was it?"

Selwyn paused. "Fifteen thousand pounds," he replied.

Beth let that figure hang in the air for a few minutes.

"And where did that sum come from?" she asked.

"You may be aware that I come from a wealthy family with a substantial art collection. I sold one of my paintings to fund the debt."

"Who did you sell the painting to?"

"There's a small art gallery in Canterbury with a partner gallery in London. I took the painting to them and they valued it at twenty thousand pounds, so that covered Barnaby's debts and helped him move on from the experience."

"Do you know how much the gallery sold the painting for?"

"Gosh no. I didn't think to ask."

"Thirty-five thousand pounds," said Beth.

"Heavens. That's quite a profit for them, isn't it?"

"Who did you deal with when you sold the painting?"

"Oh dear. Now that's a very good question. She was the gallery manager and she was a delight. An absolute delight, but I can't remember her name. How awful of me!"

"Do you know who part-owns that gallery?"

"Gosh, I have no idea. I'm not terribly business-minded I'm afraid."

"Jimmy Wheeler," said Beth. "So you see, Mr Du Pont, your path crossed Mr Wheeler's before the altercation at the homeless shelter."

"Well, I didn't know that," replied Selwyn, again looking surprised.

"What car does your old friend Felix Cavendish drive?"

"Car?" asked Selwyn. "What a strange question! Let me think. I believe it might be a Rolls Royce?"

"Yes, that's right. A Rolls Royce Dawn. He used to own a Rolls Royce Ghost. Do you remember what happened to it?"

"Heavens no. I'm afraid I have no idea."

"He gave that car to a local bookie to cover Barnaby's debts with him. That local bookie was Frankie Tanner."

Selwyn's well-practised look of surprise returned.

"So to sum up, your best friend for many decades gave a very expensive car to one of our victims to pay for a debt, and you sold an expensive painting to pay for a debt owed to another victim. Can you tell us where you were on the evening Jimmy Wheeler died, from six p.m. onwards?"

"Oh come now, Detective Chief Inspector. You can't seriously think that I am in any way involved in these murders?"

"Please answer the question, Mr Du Pont."

Selwyn turned to Jasper, who nodded.

"Mary and I normally have a roast dinner at six p.m. on Sunday nights after which, weather permitting, we enjoy an hour's walk. That's what we did on the night Mr Wheeler died. After our walk, we went home and had a quiet evening before retiring at around ten p.m."

"And where were you on the evening Frankie Tanner died, from ten p.m. onwards?"

"In bed, or on my way to bed."

"And your wife can corroborate those statements?"

"Why yes, of course," replied Selwyn.

Beth decided to close the interview to confirm his alibis before taking matters further.

"Thank you for your co-operation, Mr Du Pont. Fiona will escort you and Mr Montague to Reception," said Beth, who rose and shook hands with both men.

As Fiona was taking them to Reception, Beth walked into the viewing room to find Donald on his own.

"Well?" he asked. "What do you think?"

"I think he's lying about never having heard the victims' names before they were killed. We obviously need to speak with Mrs Du Pont to confirm his alibis, but my feeling is she'll support him. I can't see him actually killing or mutilating anyone, so if he is involved in these murders, it could be via Trevor Reed, but at this stage, we have no evidence to link them outside the homeless shelter. I'd like to put a request in for the financial investigators to check his records, to see if there are any financial transactions between Selwyn and Trevor, or if Selwyn withdrew a large sum of money in cash which he could have given to Trevor to secure his services. Are you happy for me to do that?"

Donald considered the request then nodded, and walked to the door.

"Oh, and if Selwyn Du Pont knows that you've arrested Muhammad Khan, then you've clearly got a leak in your team, Beth. Plug it."

Chapter 57

Julian answered his mobile on the third ring. "Good afternoon, darling. How are you?" he asked.

Elizabeth had no time for pleasantries. "The police have had Selwyn in for questioning," she said. "Can you believe such a thing? A respectable man of the cloth being interviewed for two murders. They're dragging the cathedral's good name through the mud. It's utterly ridiculous when this is obviously a council estate gangster problem! They're the sort of people the police should be taking off the streets."

"Two murders?" asked Julian. "What about the third murder?"

"Apparently, they've arrested the husband for his wife's murder. Or manslaughter, I believe. But going back to Selwyn, I have to say I have no confidence in this investigation or its management. What are you going to do about it?"

"Well, I'm not sure there's much I can do about it, darling. Police investigations and their operational management are matters for the chief constable, and I don't suppose he'd take too kindly to having the local MP telling him how to run his force."

"You're not just an MP, you are one of His Majesty's Secretaries of State. Surely that carries some weight? And if not, you are a strong supporter of the home secretary. Surely she can influence the running of this investigation?"

Julian was silent.

"Julian, say something!" instructed Elizbeth.

"Let me make a few phone calls," he replied, before ending the call.

***

Mary was sitting at the kitchen table hugging a mug of tea when Selwyn returned from the police station. She ran into the hallway when she heard his key in the lock, and threw herself into his arms when she saw him.

"Thank goodness you're back. I thought they were going to arrest and detain you. What did they say?"

"They know about Barnaby and both his and Felix's history with Wheeler and Tanner. They know that I gave Barnaby the money to settle his debt with Jimmy Wheeler by selling Sunset Through The Clouds. They know that Felix gave Frankie Tanner his Rolls Royce to clear Barnaby's debt with him."

"Did they know what that beast Tanner threatened to do to dear Barnaby?" asked Mary, affronted that it was Felix, not Frankie, under the spotlight.

"If they did, they didn't tell me."

"So what else did they ask you?"

"They wanted to know where I was on the evenings of both murders. I explained that we'd had dinner at around six p.m. then gone for a stroll on the night Wheeler was killed, and that we would have been either in bed or on our way to bed on the night Tanner was killed. I'm afraid they're certain to contact you to verify both events."

"Oh that's fine," said Mary, with steely resolve. "I'll tell them exactly the same as you did. I'm sorry, Selwyn, but those men deserve no mercy, and none will be shown to them."

Selwyn gave his wife a strong hug and his face changed from a look of sadness to a broad smile.

***

"Selwyn, how are you?" asked Elizabeth, when they met in the cathedral's Crypt later that day.

"I'm fine, thank you. Nothing to worry about here."

"I've told Julian about the ridiculous police action this morning, and I can assure you he's on the case. He'll speak with the chief constable and if that yields no appropriate result, then he has the ear of the home secretary. I'm so sorry that you're having to go through this. But you have your supporters, you can be confident of that."

"Thank you, Elizabeth. As the good book says, *'The Lord is my strength and my defence. Let us not become weary in doing good'*."

"Indeed," said Elizabeth. "And no one can dispute that some good has been done in this city over recent weeks."

Chapter 58

"Okay," said Beth. "It's debrief time." She updated the team on her interview with Selwyn Du Pont, then told them that she and Terry had visited the Du Pont home in the cathedral Precincts to check that his alibi was supported by his wife. It was. However, when they were in the house, she'd asked to use their bathroom and when she was upstairs, she happened to find a pot of strong sleeping tablets in the bathroom cabinet, with Mary's name on the label.

"So, although his wife confirms his version of events when she was awake, once she was asleep there could, according to Mac, have been a brass band playing in their bedroom and it wouldn't wake her, so if Selwyn was out and about after dark, he has no alibi," said Beth. "He currently has an alibi for Jimmy's murder, but we need to double-check that, and he could be in the picture for Frankie's. Clarissa – can you have another look at the external CCTV Arthur sent you, to see if you can spot any activity in the Du Pont household on the evenings of the murders? Also, we know that he and Trevor Reed spent time together at the homeless shelter, so we can't rule out that Trevor was involved in these killings, but directed by

Selwyn, not Guy. Selwyn therefore remains a suspect in our investigations. Right. What else have we got?"

"I've been in touch with Jimmy's business solicitor," replied Terry. "He confirmed that Jimmy had a separate bank account which we didn't know about, so hadn't checked. The account received regular deposits from Guy Fanshaw's Canterbury gallery, and used to receive deposits from Tanner's bookies. Taken together, these are pretty significant sums, and over the course of a few years, that's how he paid for the houses in Ickleford. Frankie's financial details have arrived, and both his homes are mortgaged, with the Chatham mortgage being particularly large. His business accounts show a notable drop in income over the last five months, which I guess explains why he was so pissed off with Jimmy's decision to move his money laundering elsewhere. There's nothing else of note for either victim."

"That's great. Thanks Terry. Any other developments?"

Fiona stood. "We've narrowed the list of those who accessed, or could have accessed, the keys to both the cathedral and St Martin's church to fourteen people. None of them have a criminal record, and we're just going through the list to try and find connections between them and the victims. We should have something for you soon."

"Is Selwyn on that list?" asked Beth.

"Yes, he is," replied Fiona.

"That's good to know. Thanks Fiona. Are there any other updates?"

There were no other contributions so Beth drew the meeting to a close.

"Okay, that's it for today apart from one thing. During his interview, Selwyn knew that someone had been arrested for Aasma's murder. How did he know about that? The arrest wasn't shared with the public until after his interview, so how did he hear about it? It's clear that someone close to this investigation has been sharing information with someone outside the investigation. I don't need to tell any of you how serious this is. Think about that and the impact it can have on our ability to solve these cases. If you want to talk to anyone, talk to me. My door is always open to all of you. But consider this a friendly warning. If it happens again, there will be a formal investigation, and you all know what the consequences of that could be."

In 1954, Canon Edward West had the idea of using the Compass Rose to symbolise the Anglican Communion across the world.

In 1988, the Canterbury Compass Rose was designed by architect Giles Blomfield and sits at the east end of the Nave in Canterbury Cathedral. It bears the inscription "The Truth Will Make You Free" in Greek.

This morning, a man knelt alone at a lectern in front of the brass design.

Once again, Geoffrey Rochester stared at the kneeling man. He felt a chill creeping from his chest to his stomach. Not again. Not another one. Surely, this wouldn't happen twice on his watch. He walked slowly towards the kneeling man and warily put a hand on his shoulder. The young man fell back as far as his hands, bound to the lectern, would allow. Geoffrey knew immediately that the kneeling man was dead, and saw that his tongue had been removed.

Geoffrey screamed again.

Chapter 59

Deputy Chief Constable Ian Merryweather was furious. After thirty-five years of unblemished service, he was less than three months from retirement, and the biggest case in his career with the East Kent Police Force had just started. The body count was growing, and the list of suspects was shrinking. Finding another body that morning was the last thing he needed.

As soon as he entered the cathedral, Ian saw Donald standing next to the Compass Rose, at the end of the long aisle in the middle of the Nave. He beckoned him. "Donald, what's happening today?" he asked.

"We've got another victim, Sir. The scene is very similar to the first murder, but we can't be certain that this is the same killer until Dr McDonald has finished her work."

"Who is the victim?"

"No one has recognised him," replied Donald. "Griswold says he's dressed in a banker's uniform – they're suited and booted at work, but they wear chinos, shirts and jackets for downtime, apparently, and she recognised his jacket as the same brand as the one her brother, a city banker, wears. She said that the jacket alone costs just short of her monthly salary, so the victim profile is an interesting one."

"Four murders in less than two weeks. I don't need to tell you how much concern this is generating, Donald. The Chief Constable is already under significant pressure from the local MP, and the Church is also expressing its concerns, both about the use of their properties as dumping grounds for murderers, and the fact that one of their clergy has been questioned in relation to the crimes. We need urgent progress, Donald. We most certainly don't need any more bodies," and with that, the DCC made his way over to speak with Emma Draper and Matthew Rye.

Donald made his way over to Beth's side as she was asking Mac if this was another victim of the Jimmy and Frankie murderer, or if it was another red herring. "There are considerable similarities between this scene and the scenes of the Wheeler and Tanner crimes but, of course, I can't confirm anything until I've taken a closer look when we get back to the mortuary. Do you have an ID on this victim, or would you like us to start the process of contacting dentists and so on?"

"If you could get the ball rolling on ID, that would be great," replied Beth. "Many thanks as always, Mac. I'll see you later for the post-mortem."

"Beth," said Donald. "A word."

They moved to a quiet area. "We need to get a grip on this case, Beth. I need to see proper progress soon. Have forensics come up with anything yet?"

"Not yet, Sir. They picked up a few fibres from both Jimmy and Frankie's coats but they're not unique so they're going to be incredibly difficult to trace. But we're working on all angles as quickly as we can," she replied, and moved over to the team.

"Okay, guys, you know we're up against it. Mac is going to help us identify the victim, but until that's done, we need to do the usual checks of the CCTV, both inside and out."

"There'll be no CCTV inside, Guv," said Ki. "The engineer arrived earlier and said they'd had to order a new part which had just arrived, so the system won't be up and running until lunchtime at the earliest."

"How convenient that the new body was dumped when the CCTV wasn't working. Again. Is there anything suspicious here, Ki, or just some dodgy kit?" asked Beth.

"The engineer won't commit, but I got the sense that he thought this wasn't a regular glitch, but a bug that could have been planted. But like I said, the implications of accusing an insider of tampering with the system would be more than just financial, so I think they're being cautious."

"Okay. Might be worth getting Elizabeth's view on that, Ki. Clarissa – please take a statement from Geoffrey then work with Jane to review the external CCTV footage within the precincts and on the streets. The rest of you should continue with your current lines of enquiry and we'll share intel at the four p.m. debrief unless there's an urgent development beforehand. Any questions?"

No questions, just a shaking of heads, so the team went their separate ways.

The ticking of the clock grew louder.

Chapter 60

When Beth walked into the squad room, she saw Jane and Clarissa hunched over a laptop screen.

"Guv," said Clarissa. "Can you come and have a look at this please?"

Beth went over to their desk and saw a dark image on screen.

"We've been looking at the footage from the streets surrounding St Martin's church on the night Frankie was killed and at 2.08 a.m., this appears."

"Is that someone pushing a wheelchair?" asked Beth.

"It certainly looks like it," replied Clarissa. "But it's not your average NHS chair, like the one Muhammad used. This looks like an all-singing all-dancing chair. I did a quick Google earlier on 'Can electric wheelchairs go up stairs?' and the answer is yes, which could be helpful if you needed support for dumping a body. But they're expensive. We're talking around thirty thousand pounds."

"Do we know where this wheelchair appeared from?" asked Beth.

"There are no CCTV cameras outside the church or on the smaller surrounding roads – that's why this footage isn't as sharp as we'd like, because we had to pull it from one of the cameras on the A257 – but we're looking for any cars that approached the smaller roads via the A257 or the A28 between midnight and 2.08 a.m. and, now that we've got a timeframe, we're going to visit the homeowners in a few of the nearby streets to see if they've got any doorcam footage that could help," replied Clarissa.

"Excellent. And can you ask traffic to send us the footage from the roads leading to and from Frankie's Canterbury flat from – what time did his drinking buddy say he'd left him at the pub, Terry?"

"Just after 11.35 p.m., Guv."

"Thanks. From eleven p.m. to three a.m. so that we can cross-match those number plates with any you find in the vicinity of St Martin's. Is there a wheelchair on the CCTV from the cathedral precincts on the night that Jimmy was murdered?"

"I'll check that next Guv," replied Clarissa.

"Great work. Thanks guys," said Beth, and moved on to see Ki.

"I've just got off the phone with Elizabeth," he told her. "According to her, the engineer doesn't know what he's talking about, as the problems with CCTV inside the cathedral are clearly the result of their useless equipment."

"Okay. But she's bound to say that, eh? Otherwise the liability for repair costs could become theirs. Thanks Ki."

Beth moved to her own desk and started to respond to emails from the comms team. She ignored the emails from the finance team, all of which looked like reminders that she had a budget, didn't she know, so could she please bear that in mind as this very difficult case progressed. *They've received notification of the first weekend of overtime then,* she thought.

After finishing with comms queries, Beth moved back to the Canterbury gallery's sales and purchase transaction logs, to search for Selwyn's name again. If he'd needed to buy a very powerful electric wheelchair, or pay an accomplice to take revenge on those who'd wronged him or the ones he cared for, he might need to release more funds from the family art stores. Beth picked up a pen and started chewing the end of it. It helped her think, she always insisted.

The Crossbow was dead, so there was no way he was involved in the most recent murder. That removed Guy from the list of suspects – he was in a cell when that murder was committed, and they still didn't have any evidence linking him directly to Trevor Reed, only a possible link via Jimmy Wheeler. To an extent, it made Selwyn a less plausible suspect if, as Beth suspected, he had paid the Crossbow to work for him, unless Selwyn had decided to personally finish the work he'd paid him to do. Again, she had no evidence to support that theory, not even another painting sold to the Canterbury gallery.

Okay. Wheelchairs, thought Beth. Who sells the really expensive ones and what sort of records do they keep for their customers? Another hour went by, as she researched the topic online. And then, Clarissa and an excited-looking Jane arrived at her office door.

"Guv," said Clarissa. "Traffic have come up trumps with the CCTV. We spotted Frankie's car turn into

Captain's Corner at 12.20 a.m. then two cars left the road between one a.m. and one thirty a.m. We followed their progress and saw one of them pull into North Holmes Road at 1.55 a.m. They could have gone from there to St Martin's Avenue, which would give them easy pavement access to the rear of St Martin's church," said Clarissa. "We've checked the database and found that the car is registered to a Leo Jenkins in Battle. Interestingly, his address is not that far from the stately home owned by the Du Pont family. I have Mr Jenkins's address here. I called him a few minutes ago, and he's at home all day and happy to talk to the police."

"Oh. Clarissa. Great work! Terry, you're with me. We're off to do Battle!"

Chapter 61

Selwyn put his mobile phone down and turned to his wife.

"There's been another murder, hasn't there," she said. As Selwyn nodded, Mary sighed then asked, "Who is it this time?"

"Identity unknown at this stage," he replied. "But the victim is young and apparently looks quite well-to-do. Roger seems to think it's the same killer, but thinks his hunting ground might have changed."

"Selwyn please!" exclaimed Mary, and sighed. "Your use of language sometimes leaves a lot to be desired! I knew this would happen. I told you, didn't I. The murders will escalate and the innocents will perish."

"Well, it's a little early to be confident that today's victim is not of the same breed as the beasts who died before, but I'm sure the police will identify him quickly, and hopefully that will put your mind at rest."

"And what do the police think? Are they any nearer finding the actual killer? Are they going to be bothering you again?" asked Mary.

"Assuming they're still looking at there being only one killer, I think they'll need to find some evidence to link me to the new victim before they can question me again, so I'm afraid we'll just have to wait and see," said Selwyn.

He moved to Mary's side and held her hands, staring into her eyes. Mary shivered. "I am not guilty of these crimes, my darling, and I have every faith in the British justice system to get their man and that's the right man, not an innocent like me."

Mary felt her heart sink.

***

Elizabeth paced across the kitchen as she waited for Julian to answer his phone. For the fifth time, the phone went into voicemail and for the fifth time, she left him a message instructing him to call her urgently.

Within a few minutes, a very tired-looking Julian walked into the door. Elizabeth's immediate concern was for his wellbeing.

"You look exhausted, darling," she said. "What have you been doing?"

"I've been awake for most of the night sorting out my Westminster affairs so that I could get back to your side as quickly as possible."

Elizabeth was comforted by his words, but immediately returned to the most recent events, and she launched into a furious tirade.

"Julian, there's been another murder and the body was, again, dumped in the cathedral. According to Selwyn's source, the victim appears to be a different age and from a different social group to Wheeler and Tanner, and Mary is terribly worried that this is an escalation which leaves every citizen in Canterbury unsafe."

Julian looked shocked. "Let me call the chief constable for an update. Mary's right. If this latest victim is not involved in the same activities as the previous victims, the public concern will be significant."

Elizabeth made them both a cup of coffee, muttering "I'm not even sure how the cathedral will recover from this latest event. Why couldn't they dump the bodies on their own estates. Honestly."

Julian put his phone down. "The Chief Constable is unavailable," he told Elizabeth. "Understandable, given the latest developments, of course."

Elizabeth suddenly spotted what looked like a small spot of blood on Julian's collar.

"Darling, is this blood?" she asked, moving towards him to get a better look.

Julian stepped away from her. "I must have cut myself shaving this morning," he replied. "I was very tired. Right. I'll get changed, then I think we need to go to the constituency office to support the staff and the voters. Come on, darling, get your glad rags on. It's showtime."

Elizabeth watched her husband move away, with a mixture of disappointment and surprise at his tone. *Showtime? That's not like him at all,* she thought.

Chapter 62

There was a buzz of excitement in the car as Terry headed towards the A252. "This is good progress, eh Guv?" asked Terry.

"It certainly is, Terry. This is one of the most positive breaks we've had on this case," replied Beth, finding the Madness song Driving in My Car on her playlist.

An hour and a half later, they arrived in the beautiful town of Battle, home to the extraordinary Battle castle and site of the famous Battle of Hastings in 1066. It took them ten minutes to find Leo Jenkins's house, but he opened the door on the first knock. A small, smart man in his seventies, he wore a shirt and tie for the occasion, and he welcomed them into his home with the offer of a coffee, which both Beth and Terry refused.

"How can I help you officers?" he asked.

"Mr Jenkins, we understand that you own a Citroen Grand C4 SpaceTourer with this registration number?" asked Terry, showing Leo a screen shot of the UK number plate taken from the CCTV footage.

"I used to own that car, yes. But I sold it several months ago. For quite a good price, actually. I sold it on eBay," replied Leo, proudly demonstrating his technical skills.

"Did you contact the DVLA to let them know that you were no longer the registered owner of this car?" asked Beth.

"No, the buyer told me he'd arrange that himself."

"What was the buyer's name?"

Leo Jenkins again had the look of a very proud man about him when he said, beaming, "It was one of the manor folk. It was Mr Selwyn."

Beth and Terry arrived back at the station a few minutes after four p.m. Terry went to make them both a coffee as Beth started the debrief.

She updated the team on the events in Battle, and the buzz of excitement transferred from Terry's car to the squad room.

"Okay, I need to discuss this development with the Super, but I think we're making real progress now. And please remember what I said about talking to others outside of this team. This information is extremely sensitive and at this stage, it's confidential to this investigation," said Beth, before going around the room asking for updates.

"Guv, I've checked the external CCTV that Arthur sent over and on the evenings of both Jimmy and Frankie's murders, Selwyn leaves his house at midnight and returns a few hours later," said Clarissa. "He walks out alone on both occasions. And there's no sign of him and Mary going for a walk together on the evening of Jimmy's murder, just Selwyn walking out of his house just before six p.m. then disappearing around the corner, out of sight of the CCTV cameras. He gets back to his house just before eight p.m."

"That's great work. Many thanks, Clarissa. Has the footage outside Shirley and Jackie's flat been sent over to us yet?" asked Beth.

"Yes, received it an hour ago. The footage supports the statement made by Jackie Wheeler, and the traffic footage I requested shows they both went directly to their own homes after leaving the flat."

"So, that's Jackie and Billy off our suspects list," said Beth. "Well done on following up with traffic." Clarissa smiled, as Fiona glowered behind her.

"Any more updates for today?" asked Beth, but there was nothing more to share. "Okay. Big thanks for all your hard work, guys. We're really making progress now. Now head off and rest up this evening. I'll see you all in the morning.

Donald sat quietly considering the latest update on Selwyn Du Pont.

"This is a very sensitive situation, Beth. I hope you've plugged your leak. We simply can't have this information slipping out to the general public. Nor can we have Mr Du Pont hearing details of this investigation before we interview him again, which we will need to do tomorrow. There are too many inconsistencies in his story to avoid that."

"I've told the team that we believe that someone is talking out of turn and that if it continues, there'll be an investigation. That should prevent Mr Du Pont getting any further updates."

"Well I hope so. This is good progress, but we need to capitalise on it. For the first time in this investigation, I feel as though we're on the front foot, and I want to keep it that way." Donald's face mellowed. "This has been quite the two weeks, Beth. You and your team have been under enormous pressure, and I am very pleased with the progress you've made this week. Hopefully, we'll be able to put this case to bed soon and if we do, your hard work won't go unnoticed."

"Thank you, Sir," said Beth, and left Donald's office with a spring in her step. Time for some fried chicken and a large glass of wine, she thought, before preparing for tomorrow's interview with Selwyn.

Chapter 63

Beth had asked Fiona to call Selwyn the previous evening to ask him to attend the station at ten a.m. He agreed, reluctantly.

At 10.05 a.m., Beth, Fiona, Selwyn, and Jasper were back in the same interview room as they'd been in just two days earlier, with Terry, Clarissa, and Donald again in the viewing room next door.

"Mr Du Pont," said Beth. "Thank you for coming in to see us this morning. Mr Montague," she acknowledged Jasper with a nod in his direction.

"I'm always very happy to help out our colleagues in the police force, but I'm afraid I'm at a loss as to what I can add to our previous discussion," said Selwyn.

"Mr Du Pont, we have found a few discrepancies in your statement, which we'd like to walk through with you."

Both Selwyn and Jasper maintained a poker face.

"At the interview on Wednesday, you told us that you and your wife eat a Sunday roast at six p.m. then go for a walk, weather permitting. You said that's what you had both done on the evening of Jimmy Wheeler's murder, and your wife confirmed that when my colleague and I visited her afterwards. Is that statement correct?"

"Why yes. To the best of my knowledge that's what we did that night. Creatures of habit and all that. Although, of course, there are times when my wife is not feeling too well – I'm sure she won't mind me telling you that she's suffered with her nerves since we lost our wee lad as a baby – so when things are difficult, I will go for a post-dinner stroll alone."

Clever Selwyn, thought Beth.

"Mr Du Pont, we have some CCTV footage here showing you leaving your house shortly before six p.m. on the evening Mr Wheeler died. You left alone and you returned to your house shortly before eight p.m." Beth showed the Selwyn and Jasper the video. "Not exactly the timings we had been told – dinner at six p.m., creatures of habit – and that could have an impact on our investigation. Can you explain this?"

"I'm afraid my wife has not been well recently. We've both been rather more concerned about her wellbeing than the practical details of our lives, which could explain any discrepancies in our recollections."

"Can you tell us where you went that evening?" asked Beth.

"Oh, now there's a question," came the reply. "I often take a walk along the Great Stour Way, so it's possible I went there. Although, it's also possible I walked up towards St Martin's hospital at the top of Littlebourne Road. There's a lovely little garden there, Webbs Garden, where I used to volunteer until age got the better of my old back," he smiled wanly. "But when my dear wife is not well, I'm afraid my concentration is entirely on her, and not on my location."

Beth realised there was no CCTV on the Great Stour way, and put her money on that being the final destination. She moved on.

"Mr Du Pont, you also told us that you and wife retire to bed at around ten p.m. every night and, again, your wife confirmed that on the evenings of both murders, you had retired together at that time. Is that correct?"

"Yes, yes that's correct but, of course, if my insomnia decides to visit, particularly when my wife is not well, then I can get up a few hours later to go for another walk to try and tire this old body enough to induce sleep."

Very clever Selwyn.

"Doesn't this disturb your wife?" asked Beth.

"Again, I'm sure my wife wouldn't mind me telling you this, she is on very strong medication to help her sleep, without which, I'm not sure she'd manage more than an hour or two every night. Fortunately, the medication is so strong that she goes to a land of absolute peace, and not even a great galumphing husband's wanderings can wake her!"

Beth paused for a moment, and looked carefully at Selwyn. His answers appeared well-rehearsed, but beneath the confident façade, Beth believed she saw some signs of concern.

"Mr Du Pont, we have footage showing you leaving your home on the nights of both murders, at around midnight, again leaving alone and returning a few hours later. Can you tell us where you went on those occasions?"

"Oh Detective Chief Inspector, you must think me a terrible nitwit, but I simply cannot answer that. As I said, when my wife is unwell, I take a number of walks which transport me to a whole other place, and it's not uncommon for me to return home without the first idea of where I've actually been. Terribly sorry."

I suspect you might very well be sorry soon, thought Beth.

"I'd like to share some more CCTV footage with you," she said to both men sitting opposite her. She turned her laptop to reveal a poor-quality clip of someone pushing a wheelchair towards St Martin's church.

"Does this footage mean anything to you?" Beth asked Selwyn.

"Oh really," said Jasper. "I can barely make out any figures in that footage let alone identify anyone from it. This is desperate stuff, Detective."

Beth didn't respond, but instead turned expectantly towards Selwyn, who merely shrugged and said, "I can tell you that the building looks like St Martin's church, and that appears to be a wheelchair being pushed towards it. As Jasper rightly says, the quality of the footage is too poor to identify who is in the chair, or indeed who is pushing it, but if it's your contention that the wheelchair pusher is me, my only reaction is that I wish I was that slender!" Selwyn chuckled, until Beth replied.

"The footage is with our digital team now, and we hope to have a clearer image of both parties soon." The atmosphere took a turn for the worse.

"Well, I can only say that I've given you as much information as I can which, I regret, is not as fulsome as I would like, but if there's nothing more, perhaps I could return to my parish duties? Unless you would like to discuss the third murder with me? Or have you concluded that the victim's profile is sufficiently different from the first two victims for there to be a different murderer?" asked Selwyn.

"That's another very interesting comment, Mr Du Pont. We haven't yet released any details of the latest victim. What makes you think the profile is different to the other victims?" asked Beth icily, acutely aware that Donald would be watching her intently through the mirror.

"Ah, again, my misunderstanding officer. Perhaps I've taken the statements of those who saw the body a step further than the evidence allowed."

Beth squeezed her hand into a ball, hoping to keep her intense frustration away from her face.

"We have just one more question for you," said Beth. She took out a number of screen shots showing a Citroen Grand C4 SpaceTourer leaving Captain's Corner, and moving towards St Martin's church on the night of Frankie Tanner's death. "This car was sold a few months ago by a Mr Leo Jenkins in Battle. He told us that he had sold the car to you. This car is now a significant part of our investigation into the death of Mr Tanner. Can you explain why it was spotted being driven from Mr Tanner's home to the church in which his body was found on the night of his murder?"

Selwyn stared at the screen shots, then stared at Beth. His face was pale, and there were beads of sweat on his forehead. After a few minutes silence, he said "I need to speak with Jasper. Alone."

Chapter 64

Donald had taken a call from the chief constable shortly before Selwyn's interview was paused. Beth was relieved to know that she wouldn't have to face any questions from him about investigation leaks before she'd had a chance to raise it with the team, and she and Fiona made their way back to the squad room.

Beth stood at the front of the room and announced loudly, "It appears that our suspect, currently our only suspect, is continuing to get information about this ongoing investigation either from someone within this room, or someone with whom one member of this team has been sharing information. You have until the end of the day to come and speak with me about it, otherwise I will launch a formal investigation."

It was then that Beth caught sight of Mac walking into the room. A rare event, Beth felt a chill move up her spine and nodded towards her office.

"Don't worry, I'm not bringing terrible news," said Mac. "On the contrary, I am the bearer of surprisingly good news! You must have friends in high places because the tox results are back already, and they show that yesterday's victim was killed with a very high dose of oramorph."

"Just like the others," said Beth.

"Just like the others," repeated Mac. "The results are not particularly surprising – we saw a puncture mark on his right shoulder at yesterday's post-mortem – but the speed of confirmation frankly was. Also, as you know, the victim's tongue had been removed. This was done after his death, and in a manner consistent with the removal of the eyes and ears of the other victims. Unfortunately, our colleagues in the forensics team have not yet replied to my many enquiries about the rope used to tie the victim to the lectern, but I can confirm that the knot was the same as the one used on Wheeler and Tanner, so I would suggest that the three victims found at the cathedral and St Martin's church were killed by the same person or persons unknown."

"Oh, that's really helpful, Mac. Thank you. Do you have a time of death for us?"

"I would estimate that the victim died between the hours of ten p.m. and two a.m."

"Thank you."

"And just to prove that it's not only bad news that comes in threes, I have an ID for you."

"Mac, you're kidding me. You star. You absolute bobby-dazzler. Thank you so, so much."

"You're very welcome. The details are in this file. Good luck. Oh, and Beth. This is a very difficult case, we're all very well aware of that, so please. Be kind to yourself."

Beth nodded, and watched her old friend leave the squad room, then picked up the file identifying their latest victim. According to one of Canterbury's leading private dentists, their patient was twenty-five-year-old Oliver Freeman. They held an address for him in one of Canterbury's most exclusive areas, and a second address in London's Canary Wharf. According to the very helpful receptionist, Oliver had had a molar removed earlier in the week, and had taken a few days to stay with his parents, Alexander and Emily, for some rest and recuperation.

A series of checks on the name revealed no new information about the victim. Not unexpected. They'd need to rely on family and friends to give them the information they needed to move forward the investigation into his death. *I'll give Selwyn and Jasper to the end of this hour before hauling them back into the interview room,* thought Beth. *We need to tie this up quickly so that we can start looking into possible motives for Oliver's murder.*

Beth looked out towards the team, all working so hard on their respective tasks. The thought that one of them was speaking out of turn and endangering progress in their investigation surprised her, as much as it angered her.

As Beth scanned the squad room, her eyes stopped with Fiona. Her body language normally suggested confidence and strength but this morning, she had an almost vulnerable air to her. Maybe she'd take Fiona with her when she went to see Oliver's family. Some time on their own in the car could be the opportunity both women needed to bring a few issues out into the open.

"Guv," said Terry, popping his head around her office door. "Selwyn and Jasper are ready for you now."

Chapter 65

Beth and Fiona entered the silent interview room. Terry, Clarissa, and Donald had retaken their seats in the viewing room. The team were ready to go.

"My client has prepared a statement which I will now read to you," said Jasper. "Mr Du Pont will take questions at the end of the statement."

Beth looked at Selwyn, but he didn't look at her. He sat forward in his seat, with his hands clasped, pressed to his mouth. Jasper looked at his laptop screen and began.

"For nearly four decades, I have been carrying out voluntary work with local homeless people. On my appointment as Canon Missioner at Canterbury Cathedral, I became an active volunteer with the charity Canterbury Cares.

Some eighteen months ago, I met a young man by the name of Trevor Reed. Since leaving the army, Trevor had spent much of his time, like so many veterans before him, struggling with his mental health and his return to non-military life.

Trevor and I spent many hours talking over a hot drink. He was a troubled young man, prone to violent outbursts – he once hit a fellow homeless person because of a perceived slight, and broke his jaw with just one punch

– and he had an abiding interest in religion. To my knowledge, he did not practice any particular faith, but in a religious education lesson during his years at secondary school, his teacher told him that Reed was a variation of Rood, a crucifix which is often found in churches. It is my belief that his teacher was trying to instil some Christian values into the boy who, by his own admission, was 'a bloody handful' when he was a pupil. Unfortunately, this connection was interpreted as a blessed calling to right the wrongs against those less able than him to take care of themselves.

Over several months, Trevor became more open about his life and his views. He told me that as a serving soldier on a number of tours of duty in the Middle East, he had been responsible for mutilating a number of insurgent corpses, for example, by removing facial features including eyes, ears, and so on. I asked him why he had behaved like this, and he said it was important that their sins in this life were visible in the next.

Trevor also told me that his Army training had given him the skills he needed to 'right the wrongs' after he'd been discharged.

He made the decision to move to Canterbury because of its obvious Christian heritage. Once here, he used old contacts to sell his 'services'. He could be hired to scare people, to harm them, and even to kill them if the motivation was right. He saw no moral difficulties here; he genuinely believed that his actions were necessary in order to protect those who could not protect themselves. It was this view that Trevor believed led Jimmy Wheeler to his door. Trevor did not believe that Mr Wheeler was in the same category as Mr Tanner. Capable of violence, undoubtedly, but capable of murder? No. Not even to protect his own life.

Trevor told me that he had been contacted by an old comrade in arms. Mr Wheeler had told this gentleman that his and his business partner's lives were in danger. The threats had come from a man called Frankie Tanner. Trevor knew of Frankie's brother, Billy, and knew the sort of violence that both he and Frankie were capable of, and he therefore had no doubt that when Mr Wheeler said he believed his life was in danger, he was correct. Trevor said that he had no qualms about killing Mr Tanner on Mr Wheeler's behalf. Mr Wheeler paid him five thousand pounds, with a further five thousand pounds to follow when the deed had been done.

This was wrong. Completely wrong. I had never encountered anything like it before. I knew I had to dissuade Trevor from carrying out the killing, and I knew that if I was unable to do so, I would have to report the incident to the police and rely upon them to intervene. It was my belief that I had been successful in my attempts to prevent Mr Tanner's death and, in order to preserve the charity's reputation as a safe haven for those in need, I made the decision, rightly or wrongly, not to discuss this with the police.

I believe that the reason Mr Wheeler appeared at Canterbury Cares on that fateful evening at the end of September is because Trevor had not returned the initial five thousand pounds to him, nor had he carried out his commitments. I saw Trevor after his shower, and explained that Mr Wheeler had been to the shelter. I urged Trevor to return the money to him, but Trevor was insistent that Mr Wheeler was also a sinner and deserved no fair treatment from him. That was the last time I saw Trevor Reed.

I am sharing this information with you because I have shared it with two dear friends of mine. I cannot, in all good conscience, not inform you of that.

One of these dear friends and I were discussing transport issues a few months ago, and he asked me if I knew of anyone selling a car that could be used to transport heavy or bulky materials in the Canterbury area. My brother's cook had told me that her brother, Mr Jenkins, was selling something on eBay that sounded ideally suited to the task, and so I bought that car on behalf of my friends, and delivered it to them the following day.

It wasn't me, Detective Chief Inspector. I haven't killed another living being in my life – I pick up spiders and carry them to the door rather than harm them in any way, so I most certainly could not harm another human being. I can only hope that the information I have shared here today will help you in your attempts to find the killer of these men. The real killer."

Jasper closed his laptop lid and stared at Beth, who let the statement hang in the air for a few minutes before turning to Selwyn and asking, "Who are your friends, Mr Du Pont?"

Selwyn looked at the table, then looked directly at her. "Julian and Elizabeth Jefferson-Briggs."

Chapter 66

"This case is getting increasingly sensitive," said Donald, when he and Beth were alone in his office. "Were the Jefferson-Briggs on your radar before Du Pont's statement?"

"No, Sir, neither Julian nor Elizabeth have been in our sights before now."

"Is their involvement in this crime plausible?"

"Well, I'd say they've got the opportunity because Elizbeth Jefferson-Briggs is a member of the cathedral's Chapter, and she's on the lists of those with access to the keys for both the cathedral and St Martin's. She's also the Chapter member with overall responsibility for IT systems, including the CCTV system which hasn't been working inside the cathedral. But we need to find a motive. The team are working on this as we speak."

"And what about the latest victim?"

"Mac and her team have identified the victim as Oliver Freeman, and Fiona and I are going to speak with his family shortly, so if there's nothing else, Sir?"

Once again, Beth was dismissed with the nod of a head.

Beth's mind was whirring as she entered the squad room, where every member of the team was working flat out on the new leads.

"Okay guys, Fiona and I are off to see Oliver Freeman's mother. We'll be back for the debrief after which I need to update the Super, so please, get me as much information as possible by then," said Beth, as she and Fiona left the room.

The University of Kent sits at the top of a small hill along a long road with exceptional views of Canterbury and its beautiful cathedral. It was here that Emily Freeman, Oliver's mother, was a professor of Actuarial Science.

As Fiona started the short journey from the station to the university, she and Beth made small talk followed by silence, before Fiona said "Beth, I've been seeing someone for a few months. He's in the same business as us, so we've been talking about our cases. I think he may be the one who's been talking to Selwyn Du Pont. I asked him last night if he knew Selwyn, and he said not personally, but his sister did. If I'd thought for one minute that Roger had been talking to Selwyn, or if he'd been talking to his sister who would have shared the information with Selwyn, I wouldn't have talked to him about this case. Not at all. I'm truly sorry, Beth."

"Roger?" asked Beth. "Not Roger Dowler, from Organised Crime?"

"Yes. Him," replied Fiona, who looked as though she was carrying the weight of the world on her shoulders.

God, thought Beth. *What a mess.* She had no doubt that Fiona had not intentionally shared information with a suspect, and all coppers needed someone to talk to who was a step away from their work but understood the pressures they were under, but nevertheless, this breach of protocol was serious. *More serious for Roger than Fiona,* thought Beth, *but still serious for both of them.*

"Thank you for telling me, Fiona. I'll have to look into this further but for now, let's focus on informing Oliver's mother about her son."

The journey was completed in silence and at the main Reception desk, they were directed to the building where an administrator showed them to Emily's office.

"Professor Freeman," said Beth, before introducing herself and Fiona. "We have a few questions about your son."

Emily Freeman looked puzzled. "He's not in any trouble, is he?" she asked with a faint Scottish accent. "He's a good lad with a heart of gold, so if you're looking into him for any reason, then I'm sure there's been a mistake."

"When did you last see your son?"

"Last night. He went out at about seven p.m. and he didn't get home until after I went to bed."

"Did you hear him get home?"

"No. I just presumed he did," replied Emily, and the realisation that Oliver wasn't in trouble with the police began to dawn on her.

"Where was your son going last night?"

"He said he was going into town to meet a few old schoolfriends of his, but he didn't specify who, he just said 'the old gang' and I didn't ask for any details. Please tell me what's happened."

"Professor Freeman, I'm so sorry to have to tell you that the body of a young man was found in Canterbury Cathedral yesterday morning, and we believe that the body is that of your son, Oliver," said Beth gently.

Emily sat silence then said, "The Cathedral? I thought he'd just gone back to London a few days early. Oh my god, was he murdered, like that other chap whose body was found in the cathedral?"

"I can confirm that the young man was murdered, and that we believe that his murder is linked to the murders of Jimmy Wheeler and Frankie Tanner," replied Beth.

"Oh god. Oh dear god. Please tell me my son was not the *'speak no evil'* victim." Emily was pleading now.

"I'm afraid that the victim's tongue has been removed," replied Beth, as Emily began to shake, with tears pouring down her cheeks.

Beth waited until Emily began to settle a little before asking, "Professor Freeman, I'm sorry to have to ask this, but did Oliver mention to you that he had received any threats? Was he scared about anything?"

Emily looked shocked. "No. He's said nothing at all."

"Has he been worried recently?"

"Not noticeably, no. Please. I really can't do this now. I need to see my son. Please take me to see my son."

Beth nodded. "Yes, of course. Is there anyone we can contact to come with you?"

"No, it's just me. My husband is at a conference in Brussels, and isn't due back until tomorrow. My mother is too old for such a traumatic task, and there are no other relatives nearby. My god. My boy. My wee laddie. My dear, darling laddie," replied Emily, her Scottish accent becoming more pronounced as the tears started to fall again.

Chapter 67

By four p.m., Beth and Fiona were back in the squad room and the daily debrief was underway.

Beth updated the team on the afternoon's events, and summed up, "Emily Freeman confirmed that the body of victim three is that of her son. When we asked about partners and friends, she said that he socialised with colleagues and a few of his old school friends, but he didn't have any close friends. Not since his best friend from school died a few years ago. It had a significant impact on Oliver's life. That friend was Matthew Jefferson-Briggs."

There was an audible collective intake of breath from the team, and Dave whistled quietly.

"Okay, this is the first proper link we have between the Jefferson-Briggs and any of our victims, even if it doesn't make any sense at the moment. I know that Selwyn told us he'd shared the stories about Jimmy and Frankie with them, but that would just be his word against theirs, and it proves nothing. What else have we got?"

Ki told the team he'd checked Jimmy's loans book but couldn't find anything relating to any Jefferson-Briggs. He'd also checked the gallery's sales and purchase records, but again there was no sign of their name.

Terry said that he'd spoken with Tracey and she couldn't find anything relating to the Jefferson-Briggs in the records for Tanner's bookies.

Dave cleared his throat and said that he'd spoken with Canterbury Council, who confirmed that there was no CCTV footage anywhere near the Jefferson-Briggs home, but he'd asked traffic to check their footage for the suspect's car in the vicinity of their new suspect's home on the nights of the murders, and he was hoping to receive a response to that request soon. He also suggested asking their neighbours if they had their own security cameras at the bottom of their driveways. Beth nodded her agreement and suggested he take Jane with him.

There were no other updates on the Oliver Freeman case, so Beth moved the conversation on to the investigation into the other murders.

"I've checked the CCTV footage in the cathedral precincts on the night of Jimmy's murder," said Clarissa. "I can't see anything resembling a wheelchair approaching the cathedral, but I spotted a car being driven into what appears to be an underground car park. This happened just after twelve thirty a.m. We weren't aware of this car park before now; Arthur didn't mention it when he was taking us on the tour of the precincts – he said he didn't think it was relevant because only substantive staff and Chapter members could access it, and he simply can't believe that anyone involved so closely with the cathedral could be involved in these murders. I can't see the full number plate, but the partial registration number matches that of the car seen leaving Frankie Tanner's home on the night of his murder."

"God almighty," said Beth. "When will people realise that it's not for them to decide what's relevant in a police investigation, it's a matter for us! Next time you see Arthur, please make sure he understands this. Okay. We need to know where the car came from."

Clarissa nodded. "I've already asked traffic to trace the car from five p.m. on the night Jimmy died. I'm hoping they'll get back to us first thing tomorrow."

It was an acknowledgment that the team would be working another weekend without being told to do so, and Beth appreciated this intervention.

"Great, thanks Clarissa. Also, Selwyn is still a suspect in this investigation, so we need to check his whereabouts when he went wandering on the nights both Jimmy and Frankie were killed. He said he might have walked towards St Martin's hospital – please get hold of the CCTV for the A257 to see if you can spot him. Okay, anything else?"

There were no other updates so Beth drew the meeting to a close and went to update Donald.

"Is it possible to identify the driver of the car from any of the CCTV footage we have?" he asked.

"I'm afraid not, Sir. The suspect has covered their appearance well, with a thick woollen hat and an equally thick woollen scarf leaving the very bare minimum of their face visible."

"And we're unable to identify the individual pushing the wheelchair towards St Martin's church?"

"I'm afraid so. The quality of the CCTV footage is very poor, and the digital team can't make it any clearer, but the team are going to carry out a door-to-door on the streets near St Martin's to see if we can get hold of any doorbell cameras. Sir, we need to look into the circumstances of Matthew Jefferson-Briggs' death. It's the only link we currently have between the Jefferson-Briggs and any of our victims."

"Yes, I understand that, Beth. I've spoken with the chief constable and the DCC, and both agree that we need a material link between the Jefferson-Briggs' and the victims, and I think the fact that Oliver Freeman was their son's best friend will be enough, but we need to make this a fact-gathering first interview, best held in an environment where they feel comfortable. Please make the arrangements to meet them at their home, and I will accompany you. Given the speed with which our victims are mounting up, please arrange to meet them tonight, if possible, or tomorrow morning at the latest."

"Yes Sir. I'll get on to it now. And I'd like to bring Terry Corfe along as well."

Donald nodded.

Chapter 68

"Who was that?" asked Elizabeth, when Julian ended the call.

"It was Detective Chief Inspector Bethany Harper. She's leading the murder inquiry. She wants to come over to speak with us about the latest victim."

"Well, it's about time the local MP was looped into this officially! What time are they arriving?"

"They should be here at about seven p.m."

The music station in Terry's car was switched off as he, Beth, and Donald made their way to the Jefferson-Briggs' home. They arrived forty minutes after leaving the station, and were greeted by Julian, who showed them into a large, plush living room. Elizabeth was standing at the mantlepiece, holding what appeared to be a large gin and tonic. She offered all three a drink, but all three refused. "No drinking on duty. How very noble," she said.

Julian quickly intervened. "Thank you very much for coming over to update us on progress with your investigation."

Beth nodded, and started the conversation. "I'm afraid we have some sad news to share with you this evening. We have identified the body found in the cathedral yesterday morning. He was Oliver Freeman."

Beth waited for the news to land, and watched their reactions carefully. Julian looked shocked to the core, Elizabeth looked mildly surprised, but Beth wondered if she almost smiled.

"Good god, not Alexander and Emily's boy? Matthew's best friend?" asked Julian.

"Yes," replied Beth. "I'm afraid so. Can you tell us a little about Oliver?"

"Yes of course," replied Julian. "Such a bright and polite young man. He was a very good friend to Matthew, especially after his accident, and he had a very bright future. I heard that he was doing very well in the city, and they had him marked as a future leader. How awful. How very, very sad." He turned to Elizabeth. "We must get in touch with Alexander and Emily to offer them as much support as they need."

"Mr Jefferson-Briggs, I'm sorry to have to ask a difficult question, but can you tell us a little about your son's accident?" asked Beth.

"Matthew's accident? Why yes, of course. Some four years ago, when Matthew was in his last year at Oxford, he did what so many young people do as the stress of their finals approach. He got very drunk one evening. Unfortunately, he made the fateful decision to go and look at the stars from the roof terrace of his shared home. We're not entirely clear on the actual events of that evening, we just know that he fell from the roof and as a consequence, received multiple, life-changing injuries."

"Oliver was with him that night," said Elizabeth. "But he failed to save him."

"That's a little harsh, darling," replied Julian. He turned to the trio and explained "Elizabeth gave up a very high-powered role in the city to care for Matthew after his accident. He was classed as an incomplete quadriplegic, which meant he had some movement in one of his arms, but he could do very little for himself. My wife was marvellous with him; she wouldn't let anyone else look after him, but Matthew was a young man who felt that his predicted bright and brilliant future had disappeared overnight. He'd gone from being an independent young man to having his mother wash and dress him every day. The depression was deep and difficult to watch. One day, when I was in Westminster and Elizabeth had gone to lunch with some friends, Oliver very kindly sat with Matthew for the afternoon. That night, Matthew managed to take the whole of his new pot of medication, and Elizabeth very sadly found his body the following morning."

"Oliver was with him that day," said Elizabeth. "But he failed to save him. Again."

"Darling that's enough," replied Julian forcefully.

Beth knew her next words would be insignificant, but nevertheless offered her sympathies. "I'm so sorry to hear that," she said, then turned directly to Elizabeth. "And I'm very sorry to hear about how difficult the whole experience must have been for you."

"Thank you, Inspector," said Julian. Elizabeth would not meet her eye and instead glared at the roaring fire.

"Did you keep in touch with Oliver after Matthew's death?" asked Beth.

"I exchanged a few text messages with him over the years, mainly wishing him a happy birthday or a Merry Christmas," said Julian.

All eyes turned to Elizabeth. "Very rarely," she replied. "Inspector, who did this? Surely by now you must have some idea, and I don't mean ridiculous ideas like good men, such as Selwyn Du Pont."

"We have been speaking with Mr Du Pont, yes," said Beth, spotting an opportunity to move the conversation on. "He told us that he recently bought a car which he delivered to you. Is that correct?"

"Yes, that's correct," replied Julian, sounding slightly puzzled.

"And that car is kept here, on your premises at all times?" asked Beth.

"Well yes, unless we need it for constituency business. That's why we bought it. We needed something a little more sturdy than our cars for taking donations to charity shops, moving party literature around, and so on," said Julian.

"Who has keys to this car?" asked Beth.

"Just my wife and me," replied Julian before turning to Elizabeth. "We should have kept the Peugeot," he said, before explaining to the others "We had a Rifter Horizon, which was excellent for transporting Matthew's wheelchair, but we sold it not long after he died."

"Sorry, to be clear, you sold the car and the wheelchair after Matthew died?" asked Beth.

"What? The wheelchair? No, that's still here, in Matthew's room. Why do you ask?" asked Julian, yet again puzzled by the direction the meeting was taking.

"Minister, could you take us to see the wheelchair?" asked Beth.

"Well yes, yes that's fine. Please follow me," replied Julian, and moved to the door. Beth and Terry followed him, with Donald and Elizabeth bringing up the rear. They moved down a long corridor and into a room which Beth presumed used to be a second living space but, with a widened door, had been adapted to be a wheelchair-accessible space for their son.

When they walked into the room, they saw an expensive wheelchair in the corner, and Beth knew immediately that the information-gathering visit had now become central to her murder inquiry. She turned to Julian and said "Mr Jefferson-Briggs, on the night that Mr Tanner was murdered, the car that Mr Du Pont delivered to you a few months ago was spotted on the route between Mr Tanner's home and the back streets near St Martin's church. Shortly afterwards, we have CCTV footage of two individuals, one pushing a wheelchair which looks very much like this one, towards the church. Can you please tell us where you were between eleven thirty p.m. and two a.m. on Thursday evening last week?"

Julian paused, realising that he had no alibi. He seemed momentarily flustered before Elizabeth's loud, hollow laugh disrupted the moment. All eyes turned to her.

She looked directly at Beth, then said,

"It wasn't him, you fool. It was me."

Chapter 69

Elizabeth turned and marched back to the large living room. The others followed and found her pouring herself another large gin and tonic. They looked at her expectantly.

She turned to Julian and said simply, "I'm sorry darling, but the game's up, as they say. They've clearly got CCTV footage which can place the car at the scene of both crimes, and soon all three, and the wheelchair at the scene of the second crime." Then, she turned to her audience and said "I have no regrets. The story is a difficult one for me, as it is for my husband, but the story needs to be told."

"In your own time, please," said Donald.

Elizabeth took a deep breath and began. "Our son, our only child, Matthew, was an intelligent, kind and caring young man but when he went to university, he became addicted to gambling. The easy availability of online gambling at the time made his descent into a great deal of debt quick and altogether far too easy. His savings dwindled to nought in a matter of months. The gambling continued and the debt built up again, and in the end, he turned to his friend, Oliver, for financial and emotional support. It has never been clear to me why he could not find that support with us." Elizabeth paused, and took a large gulp of her drink. "Oliver cleared his debt and Matthew promised to get the help he needed so that he would never be in that position again, but once the gambling industry has its claws into you, it never let's go. Matthew was hounded relentlessly, with offers of free bets, and cheap bets, and although he did well to resist in the first few months, there came a time when he could resist no more, and once again, he started building up a significant debt. This time, Oliver told him he would not provide the funds to cover that debt and suggested that Matthew seek more help. That night, it all became too much for Matthew and he drank too much then walked to the roof terrace of his home where he threw himself over the parapet. That was his first suicide attempt."

Elizabeth looked directly at Julian but he couldn't meet her eye. She returned to her audience and said, "We call the first suicide attempt an accident because we only found out what really happened about a year ago, when Oliver came to see us. He said he was riven with guilt and begged our forgiveness. Ha! Forgive the boy who had the chance to save my child? Not once, but twice?" This time, Julian stared at her. "Oliver told me a few months ago that Matthew had asked him to give him an overdose of his new medication on the day he died, but he refused. He did, however, loosen the child lock at the top of the bottle, so that Matthew could access the tablets himself that night." The anger, a deep, visceral anger seemed to consume Elizabeth. She drained her glass and poured another gin. Then she continued. "Those animals. They ruin so many lives yet they simply don't care. A few months ago, Selwyn and Mary came to dinner and he told us the shocking news about Trevor Reed – the kind of man he was, the kind of actions he took, and the most awful tale of two men who capitalised on the misery of others. Quite why Selwyn had to talk Reed out of taking the actions he'd been paid to do is beyond me, but that's the kind of man Selwyn is, which is why your interviews were, frankly, so absurd.

That was the night that my patience ran out, and I knew that I needed to take matters into my own hands. My dear, wonderful father died six months ago from complications arising from COPD. He was a wonderful, hardworking man, who saved and improved so many lives as a very talented surgeon, and these animals – Wheeler, Tanner, and the like – didn't care that they were ruining lives, and in so many cases, like that of our dear son's, taking lives. As you may already know, oramorph is used to relieve breathlessness, but my father was very stoic and, like so many other medics, would only take medication if it was absolutely necessary. As a consequence, he had quite a stockpile of oramorph at his home when he died. I had every intention of disposing of the medicine in accordance with best medical practice, but no one followed up, and it was a very busy, difficult time, and so I forgot, and the oramorph was here when Selwyn shared his tales.

It wasn't enough for me to take the lives of a few ignoble gangsters, I needed to punish them, and to punish

God himself for letting them thrive when my own loved ones were dying long, painful deaths. And so, the plan was made. Wheeler and Tanner would die, their eyes and ears removed for refusing to see or hear what suffering surrounded them, and their bodies would be found in places of immense significance to the Anglican Church. That was, of course, made easier by my association with the cathedral Chapter, both in terms of access to keys to make body disposals easier, and in terms of ensuring that any CCTV which might be present was temporarily disabled." Elizabeth smiled quietly at her own brilliance.

I had been following both men for a few weeks before killing them. They were creatures of habit, so it was easy to pinpoint the best time and place to take action. I merely drove to the best positions and waited outside my car, with the bonnet open, until they arrived. Then, I flagged them down, made an excuse about my car breaking down and could they possibly help me, and both men did. As soon as they went to look at the car's engine, I injected the oramorph. It didn't take long for it to work and, between hoisting my son from wheelchair to bed and back, and keeping up the gymnastics work which brought my husband and me together at university, it was possible for me to put their bodies in the boot of the car and, later, in the wheelchair to move them to their final destinations.

And that Freeman boy had to die too. He all but killed my child; if only he'd spoken to us when Matthew first got into difficulties, we could have stepped in to ensure he got the best help. *'The Truth Will Make You Free'.*" she said, laughing ironically. "And if he hadn't been as wicked as to open the catch on the medication bottle, Matthew would not have been able to take his own life that awful night. So, I told him to come and see me on Wednesday evening to discuss Matthew, but suggested that he tell his mother that he was seeing old friends so that he and I could speak with each other freely, but in private.

That's it, Inspector. That's what happened and why. *'Mea culpa. Mea maxima culpa.'*

Julian, will you please contact Jasper Montague and ask him to represent me. Selwyn will have his contact details. Tell Jasper that he'll find me in Canterbury police station." She turned to Beth and said, "Shall we go?"

Chapter 70

Beth sat at the front of the squad room and updated the team on the events of the previous evening. They were both shocked at the speed with which the arrest had been made, and elated that they could finally put this case to bed. Fiona, of course, had to mention the fact that "We had a suspect list as long as your arm and whose name was never on it? Elizabeth Jefferson-Briggs!" but Beth took that on the chin, in the spirit of success at solving such a complicated and high-profile case.

The evidence came trickling in over the subsequent days. Traffic cameras put the Du Pont car at each murder scene, the wheelchair was tested by forensics who found very small traces of a St Martin's-specific soil in its wheels.

A search of the Jefferson-Briggs house revealed stocks of oramorph and syringes, including, after an extensive search of the contents of two sharps boxes found in Matthew's room, three syringes with traces of the victims' DNA on the needles. They did not, however, find Jimmy's eyes, Frankie's ears, or Oliver's tongue, and despite several requests to reveal their hiding places, Elizabeth refused.

Elizabeth spoke with Jasper then said nothing more about the extraordinary events of the previous weeks.

Julian made the decision to step down from his job as an MP to give his wife the support he knew she needed. Seeing your child disabled then dying, especially by suicide, is among the most difficult things any parent can experience, and he wished he'd insisted on counselling sooner so that this mess, this awful bloody mess, could have been avoided.

Selwyn was in a state of shock and disbelief for several weeks, and blamed himself for instigating such an awful chain of events. Mary hugged him and cooked his favourite meals, and generally nursed his mental health back to wellness. She stopped asking if they could move, instead embracing the wonderful life they enjoyed in the cathedral precincts.

Beth and the team wound down their work with the Wheelers, Tanners and Freemans, leaving them to heal in their own time and in their own way. The East Kent Police Force would, however, continue to keep a close eye on the new Wheeler-Tanner crime partnership.

Donald and Ian were absolutely delighted with the arrest, and Beth was literally clapped on the back several times a day for the first few weeks.

Mac bought Beth a lasagne and garlic bread at Guiseppe's, along with several bottles of fine red wine.

And Beth finally took a week's annual leave to recover from the most extraordinary experience of her career. She and Kate went to Cardiff for the week, retracing their steps in their old haunts, and building new memories for the uncertain future ahead.

And finally, it was over. The whole sordid case. *Onwards and upwards,* thought Beth. Onwards and upwards.